His Brother's Keeper
Gay Cameron

Harlequin Books

TORONTO • NEW YORK • LONDON
AMSTERDAM • PARIS • SYDNEY • HAMBURG
STOCKHOLM • ATHENS • TOKYO • MILAN
MADRID • WARSAW • BUDAPEST • AUCKLAND

With love to my family—my husband, Chuck, and my children, Mary, Scott, Terri and Greg.

A special thanks to Harvey J. Tompkins for his valuable counsel.

ISBN 0-373-22264-5

HIS BROTHER'S KEEPER

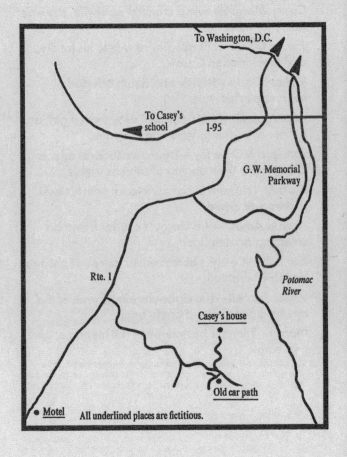

To Washington, D.C.

To Casey's school

I-95

G.W. Memorial Parkway

Rte. 1

Potomac River

Casey's house

Old car path

Motel   All underlined places are fictitious.

CAST OF CHARACTERS

Casey Michaels—As a criminal's ex-wife, she was guilty by association.

Trevor Steele—His allegiance was to his family, and that included Casey.

Richard Tapp—His life and death affected everyone in his wake.

Aunt Maude—She'd raised Casey from a girl, and left her everything, including the pain.

Jamison & Crowley—These two federal agents didn't know the meaning of citizens' rights.

Barney—He kept in constant touch with his best undercover agent.

Aretha Ames—Was Casey's courier friend an unwitting accomplice?

Jon Britt—Casey's boss seemed more uptight than his job warranted.

Victor Pernell—The cigar-chewing owner of the courier agency was a beefy boor.

Moose—Trevor's partner filled out his name, and then some.

Chapter One

He followed the car from a distance, his nerves taut but controlled, anticipation racing but subdued. The Volkswagen Bug swung left to meet the gravel drive, and Trevor Steele pulled to the shoulder. He turned off the lights and let the car idle while he watched red dots and white beams disappear through the maze of trees down the winding drive. His fingers drummed the wheel. Twice he'd been down that twisting drive unobserved. Now his waiting was over.

He cut the engine and breathed in the April night. The smell of rain and wet woods and the river nearby bathed his senses. It was a good night to find some answers.

He picked up the car phone and punched in his boss's number. "She drives like a maniac," he said.

"You're on her, then," said Barney.

"She knows the area like the back of her hand." He didn't add he'd been shadowing her for the last two weeks.

"This is a crazy scheme, Steele. If you weren't my number one agent, I'd think you were nuts." He paused. Something clanked against the phone. "Forget I said that. Look, anybody can sell those bearer bonds anywhere in the world. I don't know why she's sitting on them. If we didn't have proof that Tapp had been in the D.C. area, New York would still have this baby and we'd be free and clear. But we're not.

I could get a search warrant tomorrow, Trevor. Jamison and Crowley can be through her house in one day."

He imagined Barney leaning back in his swivel chair, his feet propped on the desk, his hand stroking his short gray beard. "What if the stolen bonds aren't in the house, Barney? What if she does know something? She'd disappear so fast we'd never lay our hands on them."

"It's a toss-up, Trevor, and you know it."

"Trust me. I'll find them." And God forbid those bumbling idiots should sniff out the bonds before he could get to her.

Barney's deep sigh whistled through the phone. "Just remember our deal. You get inside that house somehow and search it yourself from top to bottom."

"That's the plan."

"Good," said Barney, pausing. "I hate to sound like an old mother hen, but are you okay?"

"I'm okay, stop worrying."

Trevor's life had changed six weeks ago, and so had someone else's. He'd charged into a situation too quickly, and because of his poor judgment, an agent was killed. Barney told him he'd made the same choice himself in similar situations, but his words had fallen on deaf ears. Trevor was the one who'd made the wrong decision. He was the one who'd rushed into a situation without considering every possibility, and someone else had paid the price.

Yes, he was okay, more or less, but Barney believed the incident had made him decide to leave the bureau. He was wrong. It had been only one of many "last straws." There were other, more personal reasons for his decision.

"How 'bout I tear up your resignation."

"No, Barney, this is it."

"Can't blame me for trying. I don't know what the hell made you change your mind, but I'm glad you're sticking around for this case. This is a hot one. And one more thing. I mentioned agents Carl Jamison and Fred Crowley... well, they've been a bit overzealous in keeping on Michaels's tail. Between them and the police, you don't stand a chance of getting close to her when she finds out you're a fed.''

''She won't.''

He hung up the phone, then turned it off. He had no intention of telling Casey Michaels he worked for the government. And he had no intention of telling Barney why he'd changed his mind. Barney would boot him off the case in a minute if he knew.

He checked his watch. It was 9:50 p.m. He'd give her a few more minutes to get settled, then make his move. She couldn't refuse to see him, not when he told her who he was.

He switched on the interior light and picked up the computer printout to scan his file on Casey Lynn Michaels. ''Age, 28. Height, 5'8''. Business management student. Part-time courier. Background: Orphaned at age twelve; raised by aunt who died when Michaels was 24; married to Richard Tapp at 24; divorced at 26. Uncooperative. Possible suspect.'' He'd done his homework. Two weeks ago in New York he hadn't known Casey Lynn Michaels existed.

Mentally, he added beautiful, spunky and sexy as hell. That was something the computer wouldn't spit out.

He picked up a pencil and underlined ''married to Richard Tapp at 24.'' Casey Michaels would know the answers to his questions. He was betting on it.

He checked his watch again, then inched the car forward slowly onto the drive at an angle to avoid scraping the muffler. He wouldn't make that mistake again. He rolled forward another foot, then let the car settle on solid ground before pushing on.

Tall, vine-covered trees formed a canopy above him and blocked out what little light the hazy moon provided on the two-lane road behind him. His hands gripped the wheel, a response to the change in light and a sure sign of his tension. He thought about the letters he'd received from Richard Tapp two weeks ago, and his insides knotted tighter.

But something besides his own tension hung in the air tonight, some dead, heavy silence, some intangible threat that spelled danger.

He slowed the car to a creep. He'd never found a logical explanation for this sixth sense of his. Sometimes it worked, sometimes it didn't. The inconsistency made an explanation impossible. There was no physical signal, like a chill up the spine or a twitching on his neck. He just *knew*.

Years in the field had taught him to follow his instincts. He did it automatically now, just as he cut the lights automatically. The parking lights shone as faint shadows on the gravel. Inch by inch, the car moved forward. Gravel crunched beneath each turn of the wheels, piercing the deafening silence swelling and pounding in his ears. Danger dripped from every tree branch, hovered behind every shadow. He sat rigid, alert, ready to strike.

As he met the next long curve, a scream stabbed the night, a terrified, chilling scream that made his blood run cold.

He zoomed around the last curve and through the clearing to the house. Adrenaline shot through his body, pushing him to the peak of awareness. He grabbed his gun from its compartment beneath the seat.

Within seconds, he crouched beside the car, his gun in hand. He checked the clearing and clicked off the familiar shapes like a computer. A dark van, its nose barely visible, hid in the trees at the clearing's edge. Shouting drew his eyes instantly to the house. Three figures were silhouetted against the front window.

Soundlessly, he mounted the porch steps. At closer range he could define the three figures through the gauze curtains. He saw two men, one large, one small. The shorter guy had his bulky arm wrapped around Casey Michaels's throat. As if that wasn't enough, he'd twisted her arm behind her back.

He crept across the front porch, then slid along the stone wall to the door, listening to the threatening voices through the open windows. In one sweeping motion, he kicked in the door, braced his gun and shouted, "Freeze."

The short man threw the woman aside. Trevor cringed as she hit the wall. The taller one rushed him, a sneer distorting his face. Trevor fired. Blood stained the man's arm and he grabbed it in pain. Not hesitating, Trevor swiveled to find the other guy, only to catch a chair in the chest that knocked him against the wall and forced the gun from his hand. He doubled over in pain, dazed, angry, gulping for air.

He struggled to regain his footing. Nobody got the best of him, at least not without a damn good fight. He bent down to grab his gun, but the taller man kicked him to the floor. Before he could stop them, the intruders rushed out the door.

He untangled himself from the chair and an overturned table and dashed to the porch. Spinning tires spit gravel as the van sped down the drive, its taillights disappearing in the dark shadows. He ran across the clearing and fired twice. A red taillight flickered. He fired again.

He ran down the drive and raced around the first curve, looking for a hint of headlight, a shadow of taillight. The van was well out of range by now. He continued running to the end of the drive, alert, his eyes searching, the gun ready, until finally, satisfied they were gone, knowing he needed to help Casey instead of capturing the thieves, he turned and walked back to the house.

CASEY MICHAELS CROUCHED in the living room corner where she'd been thrown, stunned, immobile, afraid to move. That man who'd charged through the door—who was he? Where'd he come from? He'd startled her as much as the thugs.

A shot cracked the air. Trembling, she pressed herself close to the wall, wanting desperately for the nightmare to end. Her hands covered her injured knee, as if they could stop the swelling and throbbing. She rested her head on her good knee. Her neck hurt. Her throat burned. Everything ached. She pounded her fist on the floor again and again. Why couldn't everyone leave her alone?

This was Richard's fault. Every threat, every fear, every break-in was *his* fault. She gulped in air to clear her head, muttering and swearing that in spite of her ex-husband she would survive. She would ride out the storm, and when it was over, she would just go on with her life.

The door slammed shut. Her head shot up, and her fingers tightened on her bad knee. The man who had chased out the thieves was walking toward her.

"Are you all right?" he asked.

She nodded. "I'm okay." She didn't recognize her whispered voice.

He was a tall man with dark hair and broad shoulders. He wove his way around the overturned furniture until he stood before her. She stared at him, her breath catching in her throat.

Reflexively, she jerked back, pressing her body deeper into the corner. His soft, blue-gray eyes frowned in surprise. Eyes so like her dead ex-husband's, it was eerie.

She found her voice. "Who are you?"

He stooped beside her, keeping his distance. "Hey, I'm not going to hurt you." His frown became a smile. "My name is Trevor Steele. I heard you scream."

Steele? Not Tapp? Her fear eased and her hand loosened on her knee. She forced a return smile she didn't feel. "I'm sorry. For a second you reminded me of someone I'd rather forget."

She uncurled from her awkward position and tried to stand by putting her weight on her good leg. She felt shaky. The change in position brought a rush of blood to her swollen knee and caused her to sway.

Trevor reached out and caught her. Supporting her with one arm, he grabbed the closest chair with his free hand, turned it right-side up, and helped her sit down.

"It's my knee. I fell on my bad knee." She fumbled with the chair, feeling awkward accepting this stranger's help again. She hated feeling helpless.

"Let me take a look." He reached for her skirt.

She grabbed his wrist. "No, that's all right. Really, I'm fine." She let go abruptly, disturbed by the strange feeling in the pit of her stomach. "Look, thank you for coming to my rescue, but I just want to be alone now. You've gone to enough trouble."

She was doing her best to be cordial. The man deserved more thanks than she could possibly give right now. Every word caused fire in her throat. Her neck cramped with each turn. And the sensation in her stomach refused to go away.

He ignored her dismissal. Instead, he picked up the phone miraculously left intact on a small corner table beside her.

"What are you doing?" Renewed panic rose in her throat.

"I'm calling the police."

"Hang up the phone." She stared at his haunting eyes and willed the receiver down. The thought of another police-man tromping through her house one more time was un-bearable. "Please, no police." She pushed herself off the chair and reached for the phone, then clenched her teeth as ripples of pain shot through her leg. She caught herself before falling and managed to slide back onto the chair. "I'll call them later," she said. "Not now."

"I'll take you to the hospital, then."

He moved to help her, but she stopped him. "I'm not going to the hospital. I know what's wrong, but thanks, anyway."

His eyes caught hers with an intensity that forced her to look away. He said, "I'll get some ice." Before she could stop him, he left the room.

She leaned back in the chair and propped her leg on the bottom of the couch. Unable to avoid the destruction any longer, she glanced at the room. They'd done a thorough job. The family pictures she'd carefully arranged on the end table and hung on the wall lay smashed on the floor. Broken glass littered the rug and the floor. The lamps lay on their sides, their shades in shreds. Her books had been pulled from the shelves and thrown down. One drape had been wrenched from the rod. She felt sick in her heart as well as her body. She had to get out of the room.

Using the couch as an anchor, she pulled herself up, balanced on one leg, then closed her eyes while she adjusted to the pain. She knew if she didn't flex her leg muscles, didn't bend the bad leg at all, she could put weight on that leg long enough to take quick steps. She used the bottom frame of the couch as a crutch of sorts and leaned her way along, one small step at a time.

Her goal was the kitchen. The idea of a stranger in her kitchen, especially one that reminded her of Richard, spurred her on. With one final lunge, she grabbed for the door frame, then used the chair rail as she limped the rest of the way down the hall.

One look at the kitchen sent her heart plummeting. "What have they done!" It looked worse than the living room. She swiped at the tear rolling down her cheek and wished she could as easily stop her lower lip from trembling.

Trevor came to her side. "You don't look so hot." He righted two kitchen chairs. "Sit," he said, the command clear in his voice.

He turned away and continued putting ice onto a dish towel. She was grateful he didn't keep watching her. She didn't need his sympathy. Her whole house—her whole *life*—was in shambles. If he uttered one sympathetic word, she was sure she would crumble.

Bracing herself on the wall, then the kitchen cabinet, she maneuvered herself to the kitchen chair and propped up her leg.

Without a word, he placed an ice pack on her knee. The cold jolted her. Already her knee seemed swollen to twice its normal size. Silently, she cursed her ex-husband.

"I'm Casey Michaels. I r-really do appreciate y-your help." She heard herself stuttering. The ice was making her shiver. She wished he would leave. Misery was no stranger to her, but she wasn't used to sharing it. She could handle this problem by herself. Alone. Without any man's help. She closed her eyes and tried hard to control the shaking.

Something heavy was draped over her shoulders. Her eyes flew open to find Trevor standing beside her chair arranging an old afghan around her. The difference was immediate. Warmth spread everywhere except her knee.

"That feels good." She smiled and pulled the blanket tighter. She fought to keep her eyes open, to stop her weighted eyelids from drooping and closing. She couldn't do it. Someone had added hundred-pound weights to her lids, and the pressure was greater than she could bear.

"You've had a shock," he said. The hand gently shaking her arm got her attention and forced her to open her eyes.

He stood beside the table, a mug of steaming tea in his hand. "Here, drink this. It's hot, it's caffeine. Maybe it'll help." He set the mug on the table.

Those haunting blue-gray eyes almost made her shrink back again, but she didn't this time. She thought she'd imagined the striking similarity before. Up close like this, she could see she was right. His eyes were a duplication of her ex-husband's eyes. It was uncanny. Other than his eyes, he didn't look anything like Richard, not at all. If he did, she would have booted him out by now, knee or no knee.

She took the mug and sipped the hot, spicy tea slowly, savoring the warm liquid sliding down her throat, feeling the caffeine begin its work. Nothing had ever tasted better.

She looked around the kitchen. He was sweeping the floor. The pans and dishes were piled on the counter and table. "You don't have to do this," she said. Sitting here while a stranger cleaned her kitchen made her uncomfortable. "I'll take care of it."

The look he gave her said more than his words. "We both know you won't be cleaning up anything today."

She couldn't argue.

"What did they want?" he said, sweeping while he talked.

She didn't know how to answer him. She knew what the thugs wanted, but she couldn't tell him or anyone else. He was better off not knowing. Just chasing those two guys out of the house could bring him trouble.

"There have been a lot of burglaries around here lately."

She couldn't look him in the eye. She fiddled with the ice pack on her knee until the silence became embarrassing. When she finally glanced up, she wished she hadn't. The strange, questioning look on his face told her he knew she was lying.

But worst of all was the penetrating glare of his eyes, the piercing gaze that struck fear in her heart and reminded her he was a stranger.

Chapter Two

She felt her heart pounding in her chest until finally he broke eye contact and turned away. She waited for some retort, some scathing accusation. Or worse.

But he said nothing. Instead, he swept up the debris, emptied it into a trash bag, and pointed to the pans on the table. "Tell me where this stuff goes and I'll put it away."

She started to protest, but found she couldn't speak. He held up his hand like a policeman stopping traffic. "I know," he said, "I don't have to do this."

His eyes now held a hint of mischief, and as the tension abated between them, she felt her heartbeat slow. His words even brought a slow smile to her lips, which amazed her. Silently, she chastised herself for being paranoid.

She pointed to the cabinet beside the stove. "All of the pans and baking tins go on the shelves behind you."

He seemed to need to stay busy, like his body couldn't contain the extra energy. Broad shoulders sporting solid muscles pushed against his dark blue pullover as he placed the pans in the cabinet. The faded jeans hanging low on his hips were...sexy. That was the only word for what she saw. He turned as the thought crossed her mind, and she felt her face heat with a blush.

He stood by the pantry door at the end of the side wall. "I guess the canned food goes here in the pantry." He nodded at the closed door. Cradling stacks of cans, he looked intent, serious. He looked like he belonged in that kitchen.

She rejected the thought and said, "If there's room. The rest go in the top cabinet above the counter."

Aunt Maude had updated the kitchen a few years before she became ill. Rather than pay an exorbitant fee to have the brickwork redone in the original pantry, she had the workmen close off the back section, cellar door and all, and build a new walk-in pantry along the side wall. The storage space was limited but manageable.

As Trevor gathered the rest of the items next to her mug, she realized the throbbing in her knee had become bearable. The swelling was going down.

She was struck by how tall he was. She knew, even if she were standing, he'd tower above her by as much as eight inches. Comparing him to her ex-husband was ridiculous.

At five foot eight, she was only one inch shorter than Richard. And yet, as she watched Trevor move around the kitchen, there was a familiarity about his movements. The way he glanced at her with a raised right eyebrow was exactly what Richard used to do. His long gait across the floor duplicated her ex-husband's walk.

Of course, Richard never would have been gathering pots and cans. He would have told her there was no need to clean up, and then he would have arranged for a cleaning service the next day. Never would he have been perceptive enough to know how upset she felt with the house torn to shreds.

"There aren't many dinner plates left," he said. "I counted five."

She cringed. Five out of twelve Limoges plates left from her mother's collection.

"Where should I put them?"

His blue-gray eyes softened in understanding. The kindness in his voice helped her hide the pain of losing her mother's pride and joy. Pointing to the end cabinet in front of her, she tried to speak, but the words stuck in her throat.

He stacked the five plates in the cabinet. She watched as he picked out the remaining matching cups, saucers, luncheon and dessert plates, and placed them with the dinner plates. Three cabinets of dishes were reduced to one.

He closed the cabinet door and faced her. "How's the knee?" He lifted the ice pack and probed the injured area with a touch as light as a feather. Strange sensations skittered around her knee as his fingers moved gently from place to place. She tensed her muscles reflexively, then groaned in pain.

"Relax, okay?"

She forced herself to relax. His gentleness soothed and stimulated simultaneously. Looking up, her eyes caught his, those eyes so like Richard's, yet so different. While Richard's eyes had been cold and unfeeling, never seeing beneath the surface, Trevor's were warm and kind and penetrating, like he could see into her soul. She didn't like the idea at all.

"The swelling's not as bad now," he said.

She tried to get up, but his hand on her shoulder held her down. "You shouldn't put any weight on it yet. Sit down." He crossed the room to the stove. "More tea coming up, only this time you get the Trevor Steele special, guaranteed to cure all your ills."

His attempt to make light of the situation brought a smile to his lips, and she saw he had the most outrageously, enchanting mouth. She watched him work around the kitchen. There was much more to this man than met the eye. She'd seen him in action with the two thugs—hard, callous, unyielding, tough. Yet with her he was kind and gentle and witty. He moved with a sureness and confidence that brought order to the chaos. She could almost forget the rest of the house was torn apart.

The kitchen looked much better thanks to his efforts. If she were honest with herself, she'd admit that having him here was helping her overcome her shock. The color of his hair reminded her of the rich, dark grain of mahogany. Up close, she'd seen the slight crook in his nose where it must have been broken. But she didn't want to be honest with herself. What she wanted, what she needed, was a new life without an ex-husband named Richard Tapp.

Trevor set a fresh mug of tea in front of her. The smell of brandy wafted beneath her nose. "Some special," she said, smiling and sipping the mixture, feeling it soften the edges around her nerves.

"I always aim to please." His teasing words came out in a soft, seductive tone that contrasted with the boyish innocence on his face.

In spite of herself, she laughed. He had a way about him that made her relax and tense up at the same time. "There's beer in the refrigerator if you want one. At least there was when I left this morning."

He opened the refrigerator and took out a beer. She gave in to a quiet sigh when she saw the burglars had missed the refrigerator. For some reason, seeing the inside of the refrigerator undisturbed gave her a mental boost.

"Could you get something for me before you sit down? I could be up and around if I had my knee splint." She hadn't worn the splint in months. She hated it. But right now it would make her mobile. Worse than wearing the splint, she hated feeling helpless.

His blue-gray eyes questioned, and she added, "I tore the ligaments about eighteen months ago." She fidgeted with the ice pack. Talking about her knee made her nervous, uncomfortable. She couldn't tell him the whole truth. He was an intriguing man but he was a stranger. "I twisted it falling down a few stairs." That was close to the truth. "The doctor says the ligaments are threadbare, but under normal circumstances they hold okay."

"Knee surgery's not that complicated anymore."

"I know. I plan to have the surgery soon. As soon as I save up enough."

He set his beer on the table, narrowing his eyes. She felt uncomfortable under his close scrutiny. "The splint's upstairs in the linen closet," she said. "Would you mind?"

After he left the room, she removed the ice pack from her knee and tried placing her foot on the floor. The knee throbbed slightly, but she could walk. She took a few steps and slumped back against the stove.

Who was she kidding about the surgery? For the past two weeks her life had been in the same state as this house—falling apart, crumbling, almost destroyed. And no wonder. Millions of dollars in stolen bonds!

Only when they were found would her life return to normal. Only then would the thugs quit breaking into her house, and the "official" strongmen stop hounding her. Why everyone thought she knew where the bonds were hidden mystified her. Richard was the one who had stolen them—and she hadn't seen him in eighteen months.

She hopped to the sink and squeezed the melted ice from the dripping towel. Where was Trevor? What was taking him so long? She must be out of her mind letting a total stranger roam around her house. Maybe she'd injured more than her knee.

A sudden thought made her grab the sink for support. What if Trevor Steele knew about the bonds? What if he was upstairs now going through her room? It wouldn't be hard to find that tiny piece of incriminating evidence.

With fear in her heart, she stumbled toward the stairs. "Find it?" she called loudly.

He appeared suddenly at the head of the stairs, and they walked back to the kitchen and sat down at the table. She wrapped the splint around her leg with shaky hands. By the time she'd fastened the Velcro straps, she had herself under better control.

One glimpse at his tall body relaxing in the chair told her, no, he wasn't some secret agent or con man after the bonds. She would be able to tell.

"How can I thank you for helping me?" she said. "I don't even know who you are."

He swallowed his beer. "Not much to know. I travel a lot. Business, pleasure, you know."

"Your wife must love that." The words popped out before she could stop and think.

"There is no wife."

Was that a hint of amusement sparkling in his eyes? She lowered her own eyes, embarrassed. Probing a stranger wasn't like her. "You're here on business?"

"In a manner of speaking." He slid the beer can back and forth between his hands. "I could hear your screams all the way from the road, and I thought someone might need help."

"And you just happened to be carrying a gun."

He felt the bulge in the back waistband of his jeans. "Does it bother you? I can put it in the car."

"No," she said, waving the gesture aside, "guns don't bother me. I just find it odd that the one person who comes to help me happens to have a gun handy."

"That makes sense." He took another drink. "I earned my spending money in college working as an armed security guard. I just never got out of the habit of keeping one around."

"Lucky for me," she said, wishing they had met under different circumstances.

"I'm surprised I could hear you screaming from such a distance, though."

"I'm not. When I was a kid I used to sit on the front porch in the warm weather and listen to the neighbors fight across the road. Except for the river, it's quiet out here. My house is not as far from the road as it seems. There's just not usually anyone around to hear you."

He walked to the trash bag and pitched his can in, then turned and met her with a casual look that contradicted the warning in his voice when he said, "Your visitors will be back, you know."

He was expressing her worst fears. Refusing to meet his eyes, she picked up her mug and sipped her tea. "What makes you say that?" When he didn't answer right away, she glanced up.

His expression became deadly serious. He braced his hands on the end of the table and leaned closer. "They left empty-handed."

For a moment he didn't move, and she felt pulled in by the intense expression on his face. His penetrating glare, the twitching jaw muscle, and the determined, straight line formed by his lips revealed an uncompromising, dominating man. The moment ended, and he turned away to knot the trash bag.

"If they were looking for something specific, they didn't find it. They failed to search everywhere. Like the refrigerator and two rooms upstairs. Even your garden-type thieves would come back out of spite. It's not safe for you to stay here alone."

She wasn't sure what he was suggesting, but she didn't plan to give him the chance to be more specific. With renewed determination, she stood up and straightened to her full height to put as much pride in her stance as possible. "This is my home, Mr. Steele. No thugs are going to force me out." She limped toward the front hall. "I'd like to be alone now, if you don't mind."

When they reached the front door, she held down her temper and said, "You've been a terrific help. Not many people would have stopped. I hope the rest of your stay in the area proves better than tonight." She held out her hand.

Long, wonderful fingers wrapped all the way around her hand. She felt the slight roughness of his skin, the firmness of his grip. Ripples of pleasure danced up her arm. She withdrew her hand quickly.

"Are you sure I can't convince you to spend the night with a friend?" he said.

He towered several inches above her. When she met his gaze, she once again had that odd feeling of going back in time. Richard's eyes. "No," she said, "but thanks for your concern. I'll be okay."

"I'll check around outside the house before I leave."

She closed the door and leaned her back against the frame before realizing she'd been holding her breath. She couldn't believe she was so drawn to a man she didn't know. And she must be losing what sense she had left to let him into her home. Hadn't she learned yet that too often people are not what they seem?

She took a deep breath and bolted the door, reminding herself she hadn't exactly had a choice. At least he had chased away the two men. What if he hadn't heard her scream? What had motivated him to stop and help someone he didn't know?

She pushed the questions away to concentrate on locking up the house. She hooked the front-door chain. She checked all the downstairs windows, carefully latching each one and pulling down every shade. Slowly, she made her way up-

stairs. Tomorrow, she'd get an alarm system put in, but tonight there was one more thing she could do to help herself.

Imagining the mess in her bedroom, she walked past it to
the room Richard had rented from her aunt before they were
married. She remembered clearly the little .22 caliber pistol
he used to keep in the top dresser drawer. Since he'd bought
himself a fancier handgun after Aunt Maude died, there was
a chance the old one was still there.

She opened the door. Boxes were piled on top of boxes.
Stacks of letters sat beside an open suitcase. Trevor was
right. The thugs had missed this room. She felt a crazy kind
of peace while she walked to the dresser through a maze of
junk left lying around by her and no one else.

She reached in the deep drawer and felt her way through
an assortment of odds and ends. There it was, in the back.
Her fingers slid over Richard's initials etched in the handle. She wrapped her hand around the pistol and took it
from the drawer.

She stared at the small gun, at her hand shaking ever so
slightly. Years had passed since she'd handled a weapon. She
smiled to herself, remembering the shocked expression on
Aunt Maude's face when she told her she'd joined the high
school rifle team. Joining had been an impulsive decision,
a pure act of rebellion. The club had been fun and games,
not like her situation now. Now the gun gave her a small
edge.

She scrabbled in the drawer for ammunition, wondering
what was becoming of her life when she needed a weapon to
protect herself in her own home.

TREVOR USED HIS HEADLIGHTS to search around the house
and the surrounding woods. When he was satisfied all was
clear, he crept down the drive at a snail's pace.

A few stars studded the sky, and the moon kept drifting behind thin clouds. The night sky gave off enough light for him to see there was no subtle place to park and keep watch for the night. When he reached the end of the drive, he backed up six feet, his decision made. No one could get past him if he blocked the drive. Carefully, he angled his car across the gravel drive, turned off the lights and opened the window.

Cool air brushed his cheek. In the distance he heard the Potomac River, its soft lapping at odds with the night's violence and the confusion roiling inside him.

Tonight had been a total bust in terms of the answers he wanted, but one question had been answered before it'd been asked—Casey was in danger. He thanked his lucky stars he hadn't put off seeing her for one more night. His buddies at the bureau weren't the only ones hounding her.

Barney picked up on the second ring.

"I'm glad you called," he said. "Of course, you could have managed to do it a little earlier."

"I couldn't quite make it," said Trevor. He rubbed his bruised ribs where the chair had landed.

"Confirmation came in right after I talked to you. We got another brokerage firm that found a series of bogus bonds when they ran their audit, only they were too late. Two point five million down the drain. This one's in Chicago."

"How the hell does a guy get by with this?"

"Hey, those bogus bonds are the best fakes I've ever seen. If he's a broker, like Tapp, all he has to do is replace the real bonds with bogus bonds when no one's looking. Or, if there's no broker involved, you can pay off the couriers and make the switch in transit."

"How many does that make now? That we know about?"

"Five. New York was luckier than Chicago. The only reason they picked up on the scam this quick was because of an unscheduled audit."

"Same as the others?"

"I'd bet money on it. We've got the lab working on it now. If you ask me, the same forger did all five sets."

"Damn! What about the Middle East tip? Did that pan out?" said Trevor.

"I just got the analysis an hour ago. As near as we can figure, eight out of the last ten terrorist bombings occurred within two weeks of each switch, so based on that and the other information we have, we know where the money's going."

"Chalk one up for Jake's snitch."

"It gives us a base, anyway. The analysts are trying to trace the funds backwards. If the wrong people find the bonds Tapp stole, they'll dump them fast. There's always some sucker out there who doesn't check the list of stolen securities. What have you found out?"

"Two bruisers broke into the Michaels place tonight."

"So, they know her connection to Tapp. That's not good. Anybody you recognize?"

Barney's words made him uncomfortable as hell. "No, but they mean business." He gave him a detailed description of each man.

"I'll feed it to the computer and see what comes up. Is Ms. Michaels okay?"

Was she? Her reaction to the break-in was normal enough —scared, angry, hostile, shocked, violated. But the way she'd clung to the wall when he tried to help her seemed extreme.

"She's shaken up and her knee's hurt," he said, "but she'll be all right. She's one stubborn lady."

He smiled slightly. She would've kicked him out with the crooks if she hadn't been hurt. That stubborn streak could cost her more than she realized. If she pushed these guys too far, she was begging for trouble. Their boss would send them back to look for the bonds. The guy couldn't afford not to.

"But?"

"I don't know, Barney. I'm missing something. She was really reluctant to talk about the injury to her knee. Check out the hospital records in New York about eighteen months ago, would you? She said she hurt her knee falling down some stairs."

"What does this have to do with the case?"

He wasn't sure. Solving Casey's problems was not part of his job, he reminded himself. He was here professionally to find the bonds and personally to learn about Richard. He had to remember that.

Right. So why did the attack on her bother him so much? He could still see her face, the blood drained from her cheeks, when she'd entered the kitchen. Even then, her bullheaded pride and stubborn independence had shown through in her eyes. They'd dared him to see her as less than capable of walking to that chair.

"I don't know, Barney. Call it curiosity. And another thing. Have there been any burglaries in her area lately?"

"That's a local problem, Trevor."

"But you can find out."

"I can make a call. You think she was working with Tapp?"

"I didn't see any evidence of that. Just the opposite. She needs surgery on her knee and says she can't afford it. The bathroom ceiling leaks. The wallpaper's peeling. The whole place needs a major overhaul."

"So maybe she's not interested in redoing old houses. Maybe she has other plans for the money."

Logic told him to listen to Barney. He already knew Richard was in on the bond scam, but he couldn't believe Casey was involved. His instincts were coming through loud and clear in that respect. He wanted to trust them.

"Don't worry. I'll keep an open mind."

He turned off the phone. Twisting the keys back and forth between his fingers, he mulled over Barney's update. Whoever was running this scam was feeling pretty confident to keep pushing like this. They were bound to make a mistake soon. He reached down with his free hand to readjust the seat. The gun lay within easy reach beside him.

And how in the hell had Casey gotten mixed up with all this in the first place? Tonight had not been the time to ask her about Richard, but he was working with a short fuse and extra time he didn't have. They would meet again soon, really soon, and when they did, he would have to establish some element of trust. Fast. Without it, she would never confide in him. She was a long shot at best. The bureau had been ready to pounce right when Richard Tapp's body was found. If Richard had lived a few more weeks, he would have been brought in for questioning. Barney would have bargained with him to disclose his partners and the whereabouts of the stolen bonds.

He didn't really believe Casey could help with the first problem, but Barney was right. There was good reason to believe she might know where the bonds were hidden. He'd make sure those guys couldn't get to her before he had a chance to ask some pointed questions.

He needed Casey Michaels. She was his job.

He pulled up his jacket collar against the evening's chill and thought about why he was sitting here in a cold car, his duffel bag full of clothes on the back seat, when he could be home in a comfortable bed. Hell, for that matter, why had he been living out of his car for the last three days?

He felt responsible for her, that was why, and the feeling surprised him. He hadn't felt this protective over a woman since he'd been married, and that was so brief and so long ago, it seemed part of another life.

He told himself this irresistible urge to keep her safe was a response to her vulnerability. If she was playing games with Richard's pals, she could be putting her life on the line. She was so isolated out here, anything could happen. Or maybe this protective urge came from the relationship she knew nothing about. It made sense if he thought of it that way.

He shook his head in disgust. Who was he trying to fool? He could rationalize his behavior forever and find every excuse known to man, but it boiled down to one fact—the thought of those scums manhandling her ate at his nerves. He'd guarantee those guys would never get a chance to touch her again.

Barney had to be wrong this time. Didn't he?

Chapter Three

Monday morning brought Casey relief from a weekend spent babying her knee and cleaning up the house. The knee splint made walking awkward as she climbed the concrete steps to the courier service office, but her knee needed the support for a couple more days.

Washington, D.C., on a sunny Monday morning, with its blaring horns and masses of people, infused new energy into her bones. The usual laid-back quiet of her suburban home in its country setting contrasted sharply with the throbbing pulse of the city. She loved the difference. She often thought of buying a condo here someday, but always with the choice of escaping to her riverside home in the woods.

Cars and trucks continued to jam the streets. She paused on the steps and checked her watch. Another half hour and the traffic would thin to a steady stream. Then her job as a courier would be easier.

She reached the midway point on the steps, and the door opened at the top. Victor Pernell, her boss, surveyed the street with a frown, turned up his collar and walked down the opposite side of the broad steps.

"Good morning," she said.

He nodded slightly and kept going.

She shrugged and continued up to the office. Aretha Ames, the only other female courier, sat at the couriers' desk sorting the pickup slips. The room was large, a former sitting room, with a brick fireplace on the inside wall. Sun streaks filtered through three long windows on the opposite wall, one striking Aretha's flawless cinnamon skin.

"What's the matter with Victor?" she asked.

"Just his normal wonderful self," said Aretha, twirling her curly black hair in circles around her finger. "He got a call from New York. His brother, I think. It was a rather loud conversation from this end."

Aretha glanced at the knee splint and pushed herself back in the swivel chair. "Hey girl, what happened to you?"

Casey looked down at the splint. No one at work knew about her connection to the bogus bonds scam, and she wasn't about to tell them, not even her good friend Aretha. And Trevor Steele, well, she couldn't quite straighten out all the conflicting emotions warring inside of her when she thought of the handsome, sexy man who'd rescued her the other night.

In a light, carefree voice she said, "Oh, these crooks tried to rob me."

"You were robbed!" She rushed around the desk.

"It's okay. I don't think they took anything."

"That's awful. Are you all right?" Her eyes were filled with horror.

Casey took a deep breath. She didn't want to upset her friend, and she really didn't want to call attention to herself. In the same carefree voice she said, "Really, I'm fine."

Aretha looked down at her knee. Casey's gaze followed. Continuing in the same vein, she said, "The truth is, this Prince Charming came to my rescue, and the crooks threw me against the wall so they could escape."

"You're kidding. Prince Charming?"

"I'm serious."

"Then you're really all right?"

"I just reinjured my knee. It feels much better today."

Aretha smiled. "In that case, do you think your Prince Charming has a friend? I'm not getting anywhere with Jon."

Their new supervisor, Jon Britt, was a little older than Casey and had joined the staff a month ago. She was withholding judgment on Jon. When Aretha had asked for her opinion last week, she had to admit she found him too guarded and aloof.

"If I see him again, I'll ask him," said Casey.

Now that they were past the robbery, she let down her guard. She took out the receipts from her out-of-town pickups on Friday and deposited them in the appropriate boxes.

Aretha handed her a new stack of slips. "You sure you want these? Shouldn't you be home with that knee?"

Casey took the slips from her. "It's okay. It's healing pretty fast, and you know how much I need this job."

"Now, how did I know this was a good day to bring you a present?" said Aretha, her smile filling her face. She walked across the room to the windowsill, picked up a potted plant and handed it to Casey. "For you. I repotted my aloe plants this weekend. Next time you burn your fingers making cookies—instant cure. Just break off a stem and rub the sticky stuff over the burn. It works like a charm."

"This is beautiful," said Casey, turning the plant in her hand. "Thank you. I'll make your favorite oatmeal cookies next time." She ran her fingers over the foot-long leaves, the flat sides smooth, the edges ruffled. "I'll keep it on the windowsill until I go home. It'll look great in my kitchen."

She returned the plant to its place, thinking about the burn incident Aretha referred to. Two weeks ago, when she was baking cookies, she heard the news of Richard's death on the radio. "Richard Tapp, the former broker under investigation for his alleged involvement in the multimillion-dollar bond scandal, was found dead this morning in an abandoned garage in the city's southeast end," the local newscaster said. "The police are calling his death a suicide." She'd stood in the kitchen holding the hot tray full of cookies until it burned her hand. Richard dead? Suicide? The shock, the disbelief, had numbed her. Since that day, nothing in her life had gone right.

"You had a special request for pickup this morning," said Aretha. "Some guy with the sexiest voice I've ever heard. He wanted only Casey Michaels, no one else would do, but I don't remember which one he was."

Casey skimmed through the slips. "None of them list a courier preference," she said. She reread the one from Daren T. Smith. "Probably old Smitty pulling a joke. I'll save him until last. He always likes to talk." She put the slip aside.

She'd been promoted to part-time national courier last week and was disappointed to see that Jon had left her the local pickups today. She sighed as she mapped out her route. Whenever she ran the out-of-towners, she worked longer hours and earned more money. Her need to build up her savings quickly was even greater now with her reinjured knee.

Friday, she had flown to Philadelphia on her first out-of-towner. Friday, the thugs had broken into her house. She'd tossed that fact around in her head all weekend. Because she had returned home so late, the two men had had time to snap the lock and force their way in. The house was torn apart before she'd walked in the door. If she'd come home at the normal time, she could have kept them out, or at least given them a damn hard time, she mused as she prepared to leave.

Two hours later out on the road, she found herself behind schedule. Road construction in Foggy Bottom had slowed her down for her first pickup. Now the traffic down Pennsylvania Avenue came to a dead stop because of an entourage of stately limousines. She tapped her fingers on the steering wheel in time to the music on her radio and waited.

She knew she shouldn't be impatient. And she shouldn't feel disappointed that she was right back on the streets of Washington one working day after her promotion. Jon had promised to coordinate the out-of-towners with her class schedule when he could. Yet today's reversal seemed to fit in with her other frustrations.

Like Trevor Steele. Two of the three mornings since the break-in, she woke up with Trevor's image taunting her. Trevor checking her swollen knee with a gentleness that made her remember his magic touch, that made her forget the pain; Trevor leaning across the table and warning her the thugs would return, and the overwhelming drawing power of his eyes. In her dreams, he never reminded her of Richard, but of a compelling man with a stubborn gentleness she found attractive. The dream fragments kept flashing through her mind at odd times like now, in the middle of traffic, adding to her other frustrations.

Forty-five minutes later, she found Collins & Company right where she feared it would be, in one of the worst sections of the city. Old, run-down brick homes with thick Georgian columns and scarred, wide porches lined the block. An old man, bald and bent, sat on the crumbling steps of a house with a profusion of spring flowers blooming in pots on the porch wall. The yellows and purples brightened an otherwise dreary scene. On the street corner ahead, a group of unruly-looking kids clustered together. They eyed her as she slowed the car to check the address of the last house against the one listed on her slip. The addresses matched.

Rather than back up and stop traffic on the narrow street, she drove past the house, past the teenagers, and circled around the block. She pulled into an empty parking space two doors up from her destination.

Before stepping out of the car, she took the miniature canister from her purse. Jon insisted every courier carry a Mace-like spray. "You have an obligation to protect not only yourselves, but what you're carrying," he told them. "Good policy," she muttered, glancing at the group loitering at the corner.

No one was manning the reception counter when she walked in. She pressed the little bell by the sign that read Ring for Assistance, and waited.

The room was filled with stacks of papers and manila folders on the two desks and along the side wall. Although the house was old, the room was clean and smelled of fresh paint. Two old metal radiators painted to match the cream-colored walls stood beneath the long windows.

Still no one answered the bell. She checked her watch and was turning to go when a sudden screeching sounded from down the hall. Goose bumps puckered on her arms. She held tight to the canister.

She called out, "Is anyone here?" and stepped loudly toward the noise. Each intentional clomp with her good foot took her farther from the front door. A second screech caught her unaware. The canister dropped with a crash and rolled down the hall. Cautiously, she stooped to pick it up, wary of taking her eyes off the hall for a minute. She called out again as she moved closer to the noise. "Johnny Quick Pickup. Is anyone here?"

The narrow hallway gave her the creeps. This section of the building had not been redone. Faded floral wallpaper covered the walls of the hall. At eye level every three feet, wall sconces hung unpolished and unused.

At last she reached a door with muted light shining through the frosted glass. She hesitated, her pulse racing faster, her patience thin. She was no one's fool, she told herself, but she had a job to do. Flexible part-time jobs were hard to find. She couldn't risk unemployment.

Determined to chase away this jittery feeling, she grabbed the knob and shoved at the door. It stopped halfway, and she met the door face first. She screamed before she could stop herself.

"What the hell?" The door slammed into her again. A large man in his early twenties crawled from behind the other side. "What are you trying to do, lady, kill me?"

She held her head with one hand and the canister with the other. Only the fact that this guy was crawling on all fours stopped her from bolting back the way she'd come. When he clambered to his feet, she had second thoughts. He stood at least six feet tall and probably weighed 230 pounds, all of it muscle, from what she could judge by the faded black T-shirt stretching across his chest and straining at his biceps. His jeans were ragged and smudged with black.

She stepped back, unsure if she could make it down the hall in time. The man spooked her. "I'm sorry. I must have the wrong address."

"Casey? Is that you?" Trevor's voice sounded from inside the room behind the stubborn object that had blocked the door.

"Trevor?" He stepped into view, and she felt the tension drain from her body. Unobtrusively, she pocketed the canister as she watched his face break into a breathtaking, spontaneous smile.

"Am I glad to see you. I expected you two hours ago."

"You have a pickup?"

Another time, in another place, she wouldn't sound so curt, but these were not normal times. Seeing him reminded her of too many problems she wanted to forget. She hadn't missed the way the blue deepened in his blue-gray eyes, and she couldn't help thinking of her ex-husband. Richard's eyes used to look like that whenever his emotions were at a peak. She shuddered. Ghosts from a not-too-distant past.

"Hold on one second." He turned to the other man. "Come on, Moose, let's slide the copier back against the wall. It should work now."

She couldn't recall teasing Richard once after they were married, but she remembered telling him early on that his eyes revealed more emotion in unguarded moments than any words he ever spoke. His eyes had held that same intensity the last time she saw him, but that night his emotions had been at opposite poles to Trevor's today.

As they muscled the machine into the corner, Trevor added, "Don't go away, Casey."

His washed-out blue jeans hugged his lower body as he moved around the machine and worked at angling it into position. He wore a white dress shirt rolled up at the sleeves. The ground-in grease across the front told her he'd been working on the machine for a while.

She checked her watch again and confirmed she was running later than ever. Jon would not be pleased. "I'll wait for you at the reception counter," she said. He sent her a quizzical look, his right eyebrow arched slightly above the left one. She averted her eyes and escaped down the gloomy hall.

The day was turning into a disaster. Completing her pickups would be difficult. Seeing Trevor confused her. It made her angry that he reminded her so much of Richard. And, when she wasn't angry, she felt other emotions she didn't want to deal with. She didn't need a man in her life right now.

He followed close behind her. "It's right here somewhere." He moved behind the counter and leaned over in a way that displayed the bunched muscles in his back. "Here it is."

He placed a brown envelope on the counter. Casey took out the receipt, and he signed it. "Where should I deliver it?"

"Probably says inside." A whimsical light shone from the depths of his eyes. Reluctantly, she felt drawn to him all over again. He leaned across the counter, his chin propped in his hand. "Anyone ever tell you that you have compelling blue eyes?"

The man was flirting with her, for God's sake. She ignored his remark and lowered her eyes. Opening the envelope, she felt self-conscious and put on the spot. She removed a single sheet of paper that said, "I'm starving. How about lunch?" It was signed "Trevor" in neat, bold print.

The note took her by surprise. She was near the end of her patience. "Why did you call if you don't have a pickup?"

She didn't like the way her heart beat faster just by her being in the same room with him. She didn't like the way her breath caught when she looked at him. Complications of this sort she could do without.

He slid around the counter to her side. His arm touched her arm, and she tried to ignore the little thrill of excitement from skin touching skin.

"You have to eat sometime. There's this nice, quiet little restaurant I know with a corner table for two just waiting for us. Or we could always get hot dogs and stroll around outside the Smithsonian. I'm game if you are."

Hints of soap and grease and after-shave suffused the air. She took the receipt, and, while shoving it in her pocket, she stepped back, hoping the extra inch would give her breathing room and relief from the frustration of being near him. "Not today," she said. "I don't have time." His insistence was pushing her patience too far.

She had to make up for the time she'd already lost. And forget trying to eat lunch while sitting across the table from him. Talk about compelling eyes. No, going out to lunch was out of the question.

"And here I thought you appreciated me. I'm crushed." A hesitant smile teased the corners of his mouth.

Twinges of guilt plucked her conscience. She pushed aside her frustration and said, "We'll do it another time, honest. Everything's sort of upside down for me right now, and I need some space. You may have saved my life the other night. I owe you for that." She toyed with her keys. "How about next weekend? Will you be in town that long?"

She could do it. With a little time and a lot of regrouping, she could box up her attraction to him and set it aside long enough to repay a debt.

He moved closer. His smile was gone. His eyes had turned a cold, stormy blue. "Next weekend? How about tonight?"

Why was he pushing? What difference would a few days make? She stepped toward the door. "I'm sorry, I can't."

"And I can't wait that long, Casey. I need to talk to you now."

Something in his voice pulled her back and stopped her from walking out. When she faced him again, he was moving toward the window, his shoulders tense, his hands clenched. What was going on here?

After a long, curious pause, he said, "Three weeks ago I received a letter from your ex-husband."

She gasped. The air choked her and made any speech difficult. "You knew Richard?"

He faced her across the room. "No. That's the problem. I didn't know him." He stood ramrod straight beside a desk, his arms at his sides. His piercing blue-gray eyes sent shivers down her back.

"There was another letter, too, one from Richard's adoptive mother." He paused again and looked out the window.

She scarcely dared to breathe for fear of shattering the delicate hold she had on herself. Tension gripped the air, almost visible in its stranglehold.

He crossed the room and stood opposite her on the other side of the counter and examined her every feature, carefully, totally, while indecision flickered across his face. He settled on her eyes and gave her a searching look that spoke of a need for trust and confidence.

He backed off a step. "Come with me." He walked around the counter and led her to an office across the hall. Gently, too gently, he closed the door behind him and faced her.

Sunlight caught his hair, turning dark mahogany to a deep reddish brown. For long seconds he stood perfectly still, his hand still grasping the doorknob, his eyes cautious, hesitant, captured by a corner of the room. Something in his eyes, in his rigid stance, made her brace herself. She wanted to run.

His eyes caught hers, and the idea of flight disappeared. Quickly, he shuttered them, but not quickly enough. Instinct told her this man was hurting inside. His vulnerability appealed to her, the contrast with his physical power making him dangerously attractive.

Instinct also told her he was strong and stalwart and a man of secrets. Yet, for some reason, he wanted her to hear what he had to say. And for some reason that escaped her, she wanted to listen.

His jaw clenched, his face devoid of emotion, he seemed to be weighing the wisdom of trust. She knew the second he decided to trust her. His face remained taut, his brow was slightly creased, but his jaw relaxed and he inhaled slowly, deeply, as if these were the most difficult words he would ever utter.

Finally, in a much too quiet voice, he spoke. "Richard was my brother. My twin brother."

Chapter Four

She stood there in his office only long enough to be polite. Her legs were shaking, her palms were damp. He was telling her they had to get together tonight. Inside, she was screaming. Why hadn't Richard told her he had a twin?

"Seven o'clock, then," said Trevor as she inched toward the door. She was frantic to escape.

She drove like a maniac away from Collins & Company, away from Trevor, and away from one more stinging piece of evidence that Richard's life with her had been a farce.

He'd lied about his family like he'd lied about his work. His lies had ruined their marriage—that and her own gullibility. Until that last day, she would have believed pigs could fly if he'd said so. She'd been so damn trusting, so naive. When would the sick surprises stop, the raw pain go away?

Uncomfortable with the memories, she shifted beneath the confines of her seat belt and sped through another yellow light, oblivious to the sun shining and the horns blaring. Never again would she allow someone to make such a fool of her.

It was early evening before she returned to the empty office to drop off her receipts and pick up her plant. Driving had placated her anger and frustration, as usual. She organized her receipts quickly and deposited them in the appropriate boxes. She didn't pay much attention to Jon's voice raised in argument behind the closed door across the hall until the door opened and Jon and Victor emerged. They stopped inside the doorway when they saw her, surprised looks flashing across their faces. Victor quickly recovered.

"Ask her yourself," said Jon. He glanced at her uneasily, then tried to mask his discomfort.

"Why, Casey," said Victor Pernell in a smooth voice. "What happened to your leg?" He stared at her splint, genuine concern showing through his wrinkling forehead. His bulbous nose grew slightly redder. His cigar smoke filled the air.

She picked up her plant and moved toward the couriers' desk to retrieve her keys. "Just an old knee injury. Nothing to worry about," she said.

"I'm sorry, my dear. I hope it improves rapidly," said Victor. He stepped aside to let her pass.

Victor was about fifty, she figured. His six foot frame carried a beer belly that spilled over his belt. He always spoke in smooth, soothing tones, in a voice quiet and controlled. In contrast, his small, beady eyes darted constantly from object to object, taking in everything around him. The habit annoyed her, for it was difficult to maintain eye contact with him for any length of time.

Jon seemed agitated, shifting from one foot to the other. In spite of a day's work, he looked as fresh as he had this morning in his dark slacks, blue shirt and conservative tie.

"Did you need me for anything, Jon?" she asked.

He glanced at Victor, then said, "Can you take the shuttle to New York on Thursday?"

"I have a class on Thursday, remember? This is not a good time to miss."

He turned to Victor, whose face betrayed no emotion. Victor said, "It was my understanding you were anxious to take the out-of-town pickups and deliveries."

"That's true," she said, "but only when they don't interfere with my classes."

"I see." Victor's eyes skipped from Casey to Jon to the desk and back to Jon. "You seem to have made a mistake, Jon. Schedule Gary for the New York trip, or better yet, send Rafi. He won't turn down the extra pay."

The confusion irritated her. She and Jon had thoroughly discussed which days she was free to travel out of town. She felt the extra pay slipping away from her. "Spring break is coming up," she said. "I'll be available any day that week for the out-of-town trips."

She detected a spark of interest in Victor's eyes as his flickering gaze settled on her for longer than usual. "You'll be available," he said. "That's good, my dear." Turning to Jon he said, "Make a note of that, Jon." He walked past her to his office and closed the door.

She turned to Jon for some answers. "We'll discuss your spring break tomorrow," he said. "I can see you're on your way home." He moved from the doorway and waited for her to leave.

Once she was in her car, she dismissed the odd scene in the office. She moved her seat back until her toe barely touched the gas pedal to force herself to go slowly. It proved unnecessary, since she drove toward home through bumper-to-bumper traffic, preoccupied with thoughts of Richard and Trevor.

She needed more time to digest the fact that Richard had a twin, not an identical twin, but fraternal. She was in no hurry to meet Trevor tonight. What could she tell him about a man who was part of a past she wanted to forget?

Examining every conversation with Richard she could recall, she searched for mention of a twin. Surely she would remember.

She nosed her car up to the log barrier separating the gravel drive from her house and cringed when she saw the tulip bed to her left, mangled beyond help by the thugs' van.

She wanted to hold on to the image and the anger it provoked as she put away the dishes and straightened the house. She didn't look forward to Trevor's visit or to rehashing her life with Richard. Yet she couldn't find fault with his need to talk about a brother he'd never known. What lingered beneath her frustration was Trevor standing by the office door, trying to hide his pain, and struggling with his need to trust her. His naked vulnerability tugged at her heart.

She went upstairs to shower. When she found herself puzzling over what to wear, arranging her hair up and then down, and putting on her favorite pearl earrings, she chastised herself. How could she possibly care what Richard's brother thought of her? She dismissed the possibility that her extra care had anything to do with him. She would tell the man what she could, and that would be that.

He arrived exactly at seven wearing pressed khakis and a tailored, long-sleeved, white shirt. His paisley tie was a striking combination of browns and blues with a sprinkling of red. When he entered the hallway, the light seemed to draw forth the blue in his eyes. She led him into the living room.

"The place looks good," said Trevor. "You've done a lot of work." He sat in Aunt Maude's favorite overstuffed chair, looking at the family pictures she'd reframed and rearranged on the end table.

His comment made her smile. It was a natural, spontaneous response, and it felt good.

He picked up a small snapshot framed in old silver without a glass covering. "Is this you?" She nodded. "And this must be your family. I see the resemblance. You have the same beautiful cobalt-blue eyes."

He was holding a picture of her mom and dad and little Anne. After all these years, she still missed them. "They died in a plane crash when I was twelve."

Abruptly, she stood up. "How about a beer?"

"Sounds great."

Feeling amazingly calm and energized at the same time, she took two beers from the refrigerator and searched the cabinets for the remaining steins that had belonged to her father. Recalling her family usually made her depressed or angry, but just having Trevor notice the pictures and take an interest in them made her feel good. Aunt Maude had always been careful to avoid any reference to her family. Richard had never asked.

This pleasant feeling couldn't last. He was being exceptionally cordial and polite and seemed as reluctant as she was to spoil the mood, but they had to broach the subject of Richard sooner or later. That was why he was here, she reminded herself, not to admire her home and her family pictures.

What she wanted most was to get on with their talk so he would leave. Having him in her home disturbed her. They seemed too cozy together. He fit in too perfectly. She was enjoying his company a little too much.

Worst of all, her senses vibrated with awareness. He smelled clean and fresh, with a slight scent of musk. His bass voice stroked the chords of her soul. If suddenly her beer were to taste like heaven's honey, she wouldn't be surprised. Everything about tonight—and him—plucked just the right notes to send her senses soaring. The invisible connection between them filled her with a calming excitement. She chuckled. The contradiction pleased her.

She found the steins and filled them with beer. It was too easy to forget who he was and why he was here.

Why was he here? Maybe he wasn't Richard's twin. All she knew was what he'd told her. Maybe this twin business was a bunch of lies, but what would be the point? Was he after the bonds? Everybody else kept bugging her about them. Maybe she was getting paranoid.

Her suspicions firmly in place, she picked up the steins to carry them into the other room, and met Trevor in the doorway. "Why don't we sit in the kitchen," she said.

They sat at the table, both of them avoiding the subject that had brought them together. Her new suspicions spoiled the ambience they'd enjoyed in the living room.

After an uncomfortable silence, she said, "Look, I at least owe you this evening for helping me the other night. There's no need for some strange tale about twins."

His face froze. He set his beer on the table a little too hard. He took an envelope from his pocket and handed it to her. "I received this three days before Richard was found dead."

Hesitantly, she fingered the envelope. A knot caught in her throat.

"Take out the letter, Casey."

She lifted her eyes to his. His intense stare made her shiver. Knowing she had no choice, she opened the envelope. Her last hope of finding this twin business a hoax died as she read the letter from Richard's adoptive mother recounting his adoption as a baby.

She paused after the first page. "How could anyone leave a twin behind?"

"Read a little more. Evidently, the doctors didn't think I'd make it because I wasn't gaining any weight."

She finished reading the letter, saddened at what she read. Memories of her own family crowded her thoughts. Had her family had secrets? Her parents hadn't lived long enough for her to discover any skeletons in the closet, and Aunt Maude would never talk about the obvious, much less the hidden.

"All those years, neither one of you knew the other existed. How could a mother do that to her son?" She looked at the date on the letter. "This is dated two years ago!" Not only had Richard been alive then, they'd still been married.

Wordlessly, he handed her a folded piece of white paper. She unfolded it gingerly. It was dated six days before Richard died. She recognized the handwriting immediately. For eighteen months she'd been trying to put her marriage behind her. All the pain and humiliation, all the guilt, came rushing back at once.

Trevor,
I need your help. I'm in too deep. Meet me at Dulles Airport Wednesday night, seven o'clock.

She had no doubt the signature on the note was Richard's.

She raised her eyes to Trevor. They both knew Richard had died that day. For a moment, she tried to imagine how Trevor must feel, his frustration, his curiosity, his mourning for a brother he'd never known. "I don't know what to say."

"Richard never told you he had a twin?"

"Evidently, Richard never told me much of anything." She pushed back her chair and walked to the sink. She kept her back to him and cursed herself for her snide remark. She had to control the anger simmering inside.

She sat back down. "I'm sorry. Let's try this again."

He was running his index finger around the edge of the mug. He sat tall and rigid, staring at the table. When he raised his eyes to her, she saw his frustration, his need, and she promised herself to tell him what she could. The anger would have to wait.

"What did he tell you about his family?"

"He told me he was adopted. As far as I knew, he was an only child." She clutched the mug as the anger became pain. "Before we were married, I heard him telling my aunt about a baby sister who died of crib death."

"What about his parents? Did he ever mention them?"

His eyes never left her alone. She sipped from her mug, remembering how disappointed she'd been when Richard's parents couldn't return to the States for their wedding. At least, that's what he'd told her. Every so often, when she asked about his parents, he would mention receiving a telegram or a letter. She realized now how little she knew about his family.

"I never met his parents," she said simply.

"Do you have any pictures, you know, a family album or anything?"

She thought of the few times she and Richard had taken pictures. There had been a small shoe box full of snapshots taken before they began commuting to New York.

"No," she said, "I threw them out."

He leaned back in his chair, his face neutral. She wished with all her heart she'd known about a brother a few months ago. Trevor would've appreciated the pictures.

"I guess you've read about the investigation in the paper."

She nodded. A choking knot in her throat prevented words from forming. She clutched the mug nervously. No one knew she'd seen those bonds in Richard's briefcase. How she wished she'd never set eyes on them. Not reporting the stolen bonds made her an accessory in the scandal. Would the guilt never stop?

"Any ideas about the missing bonds?"

"No, and these federal agents keep hounding me for information, as if I know where they are." She jumped from her chair and paced the floor, her hands in fists. "How should I know where they are? I haven't seen Richard in over a year. The divorce was final six months ago. After we separated, I never saw him again."

He downed the rest of his beer and replaced the stein carefully, almost conscientiously, on the table. "I need to ask you something else."

His voice had dropped a notch. Casey felt the tension radiating from him. She stopped her pacing and sat down opposite him.

"You were Richard's wife. You probably knew him better than anyone."

"I'm beginning to believe I didn't know him at all."

"Do you think he killed himself?" There was raw pain in his voice.

"Not in my wildest imaginings can I picture him killing himself." He'd been too shallow and too filled with his own importance to take his own life. Boy, she'd learned that the hard way.

A shadow of relief crossed Trevor's face. He caught himself quickly and brought his features under control, something Richard never would have done. By now, her ex-husband would be ranting and raving and screaming offensively about the nerve of some guy to wait until he was thirty-five years old to announce they were twins.

"It must feel weird to suddenly discover you have a twin."

"Had." He frowned. "Look, I can't change the past, but if it's possible to clear Richard's name, then that's what I want to do. If it's not possible, I can at least balance the scales and do something to offset everything negative I've read in the paper."

How could she tell him his brother *had* stolen the bearer bonds and replaced them with bogus bonds? Richard had bragged about the quality of the fake bonds when she confronted him with the stolen bonds she found in his briefcase. He'd gone on and on about how easy it was for a clever broker to make the switch, that anybody in his position would be able to pull it off, if he were as smart as he was. Trevor would eventually have to face the fact that his brother was a thief.

If only she knew where they were hidden, she could help Trevor and herself at the same time. She'd looked everywhere. She'd talked to everyone she could remember who might have known Richard. Not one of them could tell her a thing.

"I was thinking," she said. "The men who keep plaguing me are convinced Richard had a very large part in the scam. What if we found the missing bonds and turned them in in his name? Would that help balance the scales?"

"I'd like to find those bonds," he said, his eyes sharp with interest. "Finding them might help me figure out what happened to him that night."

"Maybe between the two of us, we can solve the puzzle. This is not an unselfish suggestion, I'm afraid. Once the bonds surface, the flow of traffic through my house will return to normal." Was that ever an understatement.

With a lifting of his eyebrow and a broad smile on his face he said, "I'm game. More than game. It sounds like the ideal solution."

His voice held the same excitement she saw in his eyes. She liked the way his eyes shifted from intense reflection to promising hope. Something told her she liked everything about this man a little too much. She prayed this crazy scheme wasn't a mistake.

"Did Richard take everything with him when he moved out?"

Casey set the crumpled letters on the table and shifted nervously in her seat. "I moved out," she said. "Richard and I were in New York at the time. This is my family's home. Richard rented a room here from my aunt. That's how I met him. After we were married, we lived here for a while, but after my aunt died, we shuffled back and forth between here and an apartment in New York."

"So there might still be some of his things here," said Trevor.

He was difficult to read, not like the other night when he'd been so helpful and kind. "Oh, they're here all right. There's a room upstairs filled with his things, but from what I can tell so far, all of it's from before we were married. I've been sorting through it a little at a time. He wasn't the most organized person in the world."

Trevor stood, jammed his hands in his pockets and strode to the window. "I know this must be unpleasant for you, dredging up a marriage you walked out on."

"Now just a minute." She didn't like his judgmental tone.

He spun around and faced her. "You did walk out on him."

His phrasing almost made her laugh. "In a manner of speaking, and for reasons which are none of your business."

She'd never regretted the dissolution of her marriage. Why should Trevor's obvious disapproval reignite her anger?

She would make no apologies for her divorce. Maybe some day she'd forget that last, angry scene when she confronted Richard about the stolen bonds stashed in his briefcase. Maybe some day she would walk down a flight of stairs without cringing. Without feeling his hands on her back—God, without remembering the excruciating pain of her head knocking the wall and her knee twisting at odd angles.

One thing was certain. She would never forget waking up in the hospital and waiting for Richard to arrive, nor the absolute devastation she'd felt when her memory returned and she knew she never wanted to see him again.

"Casey?" He stood before her. "Hey, I'm sorry. I was way out of line. Are you all right?"

She looked up. The color of blue-gray eyes was familiar. The tenderness and regret she saw were unfamiliar. "I think you'd better leave," she said, her voice cracking and strained.

He picked up the letters from the table. Anxiety traced his face. "Can we talk again? I think your plan would work."

She felt torn between her memories of Richard and her need to find the bonds. "I just…I don't know. I don't think so."

HE STOOD ON THE FRONT porch until he heard the dead bolt slide home. Knowing she was locked in for the night would at least give him a little peace of mind. He'd blown it again, damn it. Who did he think he was, tossing out remarks about her marriage? Why did the thought of her in another man's bed grate on his nerves so? What kind of brotherly thought was that?

He got in his car and rolled down the window. The clear, balmy night suggested warmer days to come, better days, when he could tell Barney to send in his resignation, days when he could work with the kids at Collins & Company full-time. Days when he would know who he was.

How *was* he supposed to feel about the discovery of a brother, a twin, for God's sake?

Slowly, he drove away from Casey's house. When he left this morning, escaping before she caught him playing great protector at the end of the driveway, he noticed an old dirt road beyond her drive on the opposite side of the street. Blocked by a metal wire extended between two rusty posts, the private road disappeared up a hill into a stretch of woods.

He steered left at the end of Casey's drive and looked for the hidden spot. He kept telling himself keeping watch was part of his job. She might need help during the night. Those crooks would come back sooner or later.

Fifty feet beyond her drive, he spotted the old road. After breaking the wire, he coaxed his car up the relatively clear passage lined with evergreens on both sides. An old car path veered off to the right, midway up, just as he'd hoped. He nudged his car along the overgrown path until it was hidden among the trees and bushes opposite Casey's drive. He turned off the engine. With the evergreens and underbrush, no one would see the car from the road unless they looked closely.

He moved the seat back and lowered it as far as it would go. At just the right angle he could see over the windshield through a separation in the trees. He made himself comfortable while his thoughts churned in confusion. He turned on the phone and it rang immediately.

"Where the hell have you been?"

"How are you, Barney?"

"How many times do I have to tell you not to turn off your phone? I've been trying to reach you for hours." He was yelling, his voice high-pitched.

Trevor could picture his balding head growing red with frustration and wet with sweat. He would be swiping at it with his monogrammed handkerchief.

"What have you found out?" Barney asked.

"Nothing yet," said Trevor. "I need a little time—"

"We don't have a little time. I tell you, I'm getting it from all sides—the insurance company, the Securities Exchange Commission. You name it, I've got trouble with it. Did you talk to the Michaels woman?"

"I don't think she knows anything."

"Listen to me, Steele. She's got to know something. There haven't been any burglaries in her area. Those men were after the bonds. I went over the surveillance reports again. I knew there was something familiar about her address."

"I know, Barney. I read them."

"Richard Tapp was there a week before he checked himself out."

He winced at Barney's casual reference to Richard's apparent suicide. "That doesn't mean she's involved." The words came out more harshly than he intended. Barney was silent for a full minute.

"Is there something you're not telling me, Steele?"

"No, the situation's under control."

"Have you searched the house?"

"Not yet." At Barney's explosive response, Trevor jerked the phone away from his ear.

"Hell, maybe I should forget this deal we made. Maybe I should bring Michaels in for questioning and stop lilyfooting around. Otherwise, somebody's going to beat us to it."

"Don't do that, Barney."

"You won't say that if the wrong people cash in those bonds. They're worth millions, Steele."

"Give me two weeks. Let me see what I can do."

"And Trevor." Barney caught him with the receiver halfway down. "The hospital records check out—eighteen months ago, New York. She was really bashed up."

Trevor hung up the phone. He pounded his fist against the steering wheel. Bashed up? What the hell did that mean? How bashed up can you get falling down a few stairs?

The car felt claustrophobic. He climbed out and walked back and forth along the pine-needled path. He shoved his hands in his pockets. Clear in his mind was Casey, her blue eyes sparkling, her hair falling forward, that perky little nose. Those long, slim, beautiful legs that made her height so graceful. Seeing her wear the splint was bad enough. He couldn't, wouldn't, let his mind picture anything worse.

He braced himself on the side of the car. The warm spring night and the moist breeze from the river helped soothe his anger. What had happened eighteen months ago to put Casey in the hospital?

He shook his head as if to clear away the past. No one would get to her now. Not the thugs, not Barney. Maybe his protectiveness was a little heavy, not exactly brotherly. But that was too damn bad.

CASEY HOPPED DOWN the stairs from the academic building's fourth floor as quickly as possible. The splint slowed her progress. Of all the nights for the elevator to break down. She reached the third-floor landing, moved to a corner and removed the splint.

She hadn't yet gone without the splint outside her house. She tucked it under her arm and tested her knee. The pain was minor, not crippling, like before. With a sigh of satisfaction, she picked up her backpack and continued down the stairs, one at a time, holding the railing just in case.

Most of the students passed her by, skipping down the steps without a backward glance, as anxious as she was to escape academia earlier than usual. Her anxiety stemmed from more personal sources. Business management was totally removed from the reality of her life at the moment.

How could she worry about long-term goals with the ghost of her ex-husband haunting her daily?

She hadn't heard from Trevor. She couldn't erase him from her mind, no matter how hard she tried. Her conscience nipped at her for even trying. He had a right to ask about his brother, and she had a moral obligation to tell him what she could.

If only the memories weren't so painful, she wouldn't feel so reluctant to talk to him. If only he hadn't sparked her anger the other night. How would it feel knowing a newly discovered twin was a suspect in a multimillion-dollar scandal? The whole situation must be tearing him apart.

Could the two of them find the bonds if they searched for them together? Maybe the daily reminder of Richard would be worth the price to bring closure on her past.

She reached the end of the stairs, sure she must be the last student from her class to leave the building. She pushed through the heavy metal door to an overcast night laden with storm clouds. A surprising gust of wind grabbed her when she rounded the corner. Pulling her Windbreaker and keys out of her backpack, she thought of the weather differences between here and home. If the sky was overcast here, it would be filling with fog at her home by the river. She looked around the empty campus. Adjusting her backpack, she walked a bit faster toward the parking lot, her keys in her hand.

As she unlocked her car, two men approached from the adjacent lane. Only when they got closer did she realize they were the men who had trashed her house. She dropped the keys in her pocket and gripped the spray canister.

They were three cars away, one following the other. "I don't have the bonds," she said. "Can't you see that? Do you think I'd be hanging around here if I did?"

She hoped reason would convince them to leave her alone, but they never faltered, never paused. As the streetlight struck their faces, she knew nothing she said would matter. Cold, staring eyes trapped her, the tall one's gleeful, the short one's blank.

She pulled the canister from her pocket and held it up so they could see it. "This stuff really hurts...."

A wicked grin took over the taller man's lean face as his hand whipped out. She stepped back and pushed the nozzle. A soft hissing sound escaped, and the man yelled and grabbed at his eyes, cursing and yelling, falling back against his partner.

With a pounding heartbeat, she jumped in her car, slammed the door shut, pushed down the lock, and turned the ignition key in one fluid motion. The tires squealed as she backed out of the slot and tore through the lot.

When she looked in her rearview mirror, she saw the van closing in behind her.

Chapter Five

The lines at the convenience store were backed up six deep.
Trevor grabbed a soda and a bag of chips, then stood in line
for his chili dogs. He felt restless, edgy, and shuffled back
and forth on his feet. The surrounding chatter dulled after
a moment, then faded into the background. His thoughts
turned inward to a growing discomfort, an itchiness that
disturbed him. Something was wrong, but he couldn't put
his finger on what.

He paid for his food, then elbowed his way to the door.
He was anxious for the evening to end. As soon as he followed Casey home from her class tonight, he was going to
confront her about Richard, come hell or high water.

A whipping wind grabbed him as he loped across the busy
intersection. The temperature had dropped several degrees.
He walked at a fast clip, his restlessness more unsettling,
urging him on.

Something was wrong.

He was almost running by the time he reached his car, and
he wasn't sure why. He took a bite of his chili dog and
looked around. And almost choked. Casey's parking slot
was empty.

His heart pounded as he scanned the lot. Where was she? He double-checked the sections where the streetlights were out, hoping to see her dark green Bug. Nothing.

Guessing which way she might have gone was impossible. Knowing Casey, she probably picked some backwoods road home that few people used. He jumped in the car and took the quickest route to the beltway, traveling at half his desired speed and cursing at each red light.

Once he reached the beltway, he drove at breakneck speed in and out of the traffic cluttering the four lanes, and then onto the interstate. The storm hit twenty minutes later. Rain pelted the windshield, obscuring his vision. A heavy gray fog settled in.

Was she safe? Had those two guys caught up with her after all? An unfamiliar fear gripped his chest. Damn! Without a doubt, she could outwit anyone on the road, but what happened when she reached the house? Could she make it inside? With her bad knee he doubted she could even make it to the door.

He shot off of Interstate 95 and melted in with the Route 1 traffic snaking its way between stoplights. Visibility improved as he left most of the fog behind on the interstate with the wind. The storm reduced to a steady downpour.

The fear wouldn't go away. Logic told him Casey would be perfectly safe. His instincts warned of danger. Logic. Instincts. He gripped the wheel tighter and hoped his instincts were off this time.

At long last he reached her turnoff and raced down the unlit, two-lane road. Darkness closed in around him. Barely visible hills spotted with muted lights blended in a murky blur as he sped down the road. The fog thickened as he got closer to the river, its ghostly wisps getting larger and catching in his headlights.

With the gas pedal floored, he took the first wide curve and saw faint red taillights ahead of him. Two sets. The lead car hugged the tight curves and flew ahead at each hairpin turn. He'd bet it was Casey. It had to be Casey. But who was driving the other one?

As the two vehicles approached a fork in the road, he watched in awe as the dark night swallowed the lead car. The lights had been turned off! No doubts now. That had to be her. No one but Casey would take that risk. The lady was a terror on wheels. He floored the accelerator, smiling to himself as the second car turned right where it should have turned left. She'd outfoxed them. For the moment.

This was his chance. He'd been gaining on them steadily. While the second car turned around to correct the wrong turn, he willed his car faster. He reached the fork just as they did, their headlights almost blinding him. He sliced off their advantage and zoomed ahead.

Visibility was bad. He strained his eyes for movement ahead. Two high beams caught him in the mirror just as his headlights picked up Casey's car through the lazy fog. She was approaching the turnoff to her house. He increased his speed, aware that he must come to an almost complete stop to make the left turn onto her drive.

He caught up to her car a short distance from the drive and flicked his lights off and on to signal her. It didn't work. She continued to zigzag down the middle of the road, continually swerving to the left and right. He trailed right behind her, the rain washing his windshield, the road wet and slick.

Abruptly she slowed as she approached the turnoff to her house. He let up on the gas and noted the headlights coming close behind him. He slowed to ease his car onto her drive. At the last minute, Casey hit a sharp left and cut him off. Sure that he was going to hit her, he jerked the wheel to his left and, with a crunch and a thud, his front end slid into the gully. His head banged against the side window, momentarily disorienting him.

Seconds later a dark van whipped past him onto the drive.

CASEY JAMMED on the brakes and jumped from the car. Rain smacked her in the face. Wind whipped at her hair. She heard the van screech to a halt in the clearing behind her.

It was just a short distance to the house. She could still make it. Keys in hand, rain running down her neck, she scrambled over the gravel toward the front porch. The van doors slammed shut behind her. Wishing she could run, wanting so badly to turn and find them gone, she pushed herself to move faster. She ignored the slippery gravel, the new pain in her knee.

She thought she was home free when she started up the steps. Too late she remembered the warped board near the top. She slipped, her arms flailing, her keys flying. Her knee crashed against the edge and her leg collapsed. She fell, barely stopping herself from tumbling into the mud. Clutching her knee, she doubled over in pain. Water cascaded through her hair, down her arms, everywhere.

The two thugs were too close. She heard their shouts, their heavy footfalls. She pounded her fist on the step, totally frustrated. Defeat descended on her like a cloud. She looked up through the hazy fog to see the two men leaning against her car, the shorter one smirking and dripping rain from his belly, the taller one licking his lips.

A bullet shot cracked the air. "You guys got a problem?"

Trevor! His voice yelled from across the clearing. Where had he come from? Renewed hope surged through her.

The men spun around to confront him, then gawked at each other for several seconds. The short, pudgy one finally said to his partner, "Boss don't want no trouble."

The taller man raced to the van, then sneered back at his partner. "Don't stand there. Move it." They backed up in a shower of mud and gravel, then wheeled around and faced Trevor.

She watched in horror as the four-thousand pound van challenged him, dared him, machine against man. She wanted to leap to her feet and knock him out of the way, block the van, do something, because there he stood in a shooting stance, stubbornly refusing to move, his gun aimed at the van.

The revving of the engine, again and again, sent out exhaust clouds to mix with the fog. The van leaped forward suddenly, pointing straight at Trevor. The sharp blast of the gun made her heart triple its pace. Six feet from him, the van cut to the right and barreled down the drive.

He never moved, not even an inch. Was the man crazy, or just stupid? Her shoulders collapsed as the tension drained and with it what little resistance she had left.

The van lights disappeared from sight, and Trevor ran toward the porch. She tried to erase the vision from her mind, to dislodge the lump clogging her throat. His voice exploded before he reached her. "Where in the hell's your knee splint?"

"I didn't need it anymore, all right?" She stared at the gun, mesmerized by the soft glint from the handle as it caught the porch light. Richard had kept his gun in the glove compartment, the same one she'd dug out of the spare bedroom and put in the downstairs hall drawer the other night.

Guns didn't bother her, but crazy thoughts raced haphazardly through her mind as Trevor approached, as she stared at the gun, thoughts that made no sense—Friday night, skeet shooting, her flight to Philly—all of them an attempt to mask the one dominant image she couldn't face: Trevor standing ready to shoot, the huge van speeding toward him, and worst of all, the image of him broken, torn, crushed beneath the van's wheels. But here he stood in the pouring rain with his hands on his hips and a scowl on his face.

"You ask for trouble, you know that?" he said. "Anybody ever tell you you drive like a race-car driver? What are you doing, trying to win the 500?"

Anger surfaced, her only remaining defense. "You are an idiot! You could have been killed. And for what?" The lump in her throat choked her, the rain in her eyes blinded her.

Rain streamed down his face as quickly as the mix of emotions flittering across his features. Frustration, surprise, confusion, and a fierce glint she couldn't decipher. He shoved the revolver in the back of his waistband and sat on the step, totally ignoring her outburst. "Let me see."

The fire in his eyes softened as he placed his hand gently on her kneecap. His cool fingers seemed to absorb the heat radiating from her injury. "It's already swelling, but you'll live to drive again." His dark, wet hair glistened in the glow of the porch light. "Can you walk?"

His hand wrapped around her forearm, coaxing her off the step. She jerked her arm away, determined to get up on her own.

Tiny smile lines tugged at the corners of his mouth. "Anybody ever tell you you're the most stubborn..."

"My business is not your business, Mr. Steele." Remnants of fear for him fueled her anger and made her strike back.

"That's where you're wrong, sweetheart."

"Just what are you doing here, anyway? Twice when I need help, you magically appear. What's going on, mister? And don't tell me you just happened to be passing by. I might be gullible, but I'm not stupid. Why are you here?"

Trevor paused, then raced up the steps. "First, we get out of this rain. Then we'll talk."

He was right. There wasn't a dry spot on her. Her questions could wait. She scooted up the steps on her bottom. Catching hold of the porch post, she pulled herself to a standing position beside him.

"My keys, Mr. Steele? They're in the bushes. Perhaps, if it's not too much trouble, you could find them? Otherwise, we'll have to break in and trip my new burglar alarm, and I think I've had enough excitement for one night."

"And here I thought the excitement was just beginning." He winked at her and jumped off the porch to look for the keys.

She rested all of her weight on her good leg. Her anger ebbed as the blood rushed to her knee and she leaned against the post, willing the pain to stop, the nausea to pass.

"Here they are, the keys to heaven," said Trevor, smiling and chuckling and waving the keys high above his head. Rain rushed from his hair, his chin, his jacket. He took his time climbing onto the porch and then said, "I'll unlock the door. Hold on."

"I'm holding, I'm holding." She forced the words out between clenched teeth that wouldn't stop chattering. She held tightly to the post and turned her face from the sheeting rain. The rough wood grazed her cheek.

"Come on," he said. In one swooping motion he lifted her up and walked through the door.

She wrapped her arms around his neck automatically. Her head rested on his shoulder. She knew she would reject this special feeling of safety under normal circumstances. She'd felt safe and protected with Richard at first, too, and look how that had ended. Nevertheless, she wasn't about to walk, and based on his firm grip, he wasn't about to put her down.

She let the strange excitement flow through her body when her hand met the back of his neck, when her head rested so close to his heart she could hear its steady thumping. Heaven, indeed. He carried her through the hall. Still, he didn't put her down. He held her closer and marched up the stairs, down the short hall, and into her bedroom.

He lingered in the middle of her room, his chin snug against her head. "You're soaked."

She leaned her head back and looked into his eyes. They looked for a moment, mere inches apart, as if secret messages flowed eternally between them. "You may put me down," she said, fighting to hold on to her anger in self-defense.

"All right." His voice was soft and seductive. He glanced around the room, then set her gently on the dressing table chair. "You need some dry clothes." He stood solid and sure, his rugged features in total sync with the fresh rain dripping from his hair. He looked delicious.

Embarrassed and uncomfortable with her thoughts, she peeled off her jacket. Facing danger seemed to produce strange reactions in her. Delicious? Richard's brother? Forget it. "Just toss me my robe from the closet."

"Don't be a fool, Casey. You can't stay here."

Balancing on her good leg, she stood up and glared at him. "I can take care of myself, thank you, and my house. My new alarm system works fine. They won't sneak in again. In a couple of days, my knee will be fine. And I put Richard's little gun in the downstairs hall."

"Oh great! Now the lady's got a gun."

"That's right. And I do know how to use it." She limped to the bed and stood before him on both feet, her irritation building, her frustration mounting. Poking her finger at his chest, she said, "Listen one more time. I can take care of myself. I'm not leaving. You, however, *are*."

He came closer, amusement tugging at a smile. "Let's look at this another way, can we? The men will be back. That may be the only point we agree on. You know the gun won't do you one damn bit of good. If nothing else, you're determined to protect the house." He moved to the window, his back to her as he shrugged his shoulders. "There's only one solution."

"And what's that?"

"I'll have to stay."

"Yeah, right. What a jerk." She almost regretted the words as soon as she said them. It irritated her that he could be right. Until her knee improved, she couldn't move too quickly. What if they tried to break in during the night? Even if she kept the gun upstairs, she might have trouble finding it if she were awakened from a deep sleep. Could she use it if she had to? Probably not.

"I'll ignore that statement," he said. "Just direct me to a pillow and a blanket, and after I get you settled, I'll make myself comfortable on the sofa."

She didn't like the vision of him stretched out on her living room sofa. "Are you deaf? You can't stay here!"

"Have it your way." In three quick strides he was across the room and picking her up before she could stop him. And laughing, the man was laughing. "Let's go."

"Put me down." Her irritation had grown to hurricane proportions. She struggled to get free, to escape the warmth of his body touching hers, to deny the heat of her own body responding to his. Her struggle was in vain.

"Your choice," he said. "You leave the house, or you take me." His voice was light while his eyes glinted in amusement.

"All right, all right. You can stay." There. She'd said it. "Just put me down."

With deliberate slowness, he lowered her to the floor. "Don't move." He left the room and returned with a towel that he tossed to her, along with her robe. "Need any help?"

"No. Not at all." When he remained fixed to the spot, she added, "Would you leave, please? I can manage just fine."

His eyebrows lifted, a smile spread across his face. "Ten minutes is all you get. Unless you decide you want help."

Chapter Six

The door closed, and she wrestled with her own irritation and frustration for giving in to his demands, but underneath the frustration was the utter amazement that he seemed to care enough to be such a domineering pain in the neck.

But while she shed her wet clothes, an odd sort of emptiness filled the room, which struck her as rather strange. He was the first man to enter her bedroom since her marriage had ended. She thought she should feel relieved to be alone, if only for ten minutes, but she didn't.

She thought of the two men she'd dated in the past eighteen months. When she first got her job, her former supervisor arranged a dinner date for her with his cousin. The guy had been late picking her up, and then she'd ended up paying the bill because he'd misplaced his credit card.

The other guy she'd met at school. His idea of a grand evening was attending a lecture on the geophysical probability of increased seismic activity along the eastern coast of the United States. Three days later he'd continued to rave about the lecture. Neither man had appealed to her, but Trevor Steele was another matter. If he wasn't Richard's brother, she'd be tempted to compromise her newfound independence.

True to his word, he knocked on her door ten minutes later. Looping the final knot on her robe sash and finger-combing her dripping hair, she told him to come in. He'd flung a towel over his shoulder. In one hand he carried her knee splint, in the other a steaming cup of tea. The aroma of cinnamon and spice filled the room as he carried the tea to the dresser.

He must keep clothes in his car, she thought. In place of his wet clothes he wore dry jeans slung low on his hips. A deep blue T-shirt drew out the blue of his eyes. His wet hair was brushed into place, curling slightly down his neck. He looked one hundred percent male, and for a second she forgot to breathe, he looked so outrageously handsome.

He approached her and took her by the arm. "Here," he said, leading her to the bed. "Sit down. You want to take it easy on that knee."

She started to protest but decided it was easier to take his suggestion. Having family around, even though that family was Richard's brother, felt comfortable, secure. He surprised her by sitting down behind her, the towel in hand. She moved the pillows to make herself more comfortable, and he said, "Keep still a minute, will you?"

He draped the towel over her head, and with just the right amount of pressure, his fingers massaged her scalp so the towel could absorb the excess rainwater. The feel of his fingers was normal enough at first. The anxiety of the last few hours drained from her body as she closed her eyes and settled back against him. As she began to unwind, her irritation faded.

Slowly, gradually, the rubbing changed to a sensuous, rhythmic kneading that felt like heaven's caress. A new kind of tension was building. Her skin tingled as his hands worked their way back and forth and over and around. She closed her eyes and leaned into him completely, her senses awakened, her body aroused and receptive to his hands. The steady beat of his heart thumped against her back. Even through their clothes, his heat seared her body.

A whirlwind of sensations filled her mind, as she absorbed the pleasure he was giving, when, without warning, his hands stilled.

Abruptly, he stood up and walked to the dresser. "I better get out of here. And your tea's getting cold." He set the cup on the nightstand, then pulled down her comforter, and helped her move to the head of the bed. He smelled fresh and clean, like the wet, woodsy smell outside her window.

"I appreciate all of this." Nervously, she sipped her tea and watched him reach down and pull the sheet up higher. "You never did answer my question."

"What's that?"

"How you happened to be in the right place at the right time. It couldn't be coincidence, especially tonight."

He pushed away from the bed and walked across the room, his back rigid, his shoulders thrown back, but his face looked like a picture of innocence. "I've been following you."

Oh, this was just great. As if she didn't have enough problems. "Why? You just couldn't stay away from my exciting life, is that it?" She sat up straighter. "Or maybe you figured if you stuck around long enough you'd get to play Joe Hero one more time. Well, mister, your time is up."

His face was set in rigid lines of determination. "Now hold it just a minute. Let me have my say." She took a deep breath and waited for some cockeyed story. "I'm a loner, Casey. I'm not used to needing anyone's help. The other night you suggested we might help each other by looking for the bonds. And then you kicked me out."

"I did not kick you out."

"Asked me to leave. Same thing. The truth is, I need your help, and it's killing me to ask for it."

His comment made her smile inside. "Following me around in secret is a funny way to show it."

"You left me no choice."

"Why are you so anxious to find out about Richard's death? I know he was your brother, but you never even knew him. I would think you'd want to know what he was like when he was alive. And clearing his name? You don't even carry the same last name. How could the bad publicity affect you?"

She was pushing and she knew it, but she had to know why he kept popping into her life like some Prince Charming with nothing better to do.

His hands clasped behind his back, he paced the floor like a trapped animal. "You're right," he said. "The accusations can't damage me, especially since no one else knows he's my brother."

As he crossed and recrossed before the dresser lamp's glow, his features were illuminated one minute, then thrown into shadow the next.

"I lived in a lot of foster homes as a kid, but the place where I lived the longest was the Adams's. Their place wasn't much, a big old white house with drafty rooms and threadbare rugs, two acres of land full of field mice and ticks."

"Trevor, what's the point here?"

He paused in his pacing, visibly masking the myriad emotions crowding his face. "It's the brothers I remember most, that's the point. They were eight and ten."

Her curiosity peaked. "How old were you?"

"I was nine. I spent four years pretending that Carl and Curt could be my brothers."

"Did they exclude you?"

"Yes, but what I remember is how special they were to each other. They stuck together like Siamese twins. They stood up for each other. Through a nine-year-old's eyes, they were the insiders and I was the outsider."

"So you were jealous. That's understandable."

"They were family, even if their old man was a tyrant. They were important to each other. If Carl needed help, he went to Curt, and vice versa. They covered for each other. That's how they survived the old man's beatings."

His eyes darkened to a deep blue. He was silent for so long she thought he might have forgotten her. The man was driving her crazy.

She wanted to say something, anything to break the tension surrounding him, but she didn't know what. Aunt Maude had never beaten her, but she'd kept an emotional distance that made Casey wonder if she loved her. Unlike Trevor, she'd spent twelve years with warm, loving parents and a precocious little sister. The relationship she'd had with little Anne was firmly planted in her heart. Their love spurred her on, even now.

"It doesn't sound like your model family," she said. It seemed like a roundabout way to explain why he'd been following her, but his story intrigued her.

"I survived. Your place reminds me a lot of the Adams's. There was this great stream that ran through the woods a few miles from their house. That was my escape, my secret. It's probably the reason I lasted there as long as I did."

She could identify with what he was saying. Hallowing Point with its woods and river and wildlife and trees had always had the same effect on her. No matter how silent Aunt Maude became when Casey was a child, she merely had to walk out of the door and down to the river to feel alive again.

"Yes, I can see why Hallowing Point reminds you of that." She paused, then added, "It has the same effect on me."

The fact that they both needed something in their lives like Hallowing Point made her feel dangerously close to him. She took a deep breath and pushed the closeness away. She didn't want to know more about this man.

And she couldn't keep the irritation from her voice when she said, "Why are you telling me this?"

He walked to the dresser and picked up a photo of her and little Anne. His jaw muscle tightened as he examined it. "I grew up as an outsider watching family make a difference. Maybe if Richard and I had met, I could have helped him. Maybe if I'd known him ten years ago, five years ago, I wouldn't be reading about Richard Tapp, the guy involved in the bond scandal. Family can make a big difference."

"Let me get this straight. You're saying the bond business is *your* fault?"

"I'm not talking about fault, just possibilities."

She shook her head in wonder.

His eyes burned with a clear intensity in the lamp's soft glow. "Look, Casey, I don't know if I could have made a difference, but I want to find out what happened to him, and I don't think I can do it without your help. He was my family. It's that simple." A vulnerable look crept across his face.

Having grown up with Aunt Maude, she knew how it felt to feel vulnerable, to need the help of someone reluctant to give it. Aunt Maude had always been reluctant to respond to her needs. She'd had to learn to deal with her own problems, and part of that had included being honest with herself.

And in all honesty, what she felt right now for Trevor went beyond empathy and compassion. He stirred feelings in her she'd never expected to experience again. At times there seemed to be an uncanny connection between them, some meeting of the minds that was foreign to her. He seemed to sense her needs, just as she sensed his, and that frightened her.

Her instincts told her he was not like Richard, but instinct had also led her to marry a man who took her love and trust and threw them to the wind. Hadn't she vowed never again to let a man take advantage of her? Who better than Richard's brother? How could she trust her instincts where he was concerned?

She hated the battle going on within her. Her instincts told her one thing, her heart told her something else. In spite of her reservations, she knew in her heart she could never turn him away.

"All right," she said. "We'll try."

She watched his features relax and his eyes brighten in a smile, as he stood and sauntered across the room to the door. "We'll find the bonds, Casey, and I'll figure out what happened to Richard. You'd better get some sleep now, though. We'll talk in the morning." The door clicked softly behind him.

She collapsed on the pillows, exhausted from too many sleepless nights. Dear God, she hoped this wasn't a mistake. Even if she knew right now that they could find the bonds, she would still have to grin and bear it, as Aunt Maude used to say, because working with Trevor, seeing him every day, just knowing he was downstairs on her sofa for the night, had her strung tighter than a bowstring, and she had no intention of letting herself snap again.

HE COULDN'T SLEEP. For the hundredth time he turned over on the sofa and hoped the shift in position would help shift his thoughts.

His mind reeled; he visualized a picture that was a mish-mash of Casey, the letters, Richard, the Adams, but always of Casey. That beautiful lady with her sexy smile had a way of drawing him out by antagonizing him to the point of frustration, and he had a way of jumping right in.

He pictured her long, lanky body in bed surrounded by the mounds of pillows, her robe slightly askew, her creamy white breasts partially revealed. A man could confuse his priorities if he hung on to that image for long.

He tried to block it out, but another one took its place—Casey, with a forlorn look on her face, her shoulders slumped, the rain cascading through her hair as she sat on that step facing the crooks. He drew in a deep breath. Remembering those guys leaning against her car just waiting to get at her brought on its own anxiety.

What did they expect to gain by going after her? Could she know anything about the bonds? If she did know where they were hidden, she was a much better actress than he imagined. Why sit on them? Why not take off for parts unknown? Except for the house and school, she didn't appear to have any obligations or connections in the area.

Maybe she was waiting to finish school, but if she went underground and assumed another identity, the degree would be useless. Everything was connected—Casey, the letters, Richard, those crooks. He just needed the right key to unlock the answers.

Maybe she figured another two months wouldn't matter, that Richard's cohorts wouldn't wise up before then. He rolled over again and tried another position, knowing his thoughts were ridiculous. Obviously, they'd wised up already. Whoever wanted those bonds wouldn't quit until they surfaced. They must be convinced she had something to hide. Since they couldn't find them, maybe they thought they could force her hand.

That had to be the reason for their harassment. That would explain why they'd turned tail and run so easily—they were trying to frighten her into cashing the bonds.

He shifted on the couch, more uncomfortable than ever with the direction of his thoughts and the inherent conflict involved. She could have valuable information about the bonds. If so, that made her an accomplice. Hell, maybe she'd even worked out a deal with Richard to pull off the double cross.

On the other hand, he felt responsible for her. She was Richard's wife. He owed it to his brother to protect his widow. But did that hold true even if his widow was involved?

Damn! He sat up and stretched his cramped arms. The house was so quiet and still, he could hear the steady *plunk, plunk* of rainwater hitting the front porch. A few birds were awake, squawking back and forth. He switched on a lamp and read four-thirty on his watch. So much for sleep.

He pushed himself up from the sofa and stepped into his jeans, then walked over and raised the window higher. The slight breeze blowing the curtains from the sill smelled of last night's storm as it washed his face.

He remembered too vividly carrying her upstairs in his arms, her wet body against his, her arms clinging to his neck. He could still feel the imprint of her back against his chest when he dried her hair, when his body burned for things that couldn't be, and he had to leave her before doing something he'd regret.

He turned from the window. Last night had wiped his mind clean of everything but her. This wasn't helping him.

He tried to clear his thoughts as he pulled on a navy T-shirt. Damn, he'd forgotten to call Barney. His boss would once again be on his case.

Now, why hadn't he called him last night when he grabbed his duffel bag from the car? Waiting for the rain to stop before checking out the damage to his car was understandable, but how difficult would it have been to connect the phone?

He definitely was not functioning with all his faculties. It was time to get back on course.

As he walked along the gravel drive toward his car, the light from the porch followed in splintered shadows, dim but adequate until he rounded the first curve. The fog had blown itself away during the night. Rivulets of water murmured on both sides of him, draining off the storm in a steady procession to the river. He met the sweet morning smell of wet needles and decaying leaves halfway to the road and paused for a minute to let the smells surround him.

There was no doubt Hallowing Point held that special peace he'd savored at the stream. The smells were the same. The sounds were the same. Even with the conflict raging inside of him, the place offered a quiet strength.

He reached the road and found his car where he'd left it. The bright moon and star-filled sky gave off enough light for him to see that the damage was minimal. Other than a dented front fender and a jammed left door, it appeared structurally sound. If he could straighten the wheel, he might be able to force it back out of the gully.

Several attempts later, the car bumped backward onto the road. He let the engine idle while he looked again for damage. He was running his hand over the dented fender when he heard a car approaching from beyond the private road entrance, but when he searched the shadows, he saw no headlights.

The engine's putter grew louder as he continued to check the car. He looked up the road and saw the vehicle coming closer, a mere shapeless form in semidarkness. Its speed increased, then slowed to a crawl. High beams flashed before him just as he realized it was the van.

He rushed to get into his car through the passenger door. He had no intention of letting these guys escape twice.

Chapter Seven

He wasn't fast enough. As the van came even with him, it swerved to the right to crush him against his car. He jumped to the side just in time and let the curses fly. The van sped down the road.

Furious with himself for letting down his guard, he scooted over the front seat, turned the car around in Casey's drive and raced down the road after them. These two owed him some answers, and he intended to get them.

He could see the twin light beams speeding down the road and swerving around the curves. He put the pedal to the floor and pushed the car for all its worth, his anger simmering, his concentration intense, so intense he almost ignored his own thoughts.

Something was worrying around in his mind, some obvious point he'd missed. Then the obvious hit him. He'd seen only one man in the van, the driver. No one was sitting in the passenger seat. Where was the other guy? What if the driver had intentionally lured him away from the house?

An image flashed before his mind, the tall guy prancing down Casey's drive, cocky as hell that the setup had worked. And Casey, alone, unknowing.

He slammed on the brakes. Dousing the lights, he backed up to a ditch and maneuvered the car carefully to turn around on the road. The lack of light made the job twice as difficult.

He ignored the rear end tilting down and the tires spinning as they fought to grab solid ground. He had to get to Casey. He had to check the house, the property, the road, and make sure she was safe. It was part of his job, he told himself, not believing it for a minute.

With one final twist he straightened the wheel and sped back toward the house. Crazy thoughts skipped through his mind. What if she'd gone out? What if he'd left her alone overnight? Those thugs had been waiting to pounce like jackals.

He careened down the drive and raced into the house, then took the steps two at a time to the second floor. He paused outside her bedroom door. All was quiet. He didn't want to alarm her by bursting in, but he had to see for himself that she was okay. Slowly, he turned the knob and pushed the door open.

Moonlight streamed in the window. The room looked the way he'd left it last night, the closet door slightly ajar, the teacup on the nightstand. His heart slowed its beating.

His eyes strayed to the bed. She lay sleeping on her side, her bad knee propped on an extra pillow, her shoulder-length hair splayed on a pillow beneath her head. A sliver of light caught her hair, highlighting a hidden red the color of a robin's breast. She looked absolutely beautiful.

He walked soundlessly across the room, avoiding the bare floor by stepping from one scatter rug to another. He peered inside the closet.

Casey mumbled something in her sleep and turned over, and Trevor backtracked quickly, not wanting to wake her, and definitely not wanting to startle her. The shocks she'd endured in the past few days had exhausted her enough to keep her from waking easily.

Satisfied the room was empty, that no harm would come to her, he tamped down the burning urge to take one more glimpse at his brother's wife and left the room.

After one last scan of the house and the surrounding woods, he drove down the drive to check the road. The sun was rising in the east, lighting the sky and the tips of leaves. There were no signs of any vans or thugs.

What if he hadn't stayed last night? What if those guys thought he'd left? They would have thought she was alone and then tried again. In effect, his ditched car had kept her safe.

A new idea fought its way through his mind. He took a quick turn to the left, turned right up the private road and eased his car over the ruts and through the puddles to its former place opposite Casey's drive. He pulled out his gun from under the seat. His idea might work.

He climbed down the slight incline and looked back into the trees and brush for his car. At a glance he couldn't see it. It was well hidden, noticeable only to the most discerning eye. Good. Let the two thugs think he was gone. Let them come after her again. He'd be waiting for them.

He returned to the house, fixed some coffee and carried it outside to the small back porch. From here he could see the Potomac River. Sun streaks filtered through the trees, and tiny rain droplets caught up in spiderwebs glistened in the morning light. The beauty of the untamed landscape matched the beauty of the woman asleep upstairs. She belonged here, free and unfettered from the damage left behind by Richard Tapp.

He drank the steaming coffee. He hadn't meant to bare his soul to her. He hadn't thought of Carl and Curt in years, but she had that effect on him. She forced him to open doors that had been closed for years and to take a good look inside. Yes, he'd envied all the family relationships he'd viewed from the outside. He'd learned firsthand the importance of what he'd missed—a family to stick by you no matter what.

THE SMELL OF COFFEE curled around Casey's nose and nudged her awake from the best sleep she'd had in days. She stretched and was immediately hit with a blunt reminder of her sore knee, and last night. And Trevor. She groaned and quickly put on her jeans and a red T-shirt, wrapped the splint around her knee and followed the scent of coffee to the kitchen.

He was braced against the sink, absorbed in something outside the window. Bare from the waist up.

"Good morning." The words stumbled from her mouth.

He whipped around, as if she'd interrupted some private moment. Self-consciously, she sought out the coffee. She concentrated on what she was doing—finding the mug, taking it off the hook, setting it on the sink, lifting the coffeepot, pouring the hot liquid without scalding her hand. From the corner of her eye she saw him, his broad chest bare, his hair wet and tousled, his eyes a smoldering blue-gray, the color of a quiet sea at dusk. Normal concentration was impossible.

"So you're an early bird," he said.

She steadied her hand on the counter by her cup. "Not really. I don't usually have such an enticing reason to get up."

His eyes sparked with mischief. A smile spread across his face. She realized what she'd said and raised her cup and toasted him by saying, "The coffee smelled irresistible." Although she tried, she couldn't cover up her embarrassment. Already, she felt herself blushing.

He walked right up to her, his eyes never leaving hers. He was close enough for her to see the fine hairs on his chest, to smell the clean scent of him. "Not as irresistible as your blush, sweetheart," he said. He brushed her cheek with the back of his hand, a gentle, nerve-racking touch that took her breath away.

He sat down at the table. She watched his teasing smile falter, his face muscles tighten. He said, "We had unwelcome watchers overnight."

"Not the men who are after me. They came back? I slept through that? That's impossible." She had her breath now, but her cheek felt aflame where he'd touched her.

He told her what happened when he went out to move his car. She concentrated on his face, his words, the cup he held. "They're not going to give up," he said.

She walked the few steps to the counter. "More coffee?"

She refilled her cup and then topped off his. She was anxious to change the subject. She would not spend more time listening to reasons why she should leave this house to strangers. This was her home now, the only one she might ever know. It had been her parents' home, her grandparents' home, and most recently, it'd been Aunt Maude's home. She would never leave it.

"I've hidden my car across the road," he said. "If they think you're alone, they'll be more inclined to barge in. We'll be ready for them. That means I have to stick close."

"This might be a good day for me to stay home, anyway," she said, glancing at her knee.

He stared at his cup. "Do you really believe those guys are your ordinary burglars?" He raised his cup to his lips.

She couldn't ignore the slight ripple of his chest muscles when he moved his arm, his tan chest, the way the dark, sexy sprinkling of hair trailed below his waist. Who could maintain a charade when concentration was impossible?

His eyes lifted to hers and she looked away. "I want to believe that," she said, "but it's possible somebody knows about my connection to Richard and thinks I might have some information about the bonds.''

"Or the bonds themselves," he said.

She stared at him closely. "But why?"

"It's a logical conclusion."

Bare chest or no bare chest, he was beginning to sound like the government agents who kept knocking on her door. "Just what does that mean?"

He held up his hand, palm up, as if to stop her. "Whoa. I didn't say you had the bonds. I said it was logical for someone to suspect you have them."

"Sorry," she said. "That's a sensitive issue. Do you think it's possible we can find them? Everyone's looking for them. Why would we be able to find them when no one else can?"

He gave her a fixed look. "Who knows? We're not motivated by money. Maybe that'll make a difference. Are you changing your mind?"

"No. I'm just thinking we could start today. I have to call in to check the workload. If my knee can rest over the weekend, it'll heal faster. What about you? Don't you need to be somewhere?"

He got up and rinsed his cup in the sink, then spoke with his back to her. "My hours are flexible. You might say I'm in between jobs right now. I'm finishing up one job and getting ready to start a new one."

His shoulders bunched each time he moved. His voice was low, soft, and he spoke slowly, as if measuring each word.

"You were there," he said. "Collins & Company, remember? The pickup."

An image of the rundown city neighborhood flashed through her mind. She remembered. The dark hallway, the sconces on the walls. How could she ever forget where she learned Richard had a twin. "You're going to work there?"

"Yup. Ned Collins, a good friend of mine, turned it over to me a few years ago when he retired. He died last year." He turned around and leaned back against the counter, his manner changed, his eyes shifting from sadness to enthusiasm quickly.

"What is Collins & Company?"

"It's a place for kids who don't have anywhere else to go. Most of them hang out at our gym a couple of blocks away, but if they don't have a place to sleep, they can stay at the house."

"And it's yours?"

He nodded. "Ned and Allie Collins took me into their home and set me straight when I was sixteen and headed down the wrong side of the tracks. He'd founded C & C the year before."

"And you decided to pick up where he left off."

"No, actually, I was shocked to learn he wanted me to take over. I've had a resident manager running the place until now."

"Well, I wish you luck."

She finished her coffee and went to the counter to wash her cup. He stepped aside to make room for her, but not far enough away for her to miss feeling the soft down on his arm. "How about some breakfast?"

"Sounds good."

"On one condition."

"What's that?"

"Would you please put on a shirt?" When he started to laugh, she added, "It's for your own protection."

He walked over to the table, his eyes smiling and mysterious all at once. "I like taking risks," he teased.

She stumbled back against a chair. "Hey, it's your choice," she laughed, "but I only intend to feed one appetite."

He cupped her chin in his hand. Instinctively, she placed her hand on his chest. She could feel the strength of his muscles, the pounding of his heart. The racing blood through her own veins.

"Lady," he said, "you drive a hard bargain." He ran the backs of his fingers down her cheeks. "But breakfast it is. With shirt." He let his hand drop. "I'll be right back."

Her heart hammered away. Her body felt tingly and heated all over. She'd never had this reaction to a man before. His touch had her trembling. Here he was trying to help her find the missing bonds, and she was acting like some adolescent with a crush.

And for God's sake, this was Richard's twin!

HE CHUCKLED as he rifled through his duffel bag to find a shirt. So his body bothered her. Good. There really was some justice in this world, after all.

He grabbed a pullover and headed back to the kitchen, back to the sleepy-eyed beauty waiting for him. He paused by the doorway and took in the homeyness of the place. He thought of the destruction left behind by the two hoodlums. She'd done quite a job putting the pieces back together again.

The living room reflected the whole house. The room was clean and neat, but the soft green walls were dull and streaked with age. Mismatched furniture sat on a tattered, fake Oriental rug. In spite of the well-worn look, it had a warmth that appealed to him.

He straightened the sofa that had brought him so little sleep last night. Then he refolded the afghan over the back of the sofa and smoothed down the edges. Its olive green stripe blended into a navy, white and royal blue pattern that complemented the beige sofa beneath it. Allie Collins used to sit by the fire every night knitting afghans during the

short time he'd been in their foster care. Sweet old Allie. He
often wondered what path he would have chosen if he hadn't
wandered into Ned Collins's rec center to play basketball
that day.

He had been part of a family for those nineteen months.
Ned and Allie Collins had taken him in and loved him in
spite of himself. They'd treated him like a son, but he'd been
such a stubborn, rebellious teenager, he hadn't appreciated
their unselfish gift. They hadn't been blood relatives, but
they'd been the closest thing to family he'd ever known,
closer by far than Richard.

The smell of bacon and biscuits pulled him toward the
kitchen.

"You can make the orange juice," said Casey, her back
facing him. She pointed to the frozen can of juice defrost-
ing in the sink.

After he made the juice, he prepared the table. The do-
mestic scene tugged at his memories. Working in the kitchen
with Casey wasn't quite the same as the many times he'd
helped Allie years ago. The sense of well-being was the
same, but the tension between them sparked like a fire.

They sat down to eat. She avoided his eyes. When she
picked up her glass to drink her juice, it slid out of her hand
and spilled on the table. They both jumped up at the same
time.

"Sit down," he said. "I'll get some paper towels."

"No, really, I spilled it, I'll clean it up."

At last he caught her eyes with his. For one very long,
poignant moment, she held him in her steady gaze. "I'll do
it," he said.

His words broke the invisible bond between them. She
lowered herself to her chair slowly, her composure again in
place. As he hunted for something with which to clean the
table, he thought he understood. How was she going to

handle the constant reminder of a far-from-perfect marriage? Brother or no brother, Richard had had his faults. He'd read the case file. There was no need to press Casey for details.

He wiped up the spill and rejoined her at the table. She was pecking at her food with movements too precise. Her rigid back leaned slightly forward from the ladder-back chair. Something was grinding away at her.

"Do I make you nervous?" he asked.

Her eyes grazed his. She set down her fork on the edge of her plate carefully and raised her head. The pride in her face battled with the honesty in her eyes roaming the room. Those beautiful blue eyes finally settled on him.

She let out a deep sigh. "You do."

He stopped eating, pushed back his chair and stretched his legs. "Well," he said, "either we can talk about it, or we can spend the next few weeks playing cat and mouse around each other."

Her chin lifted in stubborn defiance. "All right. We can talk." She straightened the napkin in her lap several times. "Only one other man has eaten at this table with me, and you know who that was. I don't like that this bothers me, but it does."

"Do I remind you that much of Richard? I've seen his picture. I don't see that much resemblance."

She stared hard at him with all her frustration showing in the drawn lines across her forehead and the pinched creases at her eyes. "Sometimes. Little things. Some of your expressions and gestures are the same as his. It's very strange being around you."

She resumed eating. He watched her closely, looking for any telltale hint that would help him get through to her, but he ended up telling himself he was crazy for trying. Gaining her trust might be impossible. He'd be tempted to dump the case back in Jamison's and Crowley's laps if it weren't for Richard. And the woman sitting across from him.

He pulled in his chair and worked on his breakfast, thinking about the man who used to sit in this chair. Richard must have known somebody was after him. Otherwise, why suddenly send a letter to a brother who didn't know he existed? How much had Richard known about him, anyway? Had he known he was an agent? Why had he died? Not knowing was driving him crazy.

And right now Richard's ex-wife was driving him just as crazy.

He carried his dishes to Casey, who now stood at the sink. "You can still change your mind, you know."

"No," she said, "no, I can't. I want to end this thing once and for all."

She seemed less tense and more determined now that they were no longer sitting at the table. He dried the dishes as she washed them. When they were finished, she wiped her hands on the towel and placed them on her hips. "Ready?"

He sketched out a rough design of the house. She added in the nooks and crannies that weren't obvious. They tackled the upstairs first. The items accumulated through the years were stored in the smaller bedrooms.

"Let's go through the things in Richard's old room first. I've already started, as you can see." She motioned at the boxes and papers piled around the room.

He edged closer to see around her, and his arm brushed her shoulder. She stepped back. She had her reactions under control, she told herself. Just because the brief contact sent a flurry of shivers up her arm was no reason to think otherwise. What better place than Richard's former room to remind her of who he was? She followed him through the doorway.

"Why don't we split up the work," he said. "I'll take the boxes and you take the papers." He lined up all the cardboard boxes beside the bed and opened the closest one.

She found a comfortable spot in the far corner, away from the stacked boxes, away from Trevor, and started scanning each piece of paper she'd set aside.

An hour later he said, "There's nothing here that's relevant." He stood up and brushed the dust from his hands.

She barely heard him. Her eyes were fixed on the old Victorian dresser along the back wall. "I forgot about that," she said. "I've searched everywhere for the bonds, but I overlooked the storage areas."

She walked to the dresser and tried to see behind it. "Back here, Trevor. Both small bedrooms have built-in storage areas along the back walls of the house under the eaves. I can't believe I never looked in them."

But she could believe it. She'd been living with Aunt Maude for a week when she removed the mysterious wall panel on her bedroom wall and discovered the perfect hideaway for a twelve-year-old. When Aunt Maude found her, she became angry and forbade her to go there again. Her aunt blocked the entrance with the heavy dresser. She was so afraid of displeasing her aunt and losing the only family she had left, that she'd never entered it again.

"Stand back so I can move the dresser," he said. Inch by inch he nudged it aside.

"See? The doorway's like a small attic entrance," she said. "I have no idea what's in here." Their eyes locked, the communication between them silent, but real. She knew without asking that he was thinking the same thing she was. The bonds must be in the storage area. She clenched her fists and felt her spirits lift.

He leaned the panel against the side of the dresser. "It's cramped getting in," she said, "but once you're inside, you

can stand up." He stooped through the opening. "I think
there's a light switch on that left wooden beam."

Light shone from the small opening. "This may take us
all day," he called from inside.

She leaned over and stepped through the door. The room
was as she remembered it, only much, much smaller. And
Trevor was way too tall to stand upright.

The storage area was a perfect reminder that Aunt Maude
had liked everything in its place. Neat rows of boxes stacked
tightly together lined both walls, leaving a single path in the
middle that extended the length of the room.

"Why don't you stay here next to the doorway," he said.
"It's a little tight for two people, and it'll be too hard to
move around with your leg in a splint." He picked up a
small stool she remembered leaving behind years ago when
her aunt found her. "You might as well get comfortable on
this." He moved the stool beside the entrance.

She was glad to be near the doorway. The view of the
bedroom made her feel less confined, and the last thing she
wanted was to be trapped in too small a space with Trevor.

They started with the boxes closest to the door and
worked their way down the outside wall. He brought her box
after box. They'd reached the halfway mark on the first wall
when he said, "I think you'd better go through this one."
He shoved a small box in front of her.

She removed several layers of tissue paper and discovered a picture album. Holding her breath, she set the album on her lap and opened it. "Oh, Trevor, look." She
leafed through several pages. "It's all here, my parents, my
grandparents. And look," she said, pointing to a baby picture. "That's me." The next few pages were filled with pictures of her growing up. "And here's little Annie." Her
heart skipped as she went through the album. She closed it

and hugged it to her. "If nothing else comes from this mess Richard left behind, this is more than enough."

"You've never seen the album?" said Trevor.

"No, Aunt Maude wouldn't talk about my family. I was not allowed to mention them." She remembered the times she'd tried. She remembered Aunt Maude's responding silence. An orphaned twelve-year-old learns quickly, she thought.

At the shocked look on his face she added, "My aunt took me in when there was no one else, Trevor. I think she wanted me to get on with my life and leave the past behind. Besides, she was ... unusual."

"But you must have needed to talk to somebody. To lose a family and not be able to mention them? That's a cruel punishment for a kid."

He was making her uncomfortable. "I spent a lot of years feeling angry about my parents' death, and then the guilt set in. They wanted me to go with them, you know. To Chicago. But I was too busy. I had a walk-on part in a school play that Saturday night, a tiny part, really, but my first. I threw a fit and refused to go." She placed the album back in the box and looked at him sitting across from her. "I should have been with them."

He reached across the box and caught the tear forming in the corner of her eye. "I'm glad you weren't."

Their eyes held for a long, silent moment. She fought to control the flood of emotions and found it easier this time than in the past. "I've never told anyone that before."

He leaned across the short distance separating them and held her face in his hands. Gently, his lips met hers, warm, caressing lips that relieved the ache brought on by her memories, tantalizing lips that stirred the blood in her veins and cleared her mind of every thought except the delicious feelings his kiss produced. It was a kiss of compassion, she told herself, no more. Just one human being comforting another. But it felt like more.

He moved away slowly, leaving one hand to linger on the side of her face. She leaned into its warmth and savored its strength. His touch was gentle yet sure. She wanted to absorb what he offered so freely.

Quietly, he said, "I guess we'd better get back to work."

Words escaped her. Reality crept in gradually, and she lowered her eyes to the box and folded its edges closed. "Yes," she said finally, looking at the second row of unopened boxes. "I'll put this aside for later."

He reached for the box. "I'll take it to your room."

Their movements had changed, the focus had shifted, yet the magic between them remained, as if the very air they breathed had suddenly been filled with an intoxicating vapor.

She fought to break the spell. "I don't know about you, but I'm ready for some coffee."

"Sounds good." He stooped lower through the doorway and pulled out the box. "Want me to get it?"

She followed him out. "I'd rather put you to work hauling down those boxes way back in the corner. And I have to call Aretha at work."

She maneuvered her way around the small bedroom and out into the hall. Her knee had felt pretty strong this morning, considering the injury was the second one in a week. But now her legs were shaky for reasons that had nothing to do with her knee.

The taste of his lips lingered. New life flowed through her veins, and she wanted to hold on to the feeling and never let go, but her mind kept intruding. Remember who he is, it insisted. Wake up. With each step away from the storage area, she relived his warm lips on hers, and by the time she reached the kitchen, she knew her mind had joined sides with her body. She was tempted to rush back upstairs to absorb more of the magic.

Instead, she started the coffeemaker and called Aretha. "The schedule's light today, so don't worry," said Aretha. "Besides, Jon had you scheduled for an eleven o'clock shuttle to New York, and with your bad knee, that's the last type of day you need."

She heard knocking at the front door. "Look, Aretha, I'd better go. Call me if any problems come up, will you?"

She hung up the phone and went to answer the door. Certainly those two thugs wouldn't knock, would they? She peeked through the window and saw the two government officials who had plagued her in the past.

She opened the door. "Well, if it isn't my two favorite people. You're up bright and early, Mr. Jamison. And Mr. Crowley, what a pleasant surprise."

Knowing they would flash badges and talk about warrants if she refused to let them in, she motioned them inside. Carl Jamison stepped through first. He had the face of a cherub topped by nondescript, straight brown hair with a tendency to fall forward over his forehead. He walked into the living room tugging at the collar of his shirt. Fred Crowley followed, the familiar frown deepening on his pudgy face. His suit looked like it came from Saks, and when he turned to face her, he brushed imaginary lint off his sleeves.

"Please, have a seat. Can I get you some coffee?"

"This is not a social call, Ms. Michaels," said Mr. Crowley.

She hated the way he drew out the Ms. It sounded like an annoying gnat. "Of course." She took a seat on a chair in the opposite corner.

Mr. Jamison sat straight and tall on the sofa and kept looking around the room, as if searching for something. "I see you injured your knee. Is that from the break-in?"

His question caught her off guard. But of course they would know about the police report. "I have a bad knee," she said, not wanting to call attention to the break-in.

"They were looking for the bonds, weren't they?" asked Mr. Crowley. His small eyes stared at her. Mr. Crowley seemed to believe he could gain any information he wanted by intimidating her with his eyes.

"They really didn't say, Mr. Crowley."

"Really, Ms. Michaels, let's stop all this pretending," said Mr. Crowley. "We know you have the bonds." His voice was low, threatening.

She could feel her anger rising, like a full-fledged storm ready to dump its contents wherever it might land. "Is that an official charge, Mr. Crowley? Because if it is, you'd better be ready to back it up."

"Now look, Ms. Michaels, we really don't like to keep bothering you," said Mr. Jamison. "We had a man following your husband before he killed himself. Twice he came to this house. Why don't you just cooperate and we can end this matter."

She'd had enough. She stood up. "I will say this to you one more time. Listen carefully. Richard Tapp has not been my husband for six months. I have not seen him for eighteen months. I do not have the bonds. If your man followed Richard to this house, then they were both trespassing. Understand? Perhaps I'm the one who should seek legal action against you."

Mr. Crowley stood his ground. She could see the impatience in his eyes. Before he could say anything, Mr. Jamison placed himself between them and said, "Of course, that would be foolish. We're only trying to solve our problem and help you at the same time.''

"My only problem at the moment is you," she said. "If you want to help me, then go find the bonds. As you said, that would solve both our problems, wouldn't it?"

She turned toward the front door. Trevor was leaning against the wall, his arms folded in front of him, his eyes dancing, a slight smile on his lips. He nodded his head and said, "Goodbye, gentlemen."

The two men faltered momentarily, surprise evident on their faces. Their eyes locked with Trevor's, then they rushed out the door.

"So this is what you do in your spare time," he said. He hadn't moved.

Fragments of anger held her fast. She knew she needed a minute to cool down, to clear her system of yet one more intrusion from those two agents. Why couldn't they leave her alone and get on with their case? Why wouldn't they believe her?

"The coffee's ready in the kitchen," she said. She left the hall more determined than ever to locate those famous bonds.

Trevor followed her. He picked up his coffee from the counter and sat down at the table. "Friends of yours?"

"Ha! Government agents are no friends of mine. They're obnoxious, nosy, rude and interfering." She sipped at the hot coffee. "I'll find those bonds if for no other reason than to get rid of those guys."

He reached across the table and caught her hand in his. "*We'll* find the bonds." He stood up. "But not sitting here talking about it."

"You go on upstairs. I'll be there in a minute," she said. "Right after I check out my car."

"But..." He was gone before she could finish. She watched him walk down the drive from the front window, confused by his abrupt departure. Why on earth would he need to check his car?

HE WALKED AT A QUICK CLIP down the drive, repeating Casey's words one at a time with each step. "Obnoxious. Nosy. Rude. Interfering." His lips burned with the sweet nectar he'd taken from her lips. His body felt alive and ached for more. He thought of her shimmering hair, the silky strands alive in the light. When she found out he was an agent, she'd shove him out of her house and out of her life, and he wouldn't blame her. What a crazy fool he was! But not as foolish as Jamison and Crowley. He had to admire the way she'd handled those two idiots. She had them pegged right on the nose.

He climbed up the slight incline to his car hidden in the trees. A minute later he had Barney on the phone. "What's the idea of sending Jamison and Crowley in to hound Casey? You told me yourself they'd harassed her. How am I supposed to do my job with those two idiots hanging around?"

Barney said, "What am I supposed to think when I don't hear from you? Your first week is almost up."

"I need longer."

"Not unless you can report some progress. What's going on, Steele?"

"We're searching the house. No bonds yet. She doesn't have them, Barney, I'd bet my life on that. Casey doesn't know anything about those bonds." And he believed it. He knew with absolute certainty she was not involved with the stolen bonds.

"So it's Casey now, is it?" Barney chuckled.

Barney never missed a trick, and Trevor quickly tried to camouflage his growing feelings for her. "I do believe it would be a little awkward to keep calling her Ms. Michaels, don't you?"

"Your point," said Barney.

"I don't want to see Jamison and Crowley within a mile of this place. I wouldn't have been surprised if they'd blurted out, 'Hey Trev, how you doing.' That would've been real cute."

"They're good agents, Trevor."

"If they're so good, they would have found the bonds before I became involved."

"You're not forgetting you requested this assignment, are you, Steele?" Barney paused. "I'm not so sure it's their effectiveness you're worried about, but we'll let that go for now. Let me know the minute you find anything in the house."

He hung up and Trevor was left with a dial tone buzzing in his ear and the thought that getting anything by Barney had been impossible in the past. Why he thought he could fool him now, he wasn't sure. No doubt he could guess how much Casey appealed to him. Of course, there was no point in talking about an impossible situation. When she found out who he was, the point would be moot.

HE CLIMBED into the small storage area and wedged himself in between the open boxes. "Is your car okay?"

"It's well hidden. I don't think anyone saw it." He slid a box to her and opened a second one for himself. He kept his eyes more guarded than before.

"Did you hear what Mr. Jamison said? They followed Richard here. Maybe they're right about the bonds. Maybe they are in the house. Wouldn't that be ironic?"

"If they are, we'll find them."

They continued their search in silence. When they had examined all the boxes in the first storage area, they took a break for lunch, then moved into the next bedroom. Concentrating on searching box after box, Casey kept her emotions in check. Almost. She couldn't keep her eyes off the man. Even in his silence, he intrigued her. Something had changed between them, but she wasn't sure what. And he sure wasn't telling.

They were halfway down the first row of boxes in the second storage area when Trevor said, "Bingo! I've got something here. Take a look."

Chapter Eight

"The bonds?" She moved to the other end of the storage alcove next to Trevor.

"No, but these look like some kind of business papers. Are they Richard's?"

She sat down on a sturdy box, glad for the excuse to be near him, and skimmed a handful of papers. "I've never heard of these people. This is Richard's handwriting, though. These were his."

"We'll need to sort through them carefully. I'll carry the box downstairs."

They dumped the papers on the kitchen table. Receipts were thrown in with ledgers. Old postcards were mixed with bills. None of the papers seemed to be organized, so they spent the evening reading and sorting.

They were almost finished when Trevor said, "Well, what do you know." He looked at her and winked and spread out four letters in front of him. "Looks like Richard had a partner."

"What?" She scooted around the table to read the letters.

"Did he ever talk about a guy named Alcorn?"

"I've never heard of him."

"These letters don't exactly say they were partners, but I'd bet a thousand to one that's what we're looking at." He placed the four letters in a new pile and picked up another pile they'd already examined. "I want to go back over every scrap to see where the name Alcorn is mentioned. We'll check for initials, too."

"Not me," she said, stifling a yawn, exhausted from the emotional strain of the day.

"We have our work cut out for us." He picked up the first page. "We'll start looking for Alcorn tomorrow, check the phone books, make some calls. If we can find his partner, we might find the bonds."

She nodded and rubbed at her weary eyes. "I'm calling it a night," she said. He responded with a polite nod. She'd discovered he had an incredible sense of concentration, and right now he was obviously engrossed in the puzzle before him.

SHE WALKED UPSTAIRS carrying with her the pleasing picture of Trevor sitting in her kitchen reading through the papers. It felt good to be doing something to get control of her life again. It felt good having him here helping her.

If she could stay awake, she'd read her assignment for business management tonight. Before she did that, she had one essential task to perform.

She opened her top dresser drawer and took out a plain white envelope. Inside was the bond receipt she'd found in Richard's briefcase.

She fingered the envelope. No one must know she had this receipt—not the police, not the federal agents, not Trevor. This one item could prove she had prior knowledge about the bond scam. She'd be arrested and put in jail as an accomplice. Just having it in her possession would suggest she knew where the bonds were hidden, which she didn't, of course, but then, the questions would never end. No, they must never know.

She looked around the room, tamping down the temptation to burn the incriminating evidence. As long as she could find a safe place, hiding it would be the smarter choice. She pulled down an old purse from the closet shelf, unzipped it and found the tear in the lining she remembered. After folding the envelope in half, she slid it through the hole and pushed it to the bottom.

Handing over the receipt would be like putting a noose around her own neck. She *had* known what Richard was doing, and she had not reported him to the authorities. Protecting Richard like that was the final shame of her marriage.

She patted the lining back in place and held the purse up to the lamp to see if the envelope was noticeable. Satisfied that no one would think to check inside the lining of an old, beat-up purse, she zipped the purse closed and replaced it on the shelf. After she got ready for bed, she took out her business management book to read her assignment.

But keeping her emotions in check had taken its toll. She was too frustrated and exhausted to read, much less study. Instead, she lay her head back and tried to relax by constricting her muscles to the count of ten, then relaxing them to the count of five. First her feet, then her legs, and on up her body until the tension gradually subsided.

As her body relaxed, her mind opened to the emotions flowing beneath the surface. She dozed, half awake and half asleep, wrapped in the compassion of Trevor's kiss, his honest reaction to her needs, the hidden passion. She nestled down in the pillows and reveled in his seductive eyes and nerve-tingling touch.

And there she slept for the night, with the lamp burning and the book on her lap, feeling confident of a good night's sleep with someone else in the house, but ignoring the irritating little doubts whispering their warnings that things were not always as they seemed.

"I STILL SAY WE COULD TALK to all the Alcorns listed in the telephone book much faster if we split the list," said Casey. The Metropolitan Washington area seemed to be overrun with Alcorns, all of them potential clues to Richard's business, his death and the bonds.

They were driving over the Fourteenth Street bridge into Washington, D.C., to Brenda Alcorn's house, the eighth Alcorn on their list. The Potomac River churned beneath them like the feelings churning inside of her. Never had she imagined it would be so difficult to grin and bear her attraction to this man, but being closed up in a car with him complicated the problem. There was no escaping the excitement flowing through her veins, or the fluttering in her stomach. And lower.

Trevor appeared relaxed behind the wheel in a blue-striped oxford-cloth shirt and khaki pants, but his hard grip on the wheel belied his appearance. "You're the only one who knows I'm Richard's brother," he said. "I want to keep it that way. You have a legitimate reason for asking questions about your ex-husband and the missing bonds." He glanced at her. A slight smile touched his lips. "They'll open up to you."

She wasn't sure she liked this new role. When they stepped out of the car in front of the Alcorn house, her hands were clammy and a little shaky, but being free of the confining car felt wonderful.

The house was a semidetached unit in an old neighborhood. Three doors away boards covered the windows and mud puddles served as a front lawn. The Alcorn house had a trim lawn and a newly planted garden. A faded green-striped awning stretched across two front windows. Window boxes filled with plastic flowers adorned each windowsill. Steep cement steps led to the front door, and Casey pushed hard on her good leg to mount them one at a time. Another awning shaded the stoop. Trevor knocked on the door.

A thin woman about five foot two answered the door. Her eyes were red and her skin splotched. It wasn't hard to tell she'd been crying. She wore a white nylon pullover and green slacks and looked about fifty. "Yes?" she said.

Casey waited for Trevor to speak. When he didn't, she said, "Are you Mrs. Alcorn?"

Her name was Mrs. Rex Alcorn, and what could she do for them, she said. They introduced themselves and asked if she knew Richard Tapp. When she nodded yes, Casey said, "I'm Richard Tapp's ex-wife."

Brenda's face frowned in surprise as she said, "My name is Brenda. Please, come in."

She ushered them into a small, neat living room. The furniture looked worn, but everything was in place and free of dust. A cardboard copy of a Norman Rockwell painting hung without a frame above the sofa. Casey and Trevor sat on the sofa behind a coffee table overflowing with baseball cards.

Brenda stood to the side twisting a lace-trimmed hanky in her hands. "I was stunned when I read about Richard in the papers. I can't imagine him committing suicide," she said. "You must have been shocked."

She felt Trevor flinch beside her. "Did you know Richard a long time?" she asked.

"Two years," said Brenda, sitting down in the chair. She stared at a vacant spot across the room, her face a picture of sadness.

She told them of her home in Kentucky, of meeting Richard at the horse races. "He and Rex hit it off right away," she said, "and I felt good about this partnership business. I mean, Rex was a new man." Tears formed in her eyes. "I didn't know they were stealing those bonds."

Trevor reached out and patted her arm. "It'll be all right, Brenda."

She looked at him with hope and trust. "Do you think so?" She lowered her head. "No, of course. You don't know. I'm sorry." She glanced at the baseball cards on the coffee table. "Those are his, you know. I was sorting them when you knocked." She seemed to find solace from looking at the cards, for she sat up straighter and raised her chin higher. "You'll have to forgive me. Today's our thirtieth wedding anniversary. Rex loved to collect his baseball cards."

"I have a few old ones myself," said Trevor, smiling. "Rex and I will have to compare cards when he gets back."

"He'd love that," she said, her moist eyes shining.

Casey's heart warmed at how quickly Trevor had endeared himself to Brenda. His clear blue-gray eyes and his obvious interest inspired confidence and trust.

"Do you know where Rex is?" asked Brenda. "He and Richard traveled a lot, but he always called me faithfully every night."

"How long has your husband been missing?" asked Trevor.

"Over three weeks. Since the night Richard...I'm so afraid something's happened to him."

"Have you called the police?" he said.

"Oh, yes. They questioned me a long time, especially after I mentioned Richard." Abruptly, she stood up. She held herself very straight, her hands clasped in front of her. "I'm being very rude. Forgive me. Can I offer you a cup of tea?"

"That would be nice," said Casey.

After Brenda left the room, Trevor said, "She was uneasy when I mentioned the police."

"Do you blame her? It sounds like they gave her a hard time." She looked around the room. "You can't say she's living a life of luxury, though."

Brenda returned with their tea. "Did Rex ever mention anything about bonds?" said Trevor.

"No. I told the police that. I think they finally believed me. Rex never talked about business, except for Richard, of course. You see, we both felt sorry for him. Rex used to be a compulsive gambler, too, and it took him years to overcome the addiction." She brushed at her slacks. "It is an addiction, you know. A real sickness."

She looked at Casey, kindness lighting her face. "I know how hard it is to live with a man who'll do anything for betting money. That's why we were at the races. Rex and I worked out this system between us, him against me." Her face flushed slightly. "I know this sounds silly, but it seemed to be working."

Casey couldn't say a word. Richard, a compulsive gambler? Of course. It fit. First he'd gone through her aunt's money, then her money. That one fact explained so much. In the beginning of their relationship she'd sensed a reserve that didn't match the rest of his outgoing personality. Eventually, she'd accepted him as he was, or as she thought he was. If only she'd known, maybe she could have helped him. But no, Richard never would have admitted to a weakness.

Trevor was asking Brenda more questions. She reined in her emotions and memories and tried to pay attention to their conversation. Whatever he'd said had Brenda totally mesmerized. Her eyes never left his face. Casey watched him carefully for any sign of the shock she'd felt, but he appeared unaffected by this new information about Richard. His total attention was directed at Rex's wife.

Brenda rose from her chair. "He keeps his files right here." She walked to an old desk in the far corner, then turned and said, "You don't think he'd mind, do you?" Without waiting for an answer, she opened one drawer after another, muttering under her breath, until she found a large box in the bottom drawer. "Rex is a pretty organized person." She brought the box to the sofa.

Inside were file folders, each one neatly labeled in careful handwriting. Trevor leafed through the folders. He picked out several and skimmed through the papers and notes. "Is there anything else in the desk that might help?" he asked, his eyes intent and smiling.

She opened the middle drawer. "Only this." She handed him a notebook and sat down and folded her hands in her lap.

He removed a pen and notebook from his pocket and spent several minutes going through the blue notebook, occasionally stopping to copy notes. When he finished he closed the notebook and returned it and the box to the desk.

"I hope these help," said Brenda. She held out her hand to Trevor, her eyes sparkling bright with renewed enthusiasm.

"I hope so, too. Whether they do or not, we appreciate your openness, Brenda. You'll know immediately if we hear anything about Rex."

They drove away in silence. A police cruiser passed them halfway down the block, and for the first time in weeks, Casey was glad the police were close by. Their presence would give Brenda more confidence and hope.

Trevor looked completely absorbed in his thoughts as he wound his way through the short residential blocks. She was quiet herself. She kept going over their visit with Brenda.

"Get the notebook out of my right pocket, will you?" He unclipped his seat belt for easier access.

She did as he asked, both glad and sorry to pull away from him once she had the small notebook in her hand.

"See if you recognize any of the names."

She tried to focus her attention on the names, but her mind refused to leave Brenda's living room. How easily he'd won her trust. Some people inspired immediate trust in a stranger with merely a kind word or a generous gesture. Richard had been like that, especially with Aunt Maude. Five minutes after she met him, she trusted him completely.

Richard's sincerity had been a fake. For the first six months of their marriage, he'd treated her with love and respect. Gradually, though, the honeymoon had ended and he'd betrayed himself in little annoying ways that, taken individually, seemed insignificant at the time. She remembered the first night he came home in the early morning hours. Soon, late nights became entire nights; became most nights.

Now she could see that his part of their relationship had been motivated by his compulsive gambling. He'd won her trust and her aunt's trust so he could gain a new source of income to finance his sickness. Once the money ran out, he really had no use for her. Understanding this helped, but not much.

What about Trevor? Was he like his brother? He had a stubborn streak that stretched from here to China, but that didn't mean his motivation was dishonest. He'd saved her from the crooks, he'd helped put her home back together, and he'd been up front about his reasons for helping her.

Yet she'd never seen the side of him she saw today. Or had she? He'd wanted help from Brenda, and he'd played his role to the hilt—like he had with her to find out about his brother, like Richard had with both her and her aunt to increase his funds.

She shuffled through the pages of the notebook, disturbed by her thoughts. Had her experiences with Richard turned her into a cynic? Would she always suspect the worst of people?

Trevor interrupted her thoughts. "Any of them sound familiar?"

She scanned the pages quickly. "No," she said, "not one of them, but then, it's been a long time. I never knew much about Richard's friends—or his business." That was certainly true. Otherwise, what she'd found in his briefcase would not have shocked her so.

THEY SPENT A GOOD PART of the afternoon comparing Trevor's notes with the papers from the storage area. "Nothing fits," he said, pounding his fist on the kitchen table. "Nothing matches!" He pushed away from the table.

She could see his jaw muscle working overtime to contain his frustration. She felt it, too, and the disappointment. If only she'd recognized one of those names in the notebook.

He got up and stalked to the hall. "I have some things to take care of," he said. "Will you be all right for a while?"

"You go ahead," said Casey.

"Lock up," he said, "and set the alarm." He grabbed her keys from the hall table. "I'll move your car behind the house so no one will know you're here."

She fixed an early dinner of grilled cheese and soup, all the while refusing to let herself wonder where he was or what he was doing. Instead, she imagined him walking down the drive, climbing up the hill and getting into his car. He'd shown her where he'd hidden the car. It was a clever hiding place, protected, impossible to see unless you looked closely. At one time, the private road led to somebody's house.

She finished eating, went back to the storage alcove and pulled an unopened box into the bedroom. She knew he wouldn't be gone long. They were trying to lure the thugs out into the open and he would stay close, he'd said. But even after she searched three more boxes, he hadn't returned.

Darkness fell. She ambled through the house taking her time to close the blinds. She told herself she wasn't worried. He could let himself in when he got back. He'd be here soon.

But the longer she waited the more alone she felt, as if she were stranded in an isolated, deserted house. The stairs creaked and groaned as she climbed them. The wind whistled at her bedroom window. Noises that used to bring comfort echoed her loneliness and gave the night an eerie feeling.

He'd been so quiet all afternoon, so absorbed in putting the pieces together. So frustrated. The names they'd taken from Brenda's files had to lead to some answers.

She climbed into bed feeling more alone than ever. As soon as the bonds were found and the mystery was solved, he'd be gone in a flash and she'd have to deal with his absence, anyway. Might as well begin now. She couldn't need Richard's brother. Could she?

HE WATCHED THE WOODS around him turn to shadows as the sun sank in the west and darkness descended. His car was stuffy, but he didn't dare leave it. He was waiting for Barney to cross-reference the names and addresses he'd copied at Brenda Alcorn's. The bureau's high-tech computer would save him hours of time. He had a feeling the new information would lead him in the right direction. It was past time for a break in this case.

Barney might think it strange that he didn't go in and run the names himself, but he couldn't leave Casey prey to those hoodlums. She was safe. His car was still parked across from her drive. No one had come down the road since he'd been here.

Another piece of the puzzle had fallen into place, a piece he hadn't known existed. Richard was a compulsive gambler. He'd spent his life gambling himself, but not with money. Every time he went into the field, he gambled with his life.

Both he and Richard had traveled through life living on the edge. His brother died because he'd drifted too close to that edge. Trevor had already decided to back away. Their paths were crossing at an odd time. He couldn't help wondering what his life would've been like if he'd known he had a twin, someone bound to him by blood.

The ringing phone startled him. He let go of his thoughts and answered it.

"You got some relative named R. T. Steele?" Barney's gruff voice grabbed his attention.

"No, Barney. Is this a game?" he said.

Barney laughed. "That's what I'd like to know. One of the addresses is a dingy motel on the fringe of Fairfax County. Guy by the name of R. T. Steele registered three months ago. Paid up for the whole year." He read the address. Trevor found it at the top of his list and circled it.

"I'll check it out," he said.

"Probably a dead end," said Barney. Trevor thought differently. Richard's middle initial was M for Martin, not T. He'd meant for him to go there. Otherwise, why use those initials?

"You did hit the jackpot on this other one, though."
Barney read out the address of an exclusive area in D.C.
Trevor circled that one, too. "Posh, very posh. Woman
recognized Tapp from the description I gave her. He rented
the condo under the name of Jake Smith. Rather unimagi-
native, wouldn't you say? At least now we know where he
hung his hat. That's the one I want you to check, Steele.
Forget the motel."

"I'll check out the motel." No way was he turning the
motel room over to anyone else.

Silence followed. Finally, Barney said, "Suit yourself. I'll
send Crowley over to the condo."

He walked back to the house slowly, enjoying the cool
night air and Barney's good news. At last, a lead.

The house lights shone through the darkness with a welcoming warmth, and he hastened his step to tell Casey the
news. He entered the house fully expecting to find her
studying in the kitchen and felt a twinge of disappointment
when he realized she'd gone to bed.

A barely controllable urge to slip up to her bedroom and
wake her gripped him in the gut. The fantasy rolled on in his
mind as he grabbed the stair post. Her drowsy voice, those
blue eyes the color of heaven and heavy-lidded with sleep,
her mussed-up hair, her creamy breasts, all waited for his
touch. The temptation to slide in beside her would over-
whelm him.

"Damn!" He backed away from the stairs. Tomorrow
they'd have the whole day together. His news would have to
wait. There was no way he could wake her up and tell her
now without giving in to his longing.

He got a beer from the refrigerator and stretched out on
the sofa. His libido didn't understand what his mind kept
shouting—*she was his brother's wife.* Help her find the

bonds, figure out what happened to Richard, and get out. Use the new lead and make it fast.

Suddenly, an overlooked, obvious truth struck him smack in the face. He bolted from the sofa, a thin sweat forming on his brow. Thank God she was asleep. Otherwise, he would have blurted out his news point-blank, without any cover to explain how he'd obtained the information this late at night. He could hear himself now. "Yeah, I called Barney at the bureau, and he ran the addresses through the computer, and guess what?"

He paced the floor. He was losing it, no question. That tall, slender spitfire upstairs had scrambled his brain. He had to get a grip on himself. He had to recapture the intense concentration that went hand in hand with any undercover assignment. Otherwise, they would both lose.

Chapter Nine

They started on the list the next afternoon. Room 123 was an end unit in a series of connected rooms spread out behind the motel's office. Trevor had no trouble picking the lock. He turned to Casey and grinned. "Piece of cake." In spite of his lighthearted smile, she could hear the tension in his voice.

He turned the knob slowly and opened the door. "Stay back."

But she had no intention of waiting outside. Trevor had called the motel this morning and learned the room was registered to a Mr. Steele. That, combined with finding the address in Rex Alcorn's blue notebook, was too great to attribute to coincidence. They both knew Richard had rented this room.

She plowed through the doorway behind him into total darkness. When he turned on the light, an exposed bulb illuminated dull shadows in a cluttered room.

"This place smells," said Casey.

"Damn, woman, do you always do the opposite of what's asked?" His teasing eyes sent shivers down her back.

She smiled innocently and shrugged. "It's a gift."

The small room had a double bed shoved in a corner, a scarred, pine dresser beside the window, and a round table next to the tiny closet by the bathroom. The place was littered with beer cans and empty fast-food bags. She stepped to the table and found old racing forms, some plane ticket stubs, and a few hand-scribbled notes.

Recognizing the handwriting on the notes, she held up one and said, "If there was any doubt before, there isn't now. This was definitely Richard's."

Trevor pushed the door closed behind him. He didn't move. "This is how my brother lived."

She didn't miss the slight catch in his voice. His cold eyes momentarily met hers, a glimmer so like Richard's she had to stop herself from flinching.

She put her hand on his arm, hoping the contact might help ease his tension. Straining to make her voice sound light and unaffected, she cushioned her answer, since Richard had been a first-class slob. "He was not always real neat."

She thought of Trevor's duffel bag in her living room, always returned to the same spot. Each morning he straightened the sofa and washed his own dishes. What a difference between the two brothers.

She had to remember he was not only trying to find the bonds, he was discovering his twin and, perhaps, a part of himself. She wasn't sure if he'd inherited Richard's weaker traits or not, but a part of her needed to reassure him.

"From what I've seen, the two of you are very different," she said.

His hands moved slowly to her face. He was so close that his breath became hers and she was sure he would kiss her. Instead, he bent his head and touched his lips to her forehead in a long, lingering kiss. "You're a beautiful woman, Casey."

Every nerve tingled from his touch. She wanted to draw back. Who was this man who had come barging into her life? Was he the dominating, kind stranger she'd met that first night? Were his actions deceptive and manipulative, like Richard's? She couldn't let him wheedle his way into her life like Richard had. Even with these thoughts racing through her mind, she didn't back away.

His lips traced a path down the side of her face. Slowly, sensuously, his mouth met hers with warm, giving lips that melted her questions. She encircled his neck as his arms wrapped around her back, as his hands kneaded her skin and set her senses on fire. His tongue teased hers like a slow, tortuous flame.

My God! What was happening to her? She wanted to stay in his arms forever.

He ended the kiss slowly, then pulled her even closer. His cheek brushed her hair, his heart raced against her soul. With her own heart pounding against his chest, she savored the smell of him, the feel of him, the lingering honey of his lips.

He tipped up her chin and kissed her nose, his arms firmly around her waist, his arousal pressed against her, telling her what she already knew—they both wanted more. They both needed more. His eyes smoldered in passion as he reached up and pushed a stray strand of hair from her face.

"My God, woman, you're enough to drive a man crazy."

Reality slipped in slowly, like an intruder in the night. She had definitely taken leave of her senses. She shouldn't be kissing Richard's brother like this. She shouldn't feel so weak-kneed, so totally enchanted by his touch. But she couldn't deny the seductive power between them or her willing response.

Reluctantly, she separated herself from the warmth of his arms and struggled to bring herself back to their reason for being here. "Let's open the windows, get some fresh air in here."

He pulled back the curtain strips, his eyes still holding hers, and raised the tattered shades, then opened the windows.

"No maid service here," said Casey. With finger and thumb she picked up a discarded shirt from the bed.

The late afternoon sun shone on faded yellow wallpaper peeling at the edges. Cobwebs laced the ceiling corners. A slight whiff of evening air curled its way slowly around the room, and he stood for a minute, breathing in the outside world, reminding himself he could explore the past forever, but he couldn't change it.

Casey swatted at the cobwebs with a shirt, then stood with her hands on her hips surveying the room, a picture of spirit and persistence ready to take on anything. Her eyes locked with his, and for one pregnant moment the world stopped in the light of her eyes. The steady stream of tension continued to pour through his body straight to his groin.

He wanted to take that final step across the tiny room. He longed to wrap his arms around her again and very slowly, seductively, relieve her of her clothes, and just as slowly, agonizingly so, run his tongue over every inch of her lovely body until she was weak with wanting him. But he could read the withdrawal in her eyes, see the questions, the doubt.

Abruptly, she broke the eye contact and stretched toward the ceiling. He watched as two more cobwebs disappeared. "We'll start with the floor," she said.

He gave a quick nod and turned to let his body cool down. When he looked at her again, she avoided his eyes and continued swatting at cobwebs. The way she was swinging that shirt, the whole room would soon be raining dust.

He stuck his head out the window and sucked in the air. He knotted and unknotted his fists. When the snapping stopped, he straightened and said, "I'll get a flashlight from the car."

They gathered the obvious clothes and trash on the floor, then, with the help of the flashlight, pulled out the debris from underneath the bed. Gradually, the activity helped return his control.

Casey checked the dresser drawers. Trevor attacked the clothes in the closet, examining every pocket, every fold, each pants cuff and shoe.

He tried to ignore the guilt growing inside him. Richard was gone, he told himself. Besides, she was his brother's ex-wife, not his wife.

His conscience wouldn't let go. The guilt mushroomed until he had to ask himself how he could be so drawn to his brother's ex-wife right here in his brother's motel room. He felt relieved when he slipped his fingers out of the last pocket and turned his attention to the boxes on the floor.

"We'll do one at a time." He lugged the first box to the table. Dust and dirt stuck to his clammy hands.

Casey unfolded the top and found layers of newspapers covering an assortment of papers. He tossed them aside. He wasn't sure what he expected to find, but not more papers.

She grabbed a handful and shuffled through them. "These are old, Trevor. They're letters from different banks to my aunt. Here's one of her old investment statements."

"Why would he have that?"

"Richard saved everything."

Her response didn't exactly answer his question. He let it drop. He glanced at the papers as she put them on the bed and wondered why he'd spent all night getting uptight about what they'd find. What had he hoped to find, some nice little note from Richard reading, Hi, Bro'. Sorry we missed each other, but let me tell you where the bonds are hidden?

"Everything's been thrown in together," she said.

There was a tightness in her voice, a control that over-rode what could have become general hysteria at the discovery of more secrets from her past. He had to hand it to her, though, she was holding up extremely well.

"Hold on a minute. Look at this." He pulled three slim books from beneath a final layer of newspaper.

"They're ledgers," said Casey. One ledger had an X penned on the front, the second one an R, and the third one looked like a P. "What do you think the letters mean?"

"The R probably stands for Richard," he said.

"X sounds like Rex." Casey laughed, her voice music to his ears. "No, it couldn't be that simple."

He placed the books side by side on the table and compared pages with similar dates. "The figures don't match," he said. "Look, here's an entry in each book, same date, same identification, different figures."

"Search for a pattern."

They compared the next several pages. "You're right. The difference in each total is the same page after page."

She pushed back her chair and paced the room. "I think you're right about the R standing for Richard. I think he was skimming off the top of the profits. The R ledger shows the real figures. The X and P ledgers represent two other people involved in his little scam."

Cringing inside at the clearer picture of his twin, but forcing himself to remember his job with the bureau, he said, "He had to feed his addiction. You didn't know about his gambling?"

"No, but it makes sense. Aunt Maude had him working her finances two months after he rented the room from her. It irritated me at first. At the time I didn't have any background in bookkeeping or accounting, so eventually I figured she'd made the right choice."

"It's possible the ledgers tell another story," he said. "Motivation. If the authorities are wrong about Richard's death, if he was killed, then somebody discovered he was skimming and decided to put a stop to it.''

"You mean Rex?'' She sat down, her eyes focused on him.

"I doubt that. Brenda gave me the impression Rex was a follower, not a leader.''

"It's strange that he's disappeared. Maybe we should concentrate on finding Rex.''

He couldn't help laughing. "You're really getting into it, aren't you? Casey Michaels, detective at large.'' He reached out and let his fingers enclose the soft, fragile-feeling hand that minutes ago had sent flames coursing through his body. Her skin was so feminine, so soft, but when her fingers gripped his hand, he felt her strength, her pride, her bull-headed determination.

She slid her hand away. "Not me. I just want the whole mess straightened out as fast as possible so I can get back to my normal, dull life.''

"Then I'd say we have our hands full for the moment. If we don't get anywhere with the little we have, we'll concentrate on Rex. Deal?''

Mixed in with the records and notes in a paper grocery bag, they found a torn sheet of paper. "It's Richard's handwriting. Looks like he started some kind of list,'' said Casey.

He recognized one of the names from his files at work. He dug through the bag, hoping to find the missing piece. "I don't see the other half,'' he said, pocketing the list.

"Is it important?''

"Who knows. It might be.''

They tugged at another box. Casey removed the newspapers on top, and he received the shock of his life. Dozens of lose photographs lay beneath the papers.

"These were taken when Richard was a little boy." She straightened all the pictures, glancing at them briefly.

He took one photo at a time. A blond-haired little boy with Trevor's blue-gray eyes stared back at him. Richard riding a tricycle. Richard blowing out five candles. Richard before a huge house with a man and a woman holding each hand.

He couldn't put a word to how he felt. Here was his twin with the family he'd never known, the family he never would know. He experienced an instant identification with the small boy in the picture, a surprising and overwhelming connection to a past that had eluded him. The pictures made Richard real, and for a moment he again tried to imagine how his own life might have been with a brother, a twin, a family.

For him there were no childhood pictures, only cold memories of too many foster homes. None of that mattered now. He and Richard had come into the world together. They shared a common beginning that nothing could erase, and for that reason alone, the pictures caused unfamiliar, embarrassing feelings. He felt uncomfortable as hell.

He looked over at Casey. She was watching him closely. Tears moistened her eyes, and a sweet smile curved her lips. She said nothing when she placed her hand on his arm. She didn't need to. Her gentle acceptance pushed him to acknowledge what he felt—a special joy at the discovery of Richard's family, a part of him found, not lost.

He kissed her softly on the cheek. "Thank you."

She swiped at her eyes. "I didn't do anything."

But he knew she had. Her acceptance, her lack of judgment, allowed him to accept the emotion he felt.

He looked at each picture several times, then stacked them together and handed them to her.

"I'll set them on the dresser," she said. "We'll have to make you an album."

Her idea touched him and made him smile as he worked. "Here's more newspapers." He set them aside. "And something else." He took out several children's toys, some crayoned pictures and a magazine. Beneath them he found a baptismal certificate, a confirmation certificate and a high school diploma. He stared at the three papers before him.

"Is something wrong?"

"The names are different. Look at this. The high school diploma says Tapp, but the baptismal and confirmation certificates show a different last name." He recognized the new name. Anyone in his business would know it instantly as part of the sordid history of crime. But, no, it was a co-incidence, that was all.

"His mother must have remarried." When he continued to stare at the three documents, she climbed off the bed saying, "Come on. We'll take the whole box."

He began stuffing newspapers back in the box, then stopped as a headline caught his eye. He took the paper aside and scanned the article. It told of the infiltration and break-up of a national embezzling ring run by Richard's father. A second article detailed the trial.

"I don't believe this. The same damn family."

Casey peered over his shoulder. "What family? Is that his father?"

He riffled through the box for the family picture. When he found it, he held it beside the news photo. There was an age difference, of course, but the resemblance was too close not to believe these two men were the same person.

"You know these people?"

"I've heard the name."

"Could be an uncle or something. Richard never indicated his father was in trouble with the law."

But he was, thought Trevor, and that explained a lot.

"Trevor, look at the date. Richard would have been seventeen when this man went to trial." She pointed to the top of the article. "According to his diploma, he didn't finish high school until two years later. It must have been hard watching his father go through that."

He knew how it felt being the odd man out, especially as a teenager trying to find yourself. Based on Richard's activities when he died, he could only guess that perhaps he had never found himself. It looked like he'd tried to be a carbon copy of his father.

He pitched the papers in the box and let out a deep sigh as he leaned back against the wall. "You know, ever since I found out I had a twin, a small part of me envied that family scene, but not now. Not all the foster parents I knew were ideal parents, but a couple of them were really good people, special enough to make a difference, like the Collins'. Maybe Richard would have been better off left behind with me."

She closed the box and sat beside him on the bed. "We all make our choices, Trevor, regardless of our background."

He put his arm around her, absorbing her strength and support and reveling in the heat that spread through his body when he touched her. "Yeah, but every choice comes with extra baggage."

She looked up at him, her eyes wide, her lips smiling. He brushed her mouth with his, the temptation too great to resist as his need for her swept through him.

Passion flooded her eyes. Before he could kiss her again the way she deserved to be kissed, the way he longed to, she wriggled out of his arms, one hand holding his, and tugged him to his feet.

"I don't know about you, but I'm starving." As if on cue, her stomach rumbled.

He let her pull him up. He knew if they lingered any longer, dinner would be the last item on both their lists.

As he carried the first box to the trunk, he watched her climb into the front seat of the car. The cool night air stimulated his mind, as if waking him up. Casey. For the first time in his life, he questioned his ability to handle a situation alone. Having her there when he saw the pictures, when Richard became real to him, not only helped, it had been imperative. Her gentle acceptance had forced him to acknowledge the way he felt. He hadn't had to fake some macho reaction, as if he didn't care.

Had she known a part of him had yet to accept the reality of a brother out there all these years? Even he hadn't known. She trusted with her heart, not with some pretense of mind, and she spread that open trust wherever she went.

But no matter how beautiful she was, how tempting, how right, he had to keep her at a distance. Even if he could beat the guilt, there was still the matter of the bureau.

Oh, they'd find the bonds, and once they did, the system would lay bare his bureau connection. It couldn't be avoided. He'd be relieved when she knew. He hated the lies between them. But that revelation would end any fantasy about the two of them getting together.

With special care, he carried the box of Richard's childhood memories to the trunk. Precious cargo, that's what he carried. Glimpses into a past that he'd missed, a picture story of a brother he was coming to know. He'd embarked on a path of self-discovery that was slowly untangling secrets buried so deep, he'd forgotten they were there.

He closed up the motel room with a lighter spirit and a greater feeling of wholeness than any he'd ever known. He felt a new connection to his twin after seeing where he'd lived, where he'd worked, where he'd played. He couldn't define this new sense of him. It was just there, in his mind,

in his heart, in his understanding of the life Richard had
lived.

By God, he had a brother.

He rolled these thoughts around in his head as they drove
north on Route 1 amid the zooming traffic. When they
turned right at the dark road to Casey's house, they left the
confusion behind them.

He held Casey's hand as he drove. A thousand stars
lighted the sky to lead the way. It seemed a fitting celebra-
tion of the moment.

But when he steered the car around the last curve, he forgot about the stars, about Richard, about everything else.
Bouncing out the end of Casey's drive were two spears of
light.

Trevor stiffened. The vehicle sped toward them in the
opposite lane with its blinding bright beams like two sharp
blades in the night.

Chapter Ten

He reached across the seat and forced Casey's head forward. "Get down, they might see you."

"What..." Casey had no chance to question him. Her head hit her knees seconds before she heard a car speed past. Two minutes later Trevor screeched onto her drive.

"You can sit up," said Trevor. "They're gone."

He yanked the car door open and walked to the house so fast his feet threw gravel along the path. She expected the worst, but when they walked in and turned on the living room lights, the room appeared untouched.

He slammed the door shut behind them. "They were here. There's your evidence." He pointed behind the door. "Your lousy alarm system's gone."

"Damn it!" The alarm switch dangled by its wires. The gaping hole in the wall measured twice the size of the switch, not to mention the smudges left behind by the sloppy job. This was one break-in too many. She was through with tears.

She walked to the chair and threw down her purse. The anger simmering inside her reached a fast boil. "Damn it! We're going to find them. So help me, if it takes every penny I have, every single ounce of energy, they'll pay."

Trevor searched every room on the first floor. "I'll check upstairs," he said. She started to follow. "You stay put. Somebody could be up there."

"I hope so."

She followed behind him, the splint slowing her down. He glanced back once, but said nothing. She could see the anger in his eyes. She could feel her own anger building inside. This was her home, her private turf. They had no right.

The upstairs was a mess. The boxes from the storage areas were torn open, their contents strewn around the floor.

"That's it," said Trevor. "Tomorrow you install an alarm system that hooks into the police station."

"I can't afford that kind of sophisticated system."

"I'll pay for it."

"You will not." She'd priced them before. The cost had shocked her. She did a mental calculation. She would use her tuition money before she'd let Trevor pay for a new system. Without a decent system, she might not be around to worry about paying for school.

Trevor walked around the room, opening a path by sweeping things aside with his feet. "I'm not going to argue with you. You have to get one, whoever pays for it." He brushed past her, his shoulders tensed, his face frowning. "We'll discuss it after I move the car."

Left alone, she sank against the door frame, unaware of the tears spilling down her cheeks. These guys had been thorough. The contents of both dressers were thrown together with papers and letters and sentimental trinkets. She lifted the top dresser drawer. At least she'd removed Richard's gun from the drawer. For some reason, that seemed important.

HE DROVE UP THE DIRT PATH and punched in Barney's number.

"What the hell, Steele, it's Sunday night. Don't you ever quit?" said Barney.

"Last time I missed a scheduled call, you sent in the idiots," said Trevor, smiling. "I'm just following orders, Barney."

"Yeah, as usual, right? So what's going on? Good news?"

"We found some interesting ledgers at the motel. Tapp was taking them for everything he could get."

"Them? Them who?" The pitch of Barney's voice got higher as he became louder. Trevor described the three ledgers. "We're dealing with a national scam here," said Barney. "It looks like the guy decided to strike out on his own. Any clue to the *P* ledger?"

"Nothing so far."

"Ms. Michaels isn't giving anything away, huh?"

In a controlled voice, Trevor said, "She knows even less than we do." He paused. "Did you know Richard Tapp was a compulsive gambler?"

"She told you that?"

"His partner's wife mentioned it."

"Tapp had a partner? You are making progress."

"What about the gambling? It's not noted in the files."

"I'll have to ask Crowley, but it's news to me. That explains what kept him pushing for bigger and better profits."

"Rex Alcorn's the partner's name. His wife says he's been missing for three weeks. Check the local cops. They know Alcorn's connection to Tapp."

"That's great, just great. Damn bureaucratic red tape. We should already have this information. I'll put Jamison on it. Who knows, with Alcorn's connection to Tapp, we might get lucky and find Alcorn and the bonds in one sweep."

"No," said Trevor, "he doesn't fit the profile."

"Anything else? No bonds yet?"

"Another break-in at the Michaels's place. Call in some favors, will you? I want a high-tech security system in the house by the crack of dawn."

"Consider it done." Barney's yawn rumbled through the phone. "Your minute's up, Trevor. Skip the nightly calls, will you? And send me the ledgers through your usual channel."

He was ready to hang up when Barney's voice called him back. "By the way, the condo didn't pan out. Somebody beat us to it. Find them, Trevor, time's getting short." The dial tone buzzed in his ear.

Quietly, he replaced the receiver and walked toward the house. Deceiving Barney played havoc with his conscience, and his conscience was already suffering enough. He justified deceiving Casey by telling himself he was on a job, but the taste of her lips lingered to complicate the logic. He had no choice but to deceive them both. An explanation of his brother's death took priority over everything.

HE RETURNED to the small bedroom and found Casey sitting on the floor, staring at the window, tears streaming down her cheeks. His heart wrenched.

"What happened?" He sat down beside her. He'd never seen her cry. He was at a total loss. He wanted the smile back on her face, the laughter back in her voice. He longed to erase this latest break-in from her memory, to pull her close and comfort her. He gave in to the urge without a fight and put his arms around her. "Tell me what's wrong."

The quiet sobbing slowed a little. Tears continued to run down her cheeks. "I can't stand it, Trevor. It's *my* house, *my* things. And I found this." She held up a bank book. "This is the missing bank book."

She cried softly and let him hold her. Gradually, her sobbing stopped and she pulled away from him.

"This is awful. I'm so sorry." She swiped at her eyes. "I must seem like a total wimp."

"What's with this book?" He took it from her hand.

Calmer now, she said, "Aunt Maude invested the money from my parents' estate and made a small fortune. Then, I guess, she didn't trust her investments anymore. I don't know. She was a bit strange. She cashed them all in and, instead, opened three savings accounts in three different banks."

"I don't understand."

"This is the book for one of the accounts. He told me it didn't exist."

"Who?" But he knew. Before she said "Richard," he knew. Here was another lie. What type of man deceived his own wife?

"After Aunt Maude died, I tried to find the three bank books. Richard only had two, and one account was empty. He swore the third one didn't exist. But you see, Aunt Maude had told me there were three, and, damn it all, I believed *him*."

He opened the book to the first page. "This was in one of the boxes I searched. I didn't think it was important." He flipped through several pages and looked for a final balance. When he found it, his jaw dropped. The amount was staggering. "You won't have to worry about money for a while."

She handed him the withdrawal receipts. "No, you're wrong, nothing's changed. He emptied this account, too."

He looked at the figures and recalculated the balance. "Damn!"

She wiped her face with her hands and stood up. "The money's gone, Trevor. Richard claimed he spent the other money on Aunt Maude's medical expenses, when all along he probably gambled it away." She picked up the remaining papers on the floor and put them in the open box. "It's not the missing money that bothers me so much, it's the deception—and my own stupidity. I was so naive. I had no idea he spent all my family's money until after I left him."

"You trust people, Casey. It's part of your nature. You can't change that." And he felt a wrenching twist of regret deep inside.

"I don't trust so easily anymore."

She closed the box and stared at her hands twisting back and forth on its top. "This has to end. I've had it. Let somebody find the bonds—the government, those guys who keep breaking into my house, anybody."

They pushed the boxes against the wall. He followed her down the stairs in silence. Her anxiety showed through the set of her shoulders. Undaunted by the knee splint, she quickened her pace at the bottom of the stairs, her determination clear by the tilt of her head.

He felt her frustration seeping through him. He was a man who got things done, who went after what he wanted. Right now, he wanted those damn bonds found and the case settled. Damn Richard, anyway. He could only imagine the unspoken ways he must have ruined her life.

They ordered pizza and ate with a minimum amount of conversation. He kept running the case through his head, examining the known facts, and guessing at possibilities. The key seemed to be the *P* ledger. Who was *P?* What he needed was some kind of bait. If he could flush out the man at the top, maybe they'd have all the pieces.

"I want to run something past you." He pulled out two kitchen chairs.

She closed her eyes and let out a sigh. "Not tonight, Trevor. It's been a rotten day."

"Come on, sit down. Hear me out." He helped her to a chair. "Let your imagination go for a minute. What if the thugs believed some of the bonds were being cashed?

"What?" He saw a glimmer of hope reflected in those large, sad blue eyes.

"What do you think would happen?"

She sprang from her chair. "Oh my God, that's it, that's the answer." She hugged him around the neck. "I'll mortgage the house and make a huge deposit. Then I'll broadcast the fact that I'm rolling in cash."

This woman could get carried away faster than a bat in a belfry. He grabbed her wrist. "Wait a minute. That's not what I had in mind."

"But it would work. They'd come running out of the closet like that." She snapped her fingers.

"No."

She backed away and put her hands on her hips. She scowled at him, her nose wrinkling in irritation, her blue eyes growing stormy. "What do you mean, no? It's my house, my ex-husband, and my neck."

"I happen to like your neck the way it is."

That stopped her. She froze in mid-motion, her stormy eyes wider than ever. They were magnetic, intriguing to the point of clouding his judgment.

As if sensing his vulnerability, and taking advantage of his hesitation, she said, "If we can find out who Richard worked with, we can find the bonds and clear up everything."

He tore his eyes away from her. How could a man think around this woman? He paced the floor. "Right, and that's what I want to do, but not with you as bait."

"Trevor..."

"If we can find out who's involved in this scam, we can make better sense of what we know so far."

"I agree. That's my point."

"Those two troublemakers are the little guys. They do the dirty work."

"They weren't so little."

"And that's my point."

"All right, all right. So tell me your idea."

"I'll be the one to make a large deposit and brag about money."

"That's ridiculous. Why do they care if you have a lot of money?"

"I could let it be known I found the bonds in the house."

"So let me play devil's advocate for a minute, okay? How come I don't know you found some of the bonds? What do I do, just let you walk away with all that money and smile and say, 'Gee whiz, isn't this great. You found the bonds, and please, Mr. Steele, cash them in and keep the money. I don't need it. I don't even want it.' Even I wouldn't buy that, Trevor."

His logical mind knew she was right, but his heart refused to consider the other option. "It's all in how you present it. We could make it work. We could fake a fight over the bonds and somehow make ourselves a public spectacle."

"And advertise the fact that we found the bonds?"

"That was your idea, Casey. 'I'll broadcast the fact that I'm rolling in cash.' That's what you just said."

"What you're suggesting wouldn't be the same and you know it." She kept smacking her right fist into her left palm. "I've listened to your plan, Trevor, and I don't like it. I'll do this my way or not at all."

"What makes you think they couldn't find out about the mortgage loan?"

She sat down on the hard chair. "You're right. I'm just so tired of waiting for something bad to happen instead of taking the bull by the horns and making something good happen."

He felt trapped. She'd proposed a plan he knew from experience would work, as long as the loan couldn't be traced. She was at her wit's end. He wasn't sure how much more of this harassment she could take.

She looked him square in the eye, her face serious, her eyes intense. "If you have any idea that would bring this to an end, I'm game, but it has to make sense. We can't risk losing."

He didn't want to tell her the new idea forming in his mind, but he knew it would work even better than the other one. She sat tall in the chair and stopped twisting the ring around her finger, watching him, waiting, as if she knew he had more to say. After a lengthy silence, he took a deep breath and blurted out his thoughts, all the while cursing himself inside.

"I know what will work," he said. "It's dangerous. I'd have to stick to you like glue every minute of every day once the plan's in motion. No fooling around. No slips. These guys play for keeps."

She leaned back in the chair. A smile curled her lips and new life sparked her eyes. "I can make that sacrifice."

"Here's what we can do."

THE ALARM SYSTEM was installed early the next morning before Casey got up. "I'll show you how it works when we get home," said Trevor.

Sipping his coffee, he admired the way her beige slacks hugged her hips as she strolled across the kitchen. She fixed herself some tea, ignoring the perked coffee, and stood with her back to him gazing out the back door. Her shoulders seemed tense, her back rigid, not the reaction he'd expected to see when she learned her home was safe.

"How long before it's operating fully?" she asked, still watching the woods.

"I'd say," he checked his watch, "probably two hours at most. They'll code it in at the station and..." He caught himself from saying more than he should know. "At least that's what the guy said when he left."

She turned around and faced him, a slight frown on her face. "And when did you arrange all this? We were up pretty late last night."

He approached her cautiously, unsure of her mood. "An old friend of mine's in the security business. Remember I mentioned my job as a security guard? The guy I worked with eventually branched out on his own. I gave him a call last night. Since he owed me a favor, he was more than happy to oblige." Lies, when would they end? But this was close to the truth. It was the best he could do.

When she turned away from him again, he wasn't sure what to think. She pushed back her hair with a toss of her head. A sunbeam captured her hand as she lifted her cup.

"What's wrong?" The woman constantly puzzled him.

This time she swung around slowly, gracefully, the frown complete. "Nothing. Nothing at all." She placed her cup on the sink. "Except you could have waited for my decision about the new alarm, that's all."

He admired her independence, but didn't she know how vulnerable she was out here alone?

"You need it, Casey, but if you're sure you don't want it, I'll have them take it out."

"No, don't do that." She walked to the table, the creases on her forehead deeper. "I did decide to have it put in, but you didn't know that, did you?"

"Hey, look, I'm sorry I jumped the gun. I guess I'm used to doing things on my own. This system isn't foolproof, either, but it beats having nothing."

"I know. I'll stop by the bank today and transfer funds from one account to the other."

He kept the smile from his face. He'd paid for a large chunk of the expense up front. He had more money sitting around in investments and banks than he'd ever need. Then there was the inheritance from Ned. Eventually, he'd tell her, but not yet. She'd made it clear she wouldn't accept that type of help from him now.

She added, "I just wasn't prepared for anything to happen this fast."

This worried him. "When we set our plan in motion, that's when the action flies. You've got to be ready for anything."

"Then maybe it's good I'm getting some practice." Her smile cast the shadows from his heart.

She wiped her hands on the dish towel. "I have to go."

"Casey?" His eyes captured hers and held them fast. The thought of her driving off alone to work made him uptight. He took her in his arms and pulled her close. "You be careful."

She gave him a quick kiss on the cheek, her breasts soft and enticing against his chest. She raised her face, and he wanted to lose himself in her sparkling eyes, the curve of her lips, the confident tilt of her chin. "Don't worry about me," she said. "I'll be fine."

But he wasn't fine, he was going nuts. Her kiss had been innocent, but his thoughts weren't. His mouth met hers with a crushing force. So tender, so soft, her lips pressed on his. The world he knew was lost in her arms. She was strength, she was passion, she tied him in knots.

Their tongues met, and he felt her melt against him, felt her acknowledge the flames between them. He pulled her closer and gasped as her fingers trailed along his neck. He wove his fingers through her hair, wanting her, needing her, refusing to let her go. He felt lost in her softness, consumed in their passion, and when she drew back, he saw the same fire in her eyes that he felt in himself.

"I really do have to go." Her voice drifted over him like a bewitching fog.

She leaned into him one more time, and he crushed her to him, reluctant to let this end. Then she pecked him on the mouth and stepped from his arms. "I'll meet you at the deli?"

"It shouldn't take long."

Totally disoriented, he watched her drive away, then wiped his brow with his arm. Since when could a woman knock him totally senseless?

The taste of her lips lingered, the sweet smell of her haunting him as he roamed the house locking doors and checking the alarm. Finally, he gathered what he needed to put their plan in place, swearing to himself that with every bone in his body, he would keep her from harm's way.

They just had to make it through the next few hours. Apart.

Chapter Eleven

Casey paused for the red light, amazed that the whole world seemed brighter this morning. She brought her arm to her nose to savor the scent of Trevor caught in an embrace. Her heart thumped a fast beat and refused to slow down. The taste of him still felt so real, the feel of him so sure and solid. Her head was spinning, but his image was securely in place.

She smiled to herself as she wove in and out of the traffic and recalled the concerned look on his face as she left the house. He cared about her. She saw it in his eyes and felt it in his touch, and the truth of it stunned her and made the world even brighter.

But he needn't worry about her. She was used to coping by herself. She'd even learned to deal with the loneliness of living alone. Ever since she left Richard, she'd been alone. Ever since her parents died, she'd *felt* alone.

It seemed incredible to think of her life that way. Once she'd become an adult, she'd realized Aunt Maude had been incapable of unconditional love. Her own impulsiveness had baffled her aunt and driven them further apart. Because of her aunt's limitations, she'd felt left out as a child. She'd become so used to living that way that when Richard came along, she never realized he excluded her from most of his life, from most of himself.

Trevor seemed very different from his brother. Yes, there were times when his silence made her wonder what thoughts were roaming through his mind, but these silences were becoming fewer and fewer. He seemed so much a part of her already that without him following behind her, she felt that old loneliness settle over her like a blanket of thorns.

She loved his caring nature, his teasing sense of humor. She loved his arms around her, his fiery lips on hers. His touch sent her senses reeling. Just being in a room with him kept her off-balance.

Blaring horns snagged her attention. She looked up and saw the light had turned green. Behind her, the line of traffic waited impatiently. She drove one more block and parked her car.

She walked into the office to find she was expected at a staff meeting. "We never have staff meetings," she said.

"We do now," said Aretha. She sat behind a desk, busily twisting a stray black curl through her fingers. Her eyes were buried in paperwork. Casey didn't like the frown on her face.

"Did Jon mention what it's about?" she asked.

Aretha's eyes darted up quickly, then resumed their downward cast. "They're making some organizational changes."

She waited in silence for a very long minute. She and Aretha were not bosom buddies, but she thought they were friends. At lunch the other day, she'd been unusually quiet and withdrawn, not like herself at all. She'd been working two jobs this week and Casey had attributed her behavior to exhaustion, but even then, that explanation hadn't felt right. This was the first time she'd seen her since then. She was obviously hiding something.

Aretha stood up. "Okay," she said. "They're taking you off the local pickups. Jon wasn't supposed to tell me. If Victor finds out you know, Jon's name is mud."

"Why?" Casey felt a new panic. She'd have a hard time staying in the black if her income dropped. Keeping food in the house was difficult enough, not to mention saving again for her last tuition payment.

Aretha came around the desk and spoke quietly beside her. "I honestly don't know what's going on. Jon didn't say much. He seems so nervous lately, and I can't pinpoint why."

The staff meeting was brief and to the point. The part-time employees' hours were being cut because business was slow, Jon said. Casey was relegated to part-time out-of-town courier only, beginning tomorrow. The news shocked her.

She lingered to share a doughnut with Aretha. "I'm sorry, Casey. I know how much you need this job."

"Maybe the out-of-town jobs will pick up," she said. "Who knows?" The company had expanded their service to include out-of-town deliveries only recently. If business was slow locally, she had no reason to believe it was better elsewhere, but she wasn't going to say so.

"Jon's taking me to dinner tonight," said Aretha, her eyes aglow. She went into a lengthy discussion of her weekend with Jon and what had been happening in the office.

"Sounds great," said Casey, injecting an excitement in her voice she didn't feel.

Aretha had been trying to catch Jon's attention since he first walked in the office. Casey wanted to feel happy for her, but she wasn't sure she trusted Jon. He was too efficient, too organized, too dependable and too considerate to be real. No one knew better than she about deceptive first impressions. But Aretha was a smart young woman, she told herself, and certainly not as naive as Casey had been two years ago. Maybe she was wrong. Maybe Aretha's judgment of Jon would hold true. Maybe.

"Ah, Ms. Michaels." Victor seemed to appear from nowhere. "I regret the change in assignments, my dear." He broke off a bite of doughnut. His eyes flitted from the doughnut to Aretha to Casey. "It's good of you to take over the out-of-towners like this."

Jon joined them, a worried frown on his usually controlled face. "I'm sorry about the change, Casey."

"Nonsense," said Victor. "She'll have more time for her studies now. And Ms. Michaels, don't bother with the trip in each morning." He put his hand on Aretha's shoulder. "Why don't you call Ms. Ames every day or so to see if you're scheduled, instead of driving all that way to the office."

She had the distinct impression she was being dismissed without anyone telling her. "But..."

"No need to thank me," said Victor. His eyes flicked to Jon then back to Casey, where they lingered so long she thought they might bore a hole through her forehead. "I'm sure you'll find another job. You're a resourceful young lady." His smile seemed forced and calculating when he added, "Make sure you stay in touch. We need you to handle the out-of-town overflow."

"OVERFLOW MY FOOT!" she said to Trevor once she could control her anger. "One minute I have a job, the next minute I'm not sure when I'll see my next paycheck."

He took her hands in his. "You have enough to worry about with the break-ins and the stolen bonds without adding your job to the list. I'm sorry this happened."

They were sitting in a small deli not far from her office. The traffic outside the window inched along bumper-to-bumper. A steady line of customers streamed in and out, each person purchasing bags of sandwiches and trays of coffee, then skittering out the door with each hurried ring of the old-fashioned cash register. Everyone seemed to be in a rush. Like she was three hours ago. But she felt the strength in Trevor's hands, the honesty of his concern. He made her feel confident that everything would be all right.

"Didn't you say you still have the out-of-town jobs?"

"They're few and far between." She slipped her hands from his grasp and picked up her coffee. "So I guess I know what I'll be doing for the next few weeks."

"What do you mean?"

She threw her head back and stared at him, surprised that he didn't realize the magnitude of her problem. "I've got to find another job, Trevor, probably something full-time. Very few places are as flexible as the courier service. Most of them expect their part-time help to work evenings."

His back stiffened. He finished his coffee and placed his cup on the table with a precision that made her aware of the sudden change in him. Silence stretched between them until he said, "You'll have to let me help you."

Before she could reiterate her determination to do things on her own, he leaned across the table and took her hand again, his eyes a deep blue. "You can't let a few bucks stop our progress. You want those bonds as badly as I do, and if you're gone eight hours a day working, plus another two for travel, there won't be enough time left for us to finish what we've started. Come on, Casey, let's finish the job."

She held her tongue and considered what he was saying, distracted by the way his thumb wove a circle around her palm. They did seem to be getting closer to the bonds. If she stopped looking now, where would that leave her? After the large deposit he'd just made in her account, she was totally vulnerable, whether she quit now or later.

She swallowed her pride and nodded. "All right. I'll accept your help until we find the bonds, but only if I need it. This isn't charity, Trevor. You'll get every penny back."

She nibbled at her french fries and took a bite of her sandwich. Why couldn't somebody find the bonds? Why couldn't she and Trevor pursue a normal relationship? She thought of Aretha and Jon and their growing interest in each other. "Aretha said Victor was really upset when I stayed home Friday."

"Why couldn't he send someone else to New York?"

"I guess that's what he did."

"Everything's all set, by the way." He handed her a small brown envelope. She removed the deposit slip inside and stared at it. "Wow! You didn't tell me you were putting this much in my account." She folded the receipt and pushed it to the bottom of her pocket. She sent him a huge grin. "Aren't you afraid I'll take your money and run? It happens all the time in the movies."

"Yeah, but in the movies you'd be the bad guy and I'd be setting you up." They both laughed. She felt her body heat with the pleasure of being with him again.

"I trust you, Casey. You know that. You want this to end as much as I want to find some answers."

She thought about Richard's briefcase, the receipt in her old purse, and felt the guilt steal across her fingers and up her arms until it met at the top of her spine and made her shudder. "How long before the wrong people know I'm dripping in cash?"

"That depends on their bank connections."

"Oh, great. We may be sitting ducks forever."

He faced her with shadows in his eyes. "It's not too late to change your mind and drop this crazy scheme. Just say the word."

"No way. This is going to work."

A twinge of regret sprang from deep inside her. Finding the bonds seemed a step away. Trevor would uncover the sordid details of Richard's death soon and then he'd disappear from her life.

"When they discover today's deposit, those two crooks will come knocking fast and hard. You and I have to be prepared for that. So far as they know, the only place you could lay your hands on that much money is by cashing in some bonds. Once they show themselves, we'll have most of the puzzle pieces and plenty of trouble."

For a fleeting second she wanted to say, hold it. I don't like this situation any better than you do, but I love being with you. I love hearing your laughter and knowing that at the end of the day you'll be there. Your touch sets me on fire, your kisses make me tremble. Can't we freeze-frame everything just as it is?

Instead, she said, "We'll be ready and waiting."

While they finished eating, he repeated all the dangers of their plan and their need to be cautious. Casey hashed out every word spoken in the office. Trevor's protective instincts worked overtime throughout lunch until he felt like coming to blows with this Victor character. Casey's eagerness to talk things through and then let them go intrigued him. By the time they were ready to leave, her frown was gone and her eyes sparkled again.

"Sorry to dump on you like that," she said as they nudged their way through the crowd to the door. "Talking about it helped."

He took her hand, bowed, and kissed it lightly. "Consider me your official Dumpster."

Her rich, low laugh made him want to hug her close, a ridiculous urge, he thought, as they cut through the line of people waiting to get inside.

"No," she said, "you are the official mystery prince."

"Mystery prince?"

"That's the only part I left out. Aretha was dying to know who the mysterious man was who asked for me to pick up the other day. She forgot to note it on the slip. She said she called several times over the weekend, but never got an answer. Probably when we went to the motel."

"I'm beginning to understand. I think."

"I told her how you helped me that first night. I guess I called you Prince Charming."

"This is sounding better and better."

She rolled her eyes. "I exaggerated."

"And then you told her I was not only Prince Charming but also the mysterious man on the phone."

They reached her Bug, and she unlocked the door. "Why did I ever bring this up? Your ego will never be the same."

He laughed. "Then my ego thanks you." He bowed again. "Until supper?"

She punched him in the arm. "You're impossible."

He watched her drive away smiling and shaking her head. He felt ten feet tall walking across the lot to his own car. Lighthearted. Goofy. Happy. Like the man who had finally found the rainbow missing from his life.

SHE EASED ONTO HER DRIVE and stopped the car. Completing her pickups and deliveries had been more interesting than usual on her last day working the city. She'd passed the time on the road by spying on Trevor. Her eyes were still glued to her rearview mirror.

The man noticed everything, including overbearing vendors, homeless beggars, impatient pedestrians and careless drivers, and he never missed her watching him in the mirror. Anyone would think he had a trained eye. He absorbed and reacted smoothly with no change in expression. Except for twice. On two occasions drivers had dared to separate them. That's when she saw the frown wrinkle his face. Both times he swerved around quickly to the outside lane and nudged his way back in place.

Richard's brother was a good man. She had yet to find fault with him.

Had she been waiting and watching for some slip? Maybe so, she admitted. Maybe she'd prejudged him based solely on his blood tie to Richard.

As she watched him pass her driveway in the rearview mirror, as she imagined him taking his car over the worn path across the road and guiding it along the rim of the hill, she knew what her body had known all along. She could trust this man. She could depend on him. Everything he'd done since she'd met him proved his sincerity. He was nothing like his brother. For once, she would trust her instincts.

She stretched out as much as her Bug would allow, surprised at the relief she felt. The woodsy evening air brought with it a new energy that complemented her relief and made her feel at peace with herself. Amazingly, she'd blamed this absence of peace on her present situation, not knowing she'd been fighting this other battle with herself.

She trusted him. She tried on the idea like she would try on a new suit. It felt exactly right. Perfect.

She watched him clamber down the hill balancing grocery bags in both arms. He reached the bottom and glanced at her and smiled, a breathtaking smile that transformed his face and made her heart skip.

Hugging the two bags to his chest, he opened the car door.

"Let me help you," she said.

"I've got it." He climbed into the car and balanced the bags on his lap. "Let's go."

They drove down the long drive, content in their silence, while she continued to examine this new suit of trust.

"This is my night for dinner," he said, placing the bags on the kitchen table.

"You cooked the last time," she said, enjoying his light mood.

He took her by the arm and ushered her to the foot of the stairs. "This morning you had a regular job. Tonight you need pampering. Don't you have an exam to study for?"

"Really, Trevor, I'll have plenty of time to study now."

"Nope, get out of here. Go take a bath or study or read a book. Can't you see I have this great need to play chef tonight?" His easy laugh brightened the room. His eyes shone with a playful sparkle. "I'll call you when it's ready. Go on." He gave her a little nudge.

She gave in without a fight. The thought of being pampered tonight of all nights was too appealing.

After a long soak in the tub, she pulled on her robe. Faint streaks of light from the setting sun shadowed across her bed. She could smell the pines as a slight breeze ruffled the curtains at the open window.

She lay down and closed her eyes to relax for a few minutes before going downstairs. The hot water had totally relaxed her. She couldn't stop herself from drifting off to sleep.

THE DELICIOUS SCENT of beef broth and garlic stirred her senses first. She opened her eyes slowly, reluctant to let go of a sweet dream filled with Trevor and Trevor and Trevor.

He sat down beside her. Reality mixed with her dreamworld and she reached for him, took his hand in both of hers, and felt the slight roughness of skin and the strength of his fingers as they folded over hers.

A small lamp lit the darkened room. Its shadows played with the fire in his eyes and caught the highlights of his hair.

She stretched like a cat, unwilling to let go of the dream made real. She traced up the length of his arm and encircled his neck. Slowly, she pulled him down and brushed her lips on his, an innocent gesture, the melding of her dream with the reality of him beside her. Electrical charges surged through her blood, the sparks of passion beyond anything she might have dreamed. She let her hand slide away from his neck as her dreamworld faded into memory. Her aggressiveness embarrassed her.

He held her hand. Oh, so gently, his fingers caressed her chin. "Now I know you can read my mind."

Shock at her actions replaced her embarrassment. Her only experience with intimacy was with her husband. Richard had made it quite clear that only he was to initiate personal, physical contact.

But Trevor didn't seem to mind. He seemed to like it. On impulse, she reached up and ran her hand over his face, his stubbled cheeks, the crooked ridge in his nose. He didn't move, didn't speak or breathe. She found the freedom exhilarating.

He linked her hand with his and pulled her to him. "Hi, sleepyhead."

He traced his finger along her lips, her nose, across her eyes, then followed the pattern with his mouth, nipping here and licking there. Then down her neck and out to her shoulders, her robe a mere shadow of hindrance, her senses going haywire. His tasting and teasing were driving her wild.

She couldn't resist responding. She burned for the taste of him. She circled her arms around his neck and met his lips with a passion and longing born the day she met him. Her electrified senses begged for more.

He gave her more. He took her mouth with a demanding need that echoed centuries of waiting. He teetered on the edge of sanity as he lost himself in her freshness. She smelled of honey and roses and all the flowers of spring. Her sweet nectar fed his passion. He strained to hold himself in check, wanting not to frighten her, but needing her, wanting her, longing to claim her as his own, to touch, to caress, to fondle and plunder. Her hands roamed his back, strong and demanding, and caught in his hair in a sensual way that drove him crazy.

She met his plunging tongue in a seductive battle of need. He tasted and savored, then let her explore, let her instincts lead the way. She ran her tongue slowly along the edges of his teeth. Fire burned in her kiss. Still, he held back his passion, not wanting to lose this sweet torment, not daring to hope for more. My God, she was pushing him to the limit.

He took in every gasp, every moan of pleasure. He felt every move, every shift, and each touch, so that when she stiffened slightly, just a small shift in her yielding body, his senses were instinctively alerted to the outside world.

The crunch of wheels on gravel. He tore himself from her arms and cocked an ear to listen more closely. Forgetting the potential danger that lurked just beyond their grasp was easy to do when he held her in his arms, when he enjoyed her passion and ached for more.

More gravel crunched. "Did you set the alarm?" He left the bed and walked to the window, careful to keep himself hidden from view.

She pulled the sheet up to her neck. "I thought you did."

He moved closer to the window. "You expecting someone?"

"Is someone coming?" She sat up in bed and wrapped her robe tightly across her breasts.

His sudden move startled her. Before she could question him, he dashed across the room, slipped one arm behind her neck, the other beneath her knees, and in one quick swoop, lifted her off the bed.

"Trevor stop it. Put me down."

"Keep still," he growled in a whisper.

Three strides brought them to her door. Another four, down the hall.

Panic gripped her as his tense fingers dug into her skin. He was running now, as if she were fluff and feathers in his arms. Down the stairs, the front hallway, through the kitchen, out the back door.

"What is going on?" she demanded once they were outside. She wriggled in his arms.

"Damn!" His voice was gruff and anxious. Deadly eyes caught hers briefly mid-stride. "Trust me, sweetheart. We have a minute. Maybe two."

Chapter Twelve

His arms clamped her to his chest. He crashed through the trees behind her house, veering slightly to the right as he dashed ahead. She could feel the pounding of his heart, a steady bumping against her side. On he ran, away from the house.

Branches caught at her robe and tangled in her hair. The lack of a path slowed their progress. The woods were thicker now, free and untamed by human hands. There seemed no sense to the broken path he wove. Unruly vines covered clumps of trees with their roots as strong as steel. They tripped him twice, he stumbled and swore.

Behind them, she heard the back screen door bang shut. She stretched her neck to see, just as Trevor dropped to the ground. They landed on layers of damp pine needles and leaves.

When she tried to speak, he brusquely clamped his mouth on hers. She could feel his focused determination. His arms clung to her and crushed her between his body and the bed of leaves.

She surrendered to the fire fed by his body touching hers. It was crazy; it was the danger. His lips were full of need and passion. His tongue tormented, demanded, imposed.

The leaves covered them in a brown-and-green coverlet, the smell of pine disguised their scent, and the gurgle of the river hid their sighs. She felt his arousal swelling against her, like the insatiable need growing within herself, and she ached to take their passion to its natural conclusion right here on nature's bed.

His lips lessened their hold slowly at first, then suddenly his warm nectar was gone. He shifted his body to her side.

It took her several minutes to leave paradise behind. She opened her eyes to light beams tracing the trees overhead. Someone was searching the woods. For them.

"I thought we were going to bait the bad guys, then fight it out." The words spilled from her mouth in whispers. The lingering passion burning deep within her kept interfering with her brain.

The light beam arched from left to right. In the scattered shadows she could see the deadly glint in his eyes question the logic of her words.

"We don't stand a chance against six of them." He peered through the vines toward the house. "They'll know you were home, and it's not hard to figure dinner was for two."

"So what do we do?" She didn't dare move. Most likely the men's ranting and stomping around would camouflage any noise she made, but she wasn't taking any chances.

"We wait," he said. His eyes softened as he looked down at her. He gently pushed a stray strand of hair from her face. "They'll go back inside eventually. Then we'll make our move."

As he refocused on the men behind her house, a hard glint replaced the gentleness in his eyes.

The lights continued their scanning inches above their heads. She rolled over and propped her chin on her hands and watched the intruders through an opening in the vines. Trevor lay close beside her, his right leg resting over her bare thigh. Though she watched the activity, her senses burned with an awareness of his every move, of each shift in position, each breath he breathed. The heat from his body seemed to singe her.

She understood why he'd rushed her out of the house, but what now? She couldn't just give over her house to those men. Everything she owned was in there, and here she was wearing nothing but a terry-cloth robe.

Every time she tried to look at her situation logically, he inched closer. His side pressed against hers. His elbow brushed her arm. Her body betrayed her at every contact point.

Shoulder to shoulder they silently waited for the searching lights to dim and the distant voices to quiet. When the lights went out, darkness surrounded them. The screen door banged shut.

"Let's go," he said. He jumped to his feet, dragging her up with him.

When he reached to pick her up, she stopped him. "I can make it on my own."

He took her in his arms, anyway. "You're damn right you can, but we're not risking your knee. Besides, I like you in my arms."

Once again he held her close and tromped boldly through the woods. She wrapped her arms around his neck and lay her head against his chest.

He circled wide, away from the right side of the house. Every few minutes a new light beam speared the trees and they crouched down until it disappeared. He ran when the way was clear and picked his path carefully when the woods became dense. How he found his way baffled her. Even she could get lost in these woods at night, and she'd lived here most of her life. Some innate instinct drove him, and in less time than she expected, she saw a break in the trees where the road ran through.

He put her down. "You'll be all right now. Let's go. This way to the car." He grabbed her hand.

They exited the woods a short distance beyond the old car path. They scampered across the two-lane road, partially lit by a hazy moon, and climbed the grassy incline to his car. Once inside, they both let out a deep sigh.

"How long do you think they'll stay?" she said.

"We're not hanging around to find out." He started backing the car out of the woods.

"I can't just drive away and leave my entire life to those . . . those cruds." The car rolled backward a little farther. "Trevor, stop this car."

He braked abruptly. The sudden stop thrust her forward, and she caught herself on the dash.

"What do you propose? That we sit here long enough for them to find us?"

"They won't find us here." Although she said the words with confidence, she knew the men who wanted the bonds would pursue her as long as they had to, to get what they wanted. The thought made her shudder. "I need my brace, Trevor, and some clothes. Besides, where else is there to go?"

He let up on the brake, and the car continued its backward roll. "I'll take care of it."

At that same moment they saw lights flashing and searching in front of her house. He shoved the car into neutral and pulled on the hand brake. They'd rolled far enough away from the total cover of trees to be visible. She could see the narrow road down the grassy incline behind her.

Instinctively, she slid lower in her seat. "Do you think they saw us?"

He didn't answer. His eyes followed each twist of the wandering light. Interrupted by the abundance of trees, the lights skipped through the woods in broken beams. They were searching the front of her property as meticulously as they had searched the back.

He released the hand brake and, without a sideways glance, let the car roll back freely to the point of intersection. The rutted, overgrown access road jolted them to a halt.

He turned the wheel to the left and angled onto the worn car path, then drifted down to the main road. "Hold on. If they hear us, we're in for a ride."

She braced herself, ready for anything. He shifted into first and smoothly slid onto the hard surface.

The wan moon offered little help as they crept without lights down the road toward her drive. She hoped her house was set far enough away from the road that the thugs wouldn't hear the noise of the engine.

She gripped the armrest, waiting for the van to come barreling down her drive. Every muscle tightened in dreaded anticipation. She glanced at Trevor. She could barely see his profile in the dark, but she could see enough to know he never wavered, never hesitated. He was determined to outwit the men who kept plaguing them.

Slowly, they moved forward around the slight curve and past her drive, past her childhood home, past the men whose greed could destroy her very existence. When they were a safe distance from her drive, he turned on the headlights and increased his speed.

She let out a sigh and loosened her grip on the armrest. Self-consciously, she tugged at the top of her robe.

Trevor leaned back against the seat and let his shoulders ease. He looked over at her. "Sorry about the clothes."

"We were lucky to get out."

She replayed the experience in her mind and tried hard to stop the blush from creeping up her neck. She'd been too totally consumed in the driving passion of his kiss to hear the men coming. Thank God *he* hadn't been. Was this magic attraction one-sided? Had she misread him?

She put her heels up on the seat and hugged her knees to her chest. The heater ran full blast, throwing out warm air to thaw the iciness of her thoughts. The lights of the city brightened the sky as they neared Route 1, and the closer they came, the more uncomfortable she felt in nothing but her robe, the more unreal it seemed that fifteen minutes back the other way, strangers were sitting at her kitchen table helping themselves to her house and home.

"They'll be gone tomorrow," she said, as if saying it would make it so.

The brighter highway lit Trevor's face and detailed a cold determination in his eyes that made her cringe.

"I have to go back and get my clothes, Trevor." He answered her with silence. "What do you expect me to do?"

He spoke without turning away from the road. "We'll manage. I'll pick up some things for you tomorrow."

"I won't let them just take over my house."

"They already have."

When would it stop? Losing her job was bad enough. Damn Richard, anyway. "So where are we going?"

"Some place safe."

They drove to the city in silence. The night-lights and evening traffic made her feel like she was in another world. For a few moments she held on to the fantasy that all was right in her life. That she and Trevor were two ordinary people enjoying a relaxing evening out. That he suffered from the sparks between them as badly as she did. That tonight she'd return to the home she'd worked so hard to keep and tomorrow she'd report for work. That six months from now she wouldn't have to worry about her knee anymore.

But as they crossed the bridge into the District, her fantasy vanished and she concentrated on the man beside her. His continuous silence made her anxious and uncomfortable. She shifted in her seat.

"The plan worked," she said, trying to draw him out.

"Better than I expected." He glanced at her and smiled.

Trevor watched her curl one leg beneath her as she changed her position to face him. Yes, the plan had worked. They'd offered the bait, then neglected to set the trap properly.

He'd studied Barney's files. Barney suspected the embezzlement ring was deeply entrenched and widespread. He had refused to believe his brother would be involved in a professional ring of crooks. He'd been wrong, and his blindness had almost cost him the stubborn, spunky woman beside him.

Tonight proved Barney's suspicions. He'd expected two thugs to pounce when word got out about Casey's large deposit, maybe three, but not six. With a grit force that large, the organization most likely claimed a whole network of suits. He'd have to keep her as far removed from the action as possible. What the hell had he been thinking to set her up like this?

Rather than skirt the city, he steered the car downtown. He needed to be in the middle of the activity. Washington, D.C., was alive with people and traffic. By city standards, the night was young. Groups of sightseers strolled along the Washington Monument grounds. Vendors pushed their wares on the corners. Government buildings loomed large and impressive.

Escaping to the isolated setting of Casey's house at the end of each day had made him lax in his judgment. Until this case was solved, he needed the energy the city produced. He wanted the protection it offered. He would take her some place safe, and the first thing he had to do was get her there without being followed.

The stream of pedestrian traffic thinned when he left the downtown area. He wound his way around short city blocks and eventually turned left into a narrow, dark alley surrounded on both sides by small fenced yards. The homes were old, the fences mere broken relics of a more splendid age.

Casey felt the slightest trepidation. Lost in her thoughts, she hadn't paid much attention to the crooked path he wove. "Where are we?"

"You'll recognize it in a minute."

He drove slowly down the alley, then eased the car into an old brick garage. "I thought you'd rather slip in the back way." His eyes wandered to her breasts, partially exposed from the slipping robe. She pulled her robe tighter together.

A narrow sidewalk led from a garage doorway to an imposing house. It looked intimidating in the dark, its frame cast in shadows from streetlights visible between buildings. When she hesitated, he took her hand and led her forward. "Come with me. No one's going to see you."

They climbed a few steps, walked through a small screened-in porch and entered a short hallway. The first door on the left revealed a narrow staircase. "This used to be the servants' stairs," he said. "They're never used anymore, so you won't run into anybody."

Up the creaky stairs they went. When they reached the third floor, he opened another door in another hall and switched on a light. She recognized the wallpaper immediately. "Collins & Company? This is where I came for your pickup. I didn't recognize it from the alley."

He took her by the arm and led her to the first room on the left. "It's safe," he said.

His grip was unusually firm, the physical connection a lifeline. Only when he switched on the overhead light did he sever the connection.

He caught her eye and held her in a grip more overwhelming than a mere hand on her arm. He seemed to examine every detail—her face, her hair, the filthy robe cinched at her waist. Her body responded with pinpricks of awareness that followed the path of his eyes. "I'll get you some clothes," he said. But he didn't move. His eyes lingered longer in their caress before he looked away and left the room.

She hugged her arms around her to ward off the involuntary shiver and forced herself to walk to the middle of the room. The bedroom was small, but the high ceiling gave it a depth that made it seem large.

Faded ivy wallpaper surrounded her. The delicate vines were a carefree pattern on a cream-colored background. The furnishings were sparse but homey—a chiffonier, a dresser, a nightstand and a brass bed, the mattress elevated a good twelve inches off the floor and covered with a pale green chenille bedspread.

The room reminded her of home. Not the home Aunt Maude had made for her, but the home she'd known before her parents died. She turned all the way around slowly to take in the feeling of warmth emanating from the familiar decor.

Trevor walked in and held out an armful of clothes. "These will have to do. You can shower down the hall if you want. Then I'll give you the grand tour."

She took the clothes he offered, their hands brushing briefly, her stomach roiling quickly. She turned away to put them on the bed and the door clicked shut.

She let out a big breath. Staying here with Trevor was going to be difficult. At least in her own home she'd been anchored by the familiar. He'd been her shadow day and night, but during the day, she'd had driving time to recoup her defenses against the sensual onslaught constantly nipping at her body. Here, it would be different.

The music box on the nightstand caught her attention, and she picked it up. Made of delicate gold filigree rosebuds, it was a charming little music box that fit in the palm of her hand. Not expecting it to work, she felt for the knob on the bottom and wound the spring. Music from *Swan Lake* tinkled forth in melodious notes and filled the room with sunshine.

Her breath caught. She sat down on the bed. The tune was a common one played by old music boxes. It was also the tune her mother used to hum when she was her happiest.

"This is too much," she muttered. Without looking at anything else in the room, she grabbed the clothes and headed for the shower.

Ten minutes later, with the filth of the break-in washed down the drain, she felt much better. Trevor's cutoff jeans, T-shirt and old dress shirt hung on her, even after some adjustment. She gave one more tug on the cutoffs. They would have to do.

When she stepped into the hall, Trevor's eyes skimmed her body. "Those clothes have never looked better." Without waiting for more than an embarrassed thank you, he walked across the hall chuckling and motioning for her to follow.

"You're remodeling," she said.

"When I get the time."

The kitchen, the dining area and the office across the hall were functional, but the walls were stripped of wallpaper, repaired with Spackle and unpainted. Drop cloths and paint cans were crowded into corners. Her room and the hallway were the only ones untouched.

"But I've finished this one."

He led her down the hall to a large room along the front of the house. His bedroom. She swallowed to loosen the knot in her throat.

The room felt like Trevor, with a thoroughly masculine decor in beige and brown. Traditional styles reflecting traditional values were spiced up with just the right touch of intriguing color.

She walked around the room absorbing the way it felt. A border ran around the ceiling's edge, an Indian pattern in beige and brown interrupted by a cactus-like pattern of turquoise and orange. The bright colors were carried throughout the room. They were woven into the blanket at the end of his bed and splashed on the decorative pillows sitting on a chair covered with a similar pattern in muted colors. The combination fascinated her.

"I'm not quite moved in yet, but I'm getting there." He took her hand. "I'll show you the second floor."

The second floor was in the same state of repair as upstairs. A large office with a storage room and an adjoining bedroom occupied one side of the hall. Four small bedrooms ran along the other side.

"They're our emergency rooms," he said. "Sometimes these kids get kicked out of the house and have no place to stay. They only stay here one or two nights."

"Is that your office?" She pointed across the hall.

"No. That's Moose's office."

"That big guy I met?"

"Well, actually, we share both offices. He and his wife live next door. He stays in the extra room off the office whenever we have guests."

Moose was the guy she'd bumped with the door downstairs when she came for her pickup, the guy who'd scared her to death. She'd have to revise her impression of him.

They walked down to the first floor and ran into Moose in the back kitchen, a frown making his face just as fearful as ever. He was searching in a kitchen cabinet.

"Trouble?" said Trevor.

"Mina's refusing to eat again. I'm looking for that dark rice." He looked up then and noticed Casey.

Trevor nudged her forward. "I think you've met already, but we might as well make it formal. Casey, this is Moose. Moose, meet Casey. She'll be staying in the old bedroom on the third floor for a while."

Moose's entire face changed when he smiled. He held out his hand. "Welcome to C & C. Glad to have you."

"Thanks." His huge hand wrapped around hers. The firm handshake didn't surprise her. This guy had to be super strong. When she made eye contact, she saw the welcoming warmth she'd heard in his voice.

"You don't have any unusual rice hidden in those... cutoffs, do you?"

She couldn't help but laugh, and the spontaneity surprised her. The cutoffs looked ridiculous, but Moose was too polite to say so. He was a good guy. She liked him.

She turned her pockets inside out. "Nope."

"Here it is." Trevor brought out a large glass jar of dark rice from another cabinet.

Moose took the jar. "Annlyn will love you forever."

As they walked back upstairs, Trevor explained, "Mina's their foster child. She's from Vietnam."

"Where's her family?"

"Well, her mother shoved her onto an overloaded boat to Malaysia at the last minute. Moose and Annlyn sponsored her trip to the States."

"I didn't know we still had boat people coming here."

"It's not publicized much. I guess everybody got tired of hearing about them, but they're still coming."

"Where's her mother?"

"Here. Somewhere. But she's not ready to take care of a four-year-old yet."

They reached the third floor and then her room. "There's a TV on the second floor, if you want to watch something."

"No, I'm really tired. I'd only fall asleep."

"Will you be okay?"

She leaned against the door frame; suddenly every limb was exhausted. "I'll be fine."

He moved closer and ran his fingers over her chin, a light caress that made her tingle in pleasure. "You'll be safe here," he said.

"I know."

He was so close, an inch away. His eyes were filled with kindness and sparks of passion.

She knew he was going to kiss her. Any idea of resisting vanished when his lips met hers.

Chapter Thirteen

All the longing and desire within her exploded at once. She wrapped her arms around him, glorying in the feel of his body against hers, savoring the urgent message his tongue sent throughout her body.

She was on fire. He ground his hips against her, and she caught her breath as she felt his arousal, as his hips moved with hers in a rhythm as old as time. His fingers caressed her back, then slid around to her sides, the tips barely touching her breasts.

The harrowing experiences of the day melted away in his embrace, and she knew with a clarity that often escaped her that she wanted this man. She wanted him in her bed, in her body, in her heart and soul. She wanted all of him so completely, the knowledge overwhelmed her.

A new kind of urgency stirred in her blood, a need burning close to frenzy and ready to flame. Her hands worked under his shirt and across his broad shoulders, then down his muscled back. Firm. Solid. Hard as iron.

He tipped up her chin, and she saw in his eyes a desire so hot it made her heart trip. His mouth crushed hers, and all thought vanished. This was what she'd longed for, his lips on hers, demanding, captivating, his tongue seeking entrance. She opened easily, naturally, and luxuriated in the red-hot trail he left.

His hands roamed with an urgency that matched her own. He caressed her breasts, first one, then the other, and teased her nipples, already peaked with desire.

There was no defense against the burning need to touch and be touched, to take what he offered, to give what she ached to give. To want more.

His hand left her breast. He held her tight, as if willing the passion to subside. When he spoke, his voice was hot against her chest. "God, Casey, do you want this as much as I do?" He didn't wait for an answer. It was clear. He led her into the room, closed the door and took her into his arms. His breath came in ragged gasps. The pounding of his heart beat against her body till she thought it was her own.

She placed her hands on each side of his face and drew him even closer. She covered his face with kisses, then outlined his mouth with her tongue, slowly, seductively, as he inched her toward the bed.

With his lips on hers, his tongue began a gentle probing while she inched his shirt up his chest and pulled it over his head, breaking contact with his mouth only long enough to finish the deed.

She feathered her hands over his back and shoulders, down his sides, and let them slowly meet at the snap on his jeans. His gasp of pleasure encouraged her. She fumbled with the zipper, her hands shaky with this new freedom, his jeans taut with his arousal. She tugged them over his hips, and he stepped back. He yanked her shirt and T-shirt over her head. Four hands awkwardly groped in the half-light to relieve each other of their clothes, to release the barriers, to allow skin to meet skin, fire to meet fire.

He picked her up and lowered her onto the bed, his blood pounding in his veins. Every inch of him wanted her. Every part of him needed her. All reason left him. He knew only her body next to his. Every inch of her silky-soft and seductive skin added flame to his fire.

He sucked her breasts, and she arched for more. He ran his fingers lightly across her stomach, down her legs and up her thighs. Her body shuddered in release and she cried out his name. The fire in him raged beyond control as he kissed her and coaxed her over the edge again.

He entered her soft, wet body. As fire met fire, they both exploded in bursts of white-hot flame, each feeding the other, glorying in the other, until the fire consumed itself and they lay satiated, their slick, wet bodies side by side, the raging fires momentarily banked.

A NIGHT BIRD TRILLED in the outside shadows, a bird whose name she didn't know. Somehow, putting name tags on too many simple pleasures robbed them of their glory. Words could not communicate some things, like the wondrous melody so natural to the bird, like the magic feeling singing through her body.

She closed her eyes to savor every note, every pleasure, and stroked the arm draped across her waist. Trevor's body curled around hers, his breath close to her ear. "I was right, you know." His lazy voice sent tremors through her body.

"About what?" He hooked one leg across hers.

His fingers trailed a seductive circle around her breast, around and around, teasing her nipple by avoiding it. "About us. About wanting you. About imagining you here in my arms."

Her body tingled from his wandering hands, the smoldering fire ready to ignite. "It just took me longer to admit it," she said.

"You can be very hardheaded sometimes."

She gasped as his fingers found her nipple. "Is that a fact?"

"That's a fact."

"Turn around here and let me show you exactly how stubborn I can really be."

They turned in each other's arms and his mouth sought hers. Each stoked the other's fire, patiently at first, until the flames roared on their own, out of control, and they lost themselves in their fiery passion.

HER DREAMS CARRIED HER softly into the morning, and she awoke when Trevor rolled over and whispered in her ear, "Good morning, sweetheart."

She didn't move, didn't acknowledge his warmth or his tender touch when he moved the hair away from her eyes. He rolled out of bed carefully, so obviously trying not to disturb her. Even when he kissed her lightly on the cheek, she remained still and controlled her breathing to appear as if she were sleeping.

The door clicked closed. She turned over, wide-awake, and stared at the ceiling. How she ached for him again, for the kisses that sent her head spinning, for the touch that awakened her body to a new world of sensations. Most of the night seemed but a dream.

She couldn't help the memory that bombarded her mind. The consummation of her marriage had been less than satisfactory, and Richard had made sure she knew it. She'd blamed herself, her inexperience, but after last night, she knew inexperience had had little to do with the lack of satisfaction. How could she have been so naive?

She swung her legs over the side of the bed, irritated she'd let her sour marriage intrude on what could have been a beautiful morning. Richard and Trevor might be fraternal twins. They might have the same alluring eyes, some similar habits and the same easy way with people, but they were nothing alike. It was time to erase that fear from her mind. Trevor had expressed more feeling for her in a good morning kiss than Richard had in two years of marriage. It was time to separate the twins once and for all.

Determined to overcome this mind-set and this feeling of awkwardness, she pulled on Trevor's shirt and marched across the hall.

With all the creaking floorboards, there was no surprising him. She reached the doorway and took in the morning paper strewn across the small table, the smell of coffee pushing her fully awake. "Good morning."

He paused with his cup midair. "Good morning."

He smiled with his voice, his lips, his eyes, those same eyes whose passion had been her undoing last night. He'd wanted her, maybe as much as she'd wanted him. If they found the bonds today and he disappeared from her life, she'd have no regrets. She would always have last night.

He moved back his chair and motioned her in. His wavy, wet hair fell across his forehead. "Here, sit down. I'll get you some coffee."

He placed the cup before her and let his fingers trail a path around her neck. His touch taunted and teased and left no doubt how he felt about their lovemaking last night. How could she have doubted his warmth this morning?

He nuzzled her neck from behind. She leaned back into him and savored his closeness, the touch of his lips, the clean smell of his skin. A sensuous tingling electrified her every nerve ending.

"I love the way you look in the morning, so sexy with those sleepy eyes," Trevor murmured.

Morning or night, she was driving him crazy. He'd wanted to nibble her into his arms when he woke up with her sweet body next to his. He'd known she was awake. What he wasn't sure about was why she pretended to be asleep. Until this moment, he was afraid she might feel betrayed by last night. But no, her whole face had softened when she saw him.

He smoothed down her hair, then let his fingers find their way through the soft waves. When she leaned her head back and looked up at him with those bedroom eyes, he couldn't resist the invitation. He scooped her up out of the chair and carried her across the hall.

WHEN SHE AWOKE the second time, the sun bright in her eyes, Trevor was gone. She stretched like a cat, satiated, content. She hadn't realized how utterly exhausted she'd been. And never had she experienced the complete satisfaction of a well-loved woman.

She found the oversized clothes on the floor where she'd tossed them and smiled to herself as she remembered how they'd ended up there. The light shadows playing on the wall warmed the room and brought the ivy alive. Last night this room had reminded her of her childhood home. In the daylight she could see clearly that it had a charm of its own with its white chintz tiebacks and gleaming hardwood frames surrounding the windows and doors.

She was curious to see the house in the daylight and anxious to see Trevor. When she opened the door and stepped out, she almost tripped over the box on the floor. There were her clothes, folded neatly in an overflowing box with her family album on top. When had he gone back to the house?

She lifted the box, took it in her room, and emptied the contents into dresser drawers. She blushed when she saw her underwear. He'd thought of everything.

After changing again, she went searching for Trevor, but found only Moose in the house. Hours passed before Trevor returned, and when he did, she couldn't help wondering where he'd gone when he disappeared.

THE SAME QUESTION lingered in her mind over the next few days, as she got caught up in the new world around her. Collins & Company amazed her. Any youngster who needed help could find it here, whether the help came from agency referrals, from volunteers, or from Trevor and Moose and Annlyn.

Kids had been streaming in and out every afternoon for the three days she'd been here. Most of them came in with heavy chips on their shoulders, but once Trevor and Moose took them in hand, the chips fell away and their uniqueness came through.

As much as she was enjoying Collins & Company, she missed Trevor. Rarely did they find time alone. He kept disappearing for hours at a time, and when he did return, C & C kept him busy.

She washed out her cup and turned from the window. She'd enjoyed the few minutes of quiet. But not being one to waste time, she grabbed her paint shirt and headed back to the small bedroom to continue the painting she'd started two days ago.

She had finished cutting in the ceiling of one wall when Trevor walked in with a smile that lit up her heart.

He looked up at her and smiled, his eyes shining with mischief. Her hand froze in place while the paint rolled down her arm.

He could always make her smile. The view from her perch made it difficult to concentrate on what she was doing. He warmed the small room with his presence. While she fought to concentrate, he finished one side wall, then balanced his roller on the covered dresser.

"Watch out for the pictures there, under the plastic."

He moved the roller and lifted the plastic. "Where did you find these old things?"

"From the magazines in the closet. I was waiting for Moose to find me some plastic. I can trim them and cover them in heated plastic to make pictures for the guest bedrooms. Aren't they great?"

He moved to the ladder and kissed her ankle. His fingers feathered her leg, sending goose bumps on a rampage from her toes to her neck. "Not as amazing as you, sweetheart. Never as great as you."

She gulped and almost dropped the brush. Her muscles were turning to mush and there was nothing she could do to stop it.

She changed the topic to the one subject bothering her. "Any word about the ledgers?" He'd told her he had a friend who was analyzing the ledgers, but this friend was taking an awfully long time.

He shook his head. "How about the bonds?" she asked. "Any progress there?"

"Nothing important." He never missed a stroke with the roller. She could have been asking him about the weather.

She climbed down the ladder and set down her brush. "Every time I ask you that question, you answer in generalities that leave me clueless. Do you think if you don't tell me the details, I'll believe the problem's gone?" She knew he thought he was protecting her. She couldn't feel angry, but she could make him stop.

He set down his roller and let out a deep sigh. "Would that be so bad?"

"Yes! Maybe I need to stay out of sight, maybe it makes sense for you to be the one out there hunting down every clue instead of me," she said, "but I also need to know what's going on. I don't even know who you've talked to or how many names are left on that list."

"All right," he said, wiping his hands on a cloth, his forehead wrinkling in a frown. "There aren't any left. I talked to the last person yesterday. No luck."

"You talked to everyone?"

He nodded. "I couldn't locate two of them. Several people confirmed Richard's partnership with Rex, but we already knew that."

"What do we do now?" Finding the bonds seemed more hopeless than ever. There had to be a way.

He looked at her with worried eyes, the lines on his brows deep set. "Let's hope the ledger analysis gives us some leads. It should be ready any time now."

He stood so close, she could see deep in his eyes to a wellspring of pain and passion and some spark she couldn't decipher. Their power was so intense, they held her spellbound.

He took her in his arms and held her close. "We'll find the bonds, Casey, and we'll figure out what happened to Richard. Trust me."

Trevor kissed her long and hard until she felt weak in the knees again. She forgot about the bonds and his mysterious absences. His lips erased everything except the taste of his mouth and the teasing of his tongue.

They didn't hear the knock at first. "I'm not interrupting anything, am I?" said Moose. His eyes focused on the ceiling, his mouth split in a grin.

They both jumped. "Lousy timing," said Trevor.

"Sorry, boss, just thought you ought to know that's the last gallon of paint."

Trevor turned to Casey and gave her a hug. "Grab some sunglasses and that big floppy black hat downstairs, and let's go buy some paint."

"Like this?" She had paint all over her.

"Why not? You can stay in the car."

Within minutes, they stood out front by his car. "You want to drive?" he said.

"Does the sun rise each morning?" She'd been dying to get out on the road and drive off her frustration. Taking the *cause* of much of her frustration with her, well, she could handle that.

She slid into the driver's seat onto soft brown leather upholstery. It felt different from her Bug's cracked vinyl seat. She drove down the street with power humming beneath her fingers. Trevor's car would leave hers in the dust.

"The only place we can buy matching paint is on the other side of town." He gave her an address. "Do you know the place?"

"I'll find it. You don't think anyone will recognize me?"

"You wouldn't be here if I did. Those people don't know my car. Besides, I figure I needed to get you out of the house before you started painting the grass."

"You don't appreciate me."

"I do, more than you'll ever know."

His response stilled the light banter between them. He sat sideways in his seat, watching her with eyes the color of dusk. Resisting the urge to lean over and taste his lips took all her willpower. Each word, every blink of his eye, pulled her attention away from the road.

"Turn left at the next corner."

She slowed for the turn. "We'll be heading straight toward the courier service. Maybe I should stop by and see Aretha."

"You have to turn off before then." He looked out the window, then shifted in his seat. After several blocks he pointed to a tall building. "Turn here. There's a parking lot on the other side of the office building. Let's see if it's full."

There were two slots left. She parked in the closest one, next to the street.

"This will only take a few minutes," he said.

"I'll be here."

After he left the car, she watched his tall, lean body stroll around the corner. She let out a deep breath. Her frustration level measured close to a hundred percent. She couldn't believe she'd let herself become involved with him. She wasn't looking for a relationship, and even if she was, it shouldn't be with him. He'd be gone as soon as they found the bonds.

She pushed the seat back and pulled down her hat, wondering if he knew how riddled with passion she became just thinking about him. The man not only sent her senses haywire, he intrigued her. Like it or not, she was falling in love with him.

She was puzzling over this truth when he slammed into the car. "Let's get out of here."

She started the car and drove to the pay booth. He handed the man a five.

"Go, go. Forget the change."

The urgency in his voice caused her to zoom out of the lot and onto the street. In front of the building, she saw the problem. The tall, wiry guy who had broken into her house was running down the sidewalk toward the parking lot.

Chapter Fourteen

"Hold tight," she said. She sped through the yellow light and plunged ahead. The street was wide, the traffic moderate. She sped down the left lane, crossing the double line only when necessary. She passed two cars, then three. Rather than stop at the red light ahead, she swung into the left lane at the last minute and turned, leaving behind screeching tires and blaring horns.

"Is he behind us?"

"Let's not wait to find out."

She took a quick right and another left. The new street was narrow and sandwiched with parked cars. Twice she had to slow down and pull over to let on-coming cars pass.

Trevor was twisted in his seat, watching the street behind them. "Take your next right. There's a one-way street about four blocks over."

She turned at the next corner. As they crossed the third street, he saw the van.

"I know a better way." She sped down the street several more blocks. She could see the van three cars behind them in her mirror.

"Watch out for that truck!"

Illegally parked, the delivery truck blocked most of the street. Without pausing, she squeezed between it and the parked cars and raced ahead.

"My God, woman, it's a good thing I know you can drive."

"It's this car. It drives like a dream."

"The van's stuck behind the truck. I don't think he's real happy," said Trevor, as the sounds of the van's horn faded behind them.

She slowed the car as she saw the turn. The entrance to the alley was partially hidden by trash cans and old trees. The children who usually played ball there every afternoon were nowhere in sight. She drove slowly and carefully.

She'd counted ten blocks the first time she'd used the alley as a shortcut. If necessary, she could swing back onto the street at any block.

"He obviously recognized you," she said, "and now he knows your car."

"I hate to admit I didn't even get the paint."

He sounded so calm and cool, he amazed her. Her own pulse was racing from the pursuit. The adrenaline flooding her body was just now beginning to subside.

"Head straight for C & C. Moose can pick up the paint this afternoon."

Twenty minutes later, she snugged his car next to the garage wall. "Nice driving," he said as they walked through the yard to the house.

"Not exactly your leisurely Sunday morning drive."

He laughed and put his arm around her shoulder. "I agree with you there. Let's hope we can track down those guys before they catch us in another chase."

C & C was quiet when they walked in. Trevor found the keys to the center's van. "I'm going back to try and find that van."

She didn't offer to go. She'd had enough excitement for one day.

HE RETURNED TO C & C a few hours later. His attempt had resulted in zero. His calls to Barney hadn't paid off any better. Barney was canceling the surveillance on Casey's house, the computer had no record of the two men in the van, and the ledger analysis still wasn't ready. He was fast running out of options, and he wasn't happy about it. Something had to break soon.

From inside the screen porch, he watched Casey work with Mina in the backyard. The afternoon sun caught at her hair and highlighted the hidden auburn whenever she turned her head. Her eyes sparked with concentration and total devotion to the small child beside her. That smile lit up the yard.

He was so tempted to walk out and join her, to give in to the yearning to be near her. He wanted to smell her scent and touch her hand. He longed to do more than that.

But he wouldn't. He'd blown it this morning. His top priority was Casey's safety. He hadn't even told Barney where they were staying. Giving in to his need to be with her had cost them one more pound of freedom this morning. He'd jeopardized her safety. He didn't think straight when he was around her. If ever he needed to stay in control, it was now.

He watched as she helped Mina add a bead to the string. Her relationship with Mina was the most amazing of all. This little Vietnamese girl shied away from most people, including him. Thanks to Casey, she'd spoken to him for the first time, but she wouldn't let him get close enough to touch her, not even to shake her hand. With Casey's help, Mina would be a much more confident little girl by the time her mother was ready to take her to her new home.

Casey was running to the porch, laughing and calling back to Mina. She rushed through the screen door and stopped when she saw him, her eyes wide with surprise. "You're back. Did you find them?"

"Not a trace."

God, she looked great all breathless and flushed. It was probably from playing in the sun with Mina, but he wished it was from him.

"Maybe we should report this to the police. I never heard a word from them after they talked to me about the break-in. Wouldn't they want to know we saw them?"

He studied her carefully. "I thought you didn't like the police."

"At least they're a lot more pleasant than those federal agents. You remember them. Mr. Crowley and Mr. Jamison? I wouldn't call those two if my life depended on it."

"I can call them." He tore his eyes away from her and watched Mina. Her words stung like acid on an open wound, and it was his own fault. "We don't have much to tell them, though, only that we saw them."

"They were chasing us."

"The police will want to know why."

"So just tell them we don't know."

"They'll also need a name and address."

"Oh. Maybe we better wait."

"We can give it a few days. If nothing breaks by then, we'll call them."

She took him in from head to foot. What a surprise to find him on the porch. He had on khaki shorts and a black T-shirt with some kind of logo on the front.

He glanced at her with steel gray eyes. His face could have been made of stone, except for the slight movement of his jaw. She scrunched up her bare toes. She flexed her fingers. Her heart kept pounding in her chest, waiting for the closeness she'd felt between them before. "You want to make necklaces with us?"

He shook his head. He'd closed himself off from her. She couldn't get through that thick, stubborn streak of his.

"About this morning," she said.

"It shouldn't have happened," he said, the blue of his eyes showing through the gray. "I'm sorry I put you in danger again."

So that was the problem. "I didn't have to go, you know." She tightened the knot in her shirttail. "Any news in the mail?"

His eyes never strayed from her. "No, but don't worry. We'll hear soon. The ledgers will give us what we need."

Why wouldn't her feet move? All she wanted was a knife or a pair of scissors, then she could be on her way. But she stayed where she was, drinking in the teasing scent of him and fighting the urge to move closer, to run her fingers down his arms, to lift her lips and brush his mouth. To feel his arms around her body.

He pointed at Mina. "I think someone's waiting for you."

Mina. She'd forgotten about Mina.

He smiled slightly, then turned to walk down the hall, his shoulders thrown back, his spine rigid. The strain was catching up to both of them. There had to be something she could do. Suddenly, a picture of the incriminating receipt flashed before her mind. There had been a name at the bottom. What was it?

AFTER MINA LEFT with Annlyn for her doctor's appointment, they walked to the gym together. Trevor took a few steps toward the basketball court and turned back with a wink. She let the warmth spread through her and sent him a smile in return, but she felt sadness intrude on the warm feeling. His effort to mask his frustration hadn't worked.

She saw it in his eyes, in his stance. He walked across the gym with tense shoulders and determination in his gait.

She did her warm-up exercises, then started with the exercise bike, thankful to be working out again. Her knee felt strong, but she would have to be careful. She watched Trevor, loving the way his muscles rippled smoothly as he reached and stretched and stuffed the ball through the hoop. He was quick. He could pivot on a dime and spin back around and score faster than a blink, as one of the kids kept saying.

Finished with the bike, she moved across the room to the weight machines, her mind filled with his image. Making love with Trevor was the most incredible experience of her life. The magic lingered throughout each day. But the dark cloud in her mind grew larger as the afternoon progressed. He'd been open and honest with her about his feelings and about why he was helping her look for the bonds. Thinking about his openness pricked at her conscience.

She started with the closest weight machine. The ominous cloud hovered closer. Here she was accepting the trust he gave so freely and glorying in his lovemaking. At the same time, she withheld the one piece of information that might help him resolve what he needed to know about his brother. She now knew how it felt to be a traitor. Trevor gave her sunshine and hope, and she was repaying him by deceiving him. The thought made her feel ugly inside. Wasn't that what Richard had done to her?

She strapped herself into the next machine and closed her eyes while lifting the weights over her head. She visualized the receipt she'd hidden in the old purse and tried to see the signature at the bottom.

It was no use. She'd been so intent on hiding the receipt, she'd paid little attention to the name.

She wanted to reason away the consuming guilt. She tried to believe they would figure this out without that name. She couldn't bear to destroy the growing relationship between them. Pushing him away was unthinkable, and telling him what she knew would do just that.

She completed her workout and wiped the perspiration from her face, the dark cloud of guilt in place. She watched him approach. His body glistened, his muscles stretching as he pulled on a shirt.

He came up beside her, his eyes capturing hers, then taking her in from head to toe. A well of desire sprang from deep within her, a need so great she felt afraid to reach out her hand and touch his arm. But she couldn't trust herself to stop there, gym or no gym.

He edged closer and whispered in her ear, "Hi gorgeous." His voice was husky, seductive, tempting her to turn her head a mere fraction and brush those lips that brought her so much pleasure.

At a leisurely pace, they walked hand in hand back to C & C.

"Hey Trev," said Moose as they walked in the door. "Your call came in. You can pick them up tomorrow morning."

"The ledgers?" asked Casey.

"The same," said Trevor, his face more relaxed than she'd seen it in days.

THAT EVENING, she lay wrapped in his arms, her soft breasts against his chest. Their legs were entwined as though they were one. He nuzzled her neck and worked his way up to her ear, then nibbled playfully at the lobe. Her sudden intake of breath made him smile.

"I hear somebody downstairs," she said, her whispered words music in his ear.

"Umm. Just Moose locking up before he goes home."

God, she made him feel good. He wanted to block out the rest of the world. He longed to tell her how right they were together, how much he needed her in his arms, in his life.

The fact that she used to be Richard's wife didn't seem to matter now. He could only guess when he'd stopped forcing himself to see her in that role. That first night he made love to her would be his first guess, the night when he thought he might lose her, when she gave herself so completely that he lost himself in her softness and gained heaven in return.

Seeing her as Richard's ex-wife had been a stopgap measure, at best. Deep down inside, he'd always known that. It had given him the excuse he needed to stay away from her, because once the bonds were found, she would learn his true identity and it wouldn't matter how he saw her.

It was tempting to dismiss the importance of the ledgers. But, he couldn't hide her forever. Someone was bound to trace them to C & C eventually. He had no choice but to go get the ledgers in the morning. "Damn," Trevor muttered aloud without thinking.

"We can just ignore him," she said, snuggling closer.

She'd misunderstood him. It was just as well. He treasured the little time they had left. And when his time was up? He refused to think beyond tonight.

TREVOR WAS GONE when she got up in the morning. She planned to keep her mind off the ledgers and the bonds by finishing up her painting.

"The paint's in the basement," said Moose as he ushered a young teenager out the door. "I'll be at the gym if you need me. Don't answer the phones, the machine's on."

She hadn't been in the basement yet. She crept down the narrow passage carefully, unsure of the steps.

She reached the concrete floor, and the smell hit her immediately, that old, familiar, damp mustiness from years ago. As she made her way around the crowded room, she recalled the cellar of her childhood and the many times she'd sneaked past her mother into the pantry and down the cellar stairs to play. It had been such a wonderful place, filled with surprise boxes, as her grandfather used to call them. Her mother used to laugh at her grandfather's eccentric habit of storing old clothes and trinkets in boxes down there, instead of throwing them away.

She spotted the paint in the corner and found a gallon that matched the color they were using in the bedroom. She carried it halfway to the stairs before it hit her. The smell. The cellar. She dropped the paint. My God! She'd forgotten to search her cellar.

She raced up the stairs, the light dawning in her mind as it brightened in the stairwell. Of course. What a perfect place to hide something you didn't want anyone to find. Since Aunt Maude had closed off the cellar stairs in the pantry, no one could get to it from the house. The only entrance was outside, the doors flush with the ground and usually covered with leaves. And she'd shown it to Richard.

She danced off to her room and shed her orange T-shirt and replaced it with a dark blue one, something less noticeable. At the last second, she pulled on the floppy black felt hat and tucked her hair up under the wide brim. The dark shirt and hat, and then a pair of plain sunglasses, should prevent anyone from recognizing her.

She stepped out the back door to get her car, then stopped. Those men would recognize her car. Trevor's, too. Without hesitating, she returned to the house, picked up the keys to Moose's car and drove off down the alley. No one would recognize this car. She would be safe.

Light traffic made driving easier. A dark and threatening sky hid the sun and the ominous cloud cover pressed down upon her. She took off her sunglasses and turned on her lights. Even the thick, heavy air blowing in the window couldn't dampen her spirits, not when she was positive she'd find the bonds.

She crossed the bridge into Virginia and picked up the parkway. Guilt gnawed at her conscience. The receipt. Why hadn't she told Trevor what she knew? It wasn't much, only that, yes, Richard *was* involved in some illegal bond business. She knew the answer, though. Giving him that information would solve nothing. Both of them were assuming Richard had been involved in the embezzling ring. Only if she could counterbalance her confession with the bonds would the telling be worth it.

She outran the storm but not the overcast skies. As she turned off Route 1, the dismal day surrounded her. The gloom couldn't dampen her mood, however. She would get rid of this guilt when she found the bonds. She loved Trevor with all her heart, and the idea of clearing the air and moving beyond today lifted her spirits even higher.

She stopped at the entrance to her house, knowing she should drive the short distance to the car path. Yet it seemed silly to waste the extra time walking down her long drive. She needed only four minutes to get the receipt from her closet and check the cellar, less time than it would take to reach the house from the road on foot.

She eased Moose's car onto her drive and made her way slowly. The trees overhead blocked the meager light from the gloomy sky. She was driving through a winding tunnel with gravel on the ground and wispy tree branches overhead. Each new curve greeted her with thick, twisted branches that looked like they wanted to grab her and hold her back. She ignored the shadowy threat and coasted up to the front of her house and got out of the car.

She noticed the drawn curtains across the front window, evidence that Trevor and Moose had cleaned up the place when they picked up her clothes. She hated to think about what the house had looked like after those six men had gotten through with it.

Before she had time to visualize the worst, the rain came and soaked her immediately. She ran for the porch, careful to step lightly on the slippery steps.

She wiped her eyes, removed the floppy hat and shook off the puddles of water. She didn't worry about the rest of her. She'd be back out in the rain by the cellar door in minutes once she got the receipt.

She let herself in the front door and automatically reached to shut off the alarm. The hole in the wall stared back at her. Why did they blatantly destroy things? Why couldn't they simply cut the wires?

Shaking away the dread that was pushing its way into her imagination, she walked into the living room. It was pretty much the way she'd left it, but it didn't feel the same. She'd expected a rush of that warm feeling she used to get when she returned home from work at night, but that sense of belonging had changed.

She rushed upstairs. The misplaced articles in the hall made her hesitate. Of course the house was empty. No one was here. She pushed aside her discomfort and entered her bedroom. It looked the same. It didn't feel the same. Quickly, she retrieved the receipt.

She struggled to subdue the growing feeling of loss as she ran back to the first floor. She stood at the bottom of the stairs looking around, as if seeing her home for the first time. With new eyes she noted the shabbiness, the worn furniture and faded drapes. No matter how long she looked, the old, comfortable feeling, the one that had always reassured her she was safe from the outside world, was gone.

This had been a happy home when her parents were alive. She remembered the disagreement her parents had the day they left for the last time. Her mother thought she should go with them. Always the philosopher, her father had argued, "She's a teenager now. We have to let her make her own choices. It's good her world's expanding."

She hadn't thought about her father's words in years, but she thought about them now. They sounded over and over in her head as she looked for an umbrella. That was the difference. That was the answer to this change she felt. Her world had expanded and grown beyond the confines of these four walls, beyond Aunt Maude, beyond Richard. Finally.

She had started to live again. Trevor had made it possible for her world to grow. The dramatic changes in her life amazed her when she thought about them. The bond scam, the accusations and the intrusions had forced her out of her self-conscious shell. She smiled as she thought about Trevor, about Collins & Company. She liked these changes.

Rain beat against the windows as she rummaged through the hall closet. She would be glad to get out of here. The house was depressing.

She closed the closet door, umbrella in hand, just as the front door crashed open. Before she could turn around, someone grabbed her from behind.

Chapter Fifteen

She struggled to pull free. Adrenaline pumped in her veins. In one violent twist that almost wrenched her shoulder, she loosened the man's hold on her.

Frantically, she reached forward, fighting to stay free of his grasp. She had to get the gun. It was right next to her, in the gateleg table. In the drawer. She had to get to it.

He locked his arms around her. She lifted her foot as high as she could and stomped on the man's foot with her heel. He moaned in pain. His grip remained firm. In one violent shove, he pushed her down the hall and into the living room.

Victor Pernell, her boss, was making himself comfortable in Aunt Maude's favorite overstuffed chair. The pungent smell of cigar smoke filled the room. "Victor?"

"Sit down, Ms. Michaels. I'm so glad you've finally graced us with your presence." He waved his hand in a casual gesture. "She almost bested you, didn't she, Wally?" he chortled. "Stop whining like a baby. You and Burt get the window. Do I have to tell you everything?"

"No, boss."

Confusion flooded her mind. Awkwardly, she stumbled to a chair. "What are you doing in my house?"

But she needn't have asked. The two thugs who'd been after her for so long brushed past her chair with a blanket and began draping it across the window. "You!" She jumped to her feet. "All of you! Get out!"

Burt was on her so fast she never saw him coming. "Sit down, lady." He pushed her into the chair. Victor's mouth turned up in a crooked grin.

She held her tongue and sat back in the chair. Fear crept in slowly, as though her mind kept fighting to ignore the obvious. Her hands trembled. She resisted the urge to hug her arms around her, knowing that small gesture would give Victor too much satisfaction.

"What do you want, Victor?" She said it slowly, deliberately. Her teeth kept trying to chatter, maybe from the cold seeping through her wet clothes into her skin, maybe from fear. Probably both. She tightened her jaw and stared at him.

"Why, you know what I want," he said. He paused while his eyes darted from the shaded window, to Wally leaning against the door frame, to her. "The same thing you came back to get." Wally and Burt walked toward her.

"I don't have the bonds." Her voice sounded weak, even to her. She sat up straighter and glared at him to try to counteract the sign of weakness.

"Now, now, let's not go backwards. We both know that's not true, my dear. Well, not quite true."

"What are you talking about?"

"You made a rather large deposit not long ago, so obviously some of the bonds have been cashed. Where are the others, Casey?"

She forced her eyes not to waver from his. "That's why you fired me, isn't it. So I'd have to cash in the bonds to survive. Well, guess what? I don't have them."

He stood up abruptly and walked across the room. He leaned over until he was an inch from her face. His cigar-breath bombarded her nostrils.

"Understand this, young lady. We're through playing your games. We want some answers. About Richard. About his buddy, Rex. About your newest companion, Trevor Steele, is it? But most important of all, you will tell me where the bonds are. We already know they're here, in this house, and no one—not you, not me, not my friends here—no one is leaving until those bonds are in my hands." He smacked his hands together.

The clap made her jump. Cigar ash spilled in her lap before he removed the chewed, wet stub and flipped it onto the rug. He turned to Burt with an angry scowl on his face. "Tie her up."

Everything was making sense now. "And the trips out of town? You wanted to search my house, didn't you? Only I spoiled your plans by coming home early. Too bad."

Burt whipped a gag on her mouth. He led her to the kitchen and tied her hands and feet and roped her to a chair. She didn't recognize her own kitchen. The three of them had been helping themselves to her food. Dirty plates littered the sink and counter. The table was covered with whiskey and wine bottles and the room smelled sour. The faded green linoleum had ugly brown smudges from all the crushed cigarette butts.

The rope around her waist and chest pinched the air from her lungs and left her no room to move. Her fingers were already growing numb.

Before they blindfolded her, Victor said, "I'm at the end of my patience, Ms. Michaels. The very end. I'm doing this for your own good, to allow you time to think things through. Carefully consider your choices."

They left her alone in the kitchen. She heard them tromping up the stairs, mumbling under their breath.

Thinking of Trevor kept her sane. She wanted to escape to some fantasyland and pretend none of this was happening, but she hurt too much to indulge herself for long. Her shoulders ached. The coarse rope cut into her skin. She kept shifting and moving, trying to loosen the ropes, but they tightened with every effort. She could hear the men tearing the upstairs apart.

She had to get free. Trevor would look for her, and eventually he'd come here. Oh, God help him, he'd be walking into a trap. She didn't want to think about what they'd do to him.

She heard heavy footsteps coming down the stairs and into the kitchen. Light filtered through her blindfold before someone removed it. The stinging glare forced her eyes shut. When she opened them, Victor stood beside the table pouring himself a glass of wine.

He stared at her unflinchingly, a new cigar trapped between his fingers as he passed the wine beneath his nose and took a sip. "You have excellent taste in wine, my dear. I hope you've considered applying that same good judgment to your current situation."

She stared straight ahead, refusing to give him the satisfaction of watching his show. And it was a show, a put-on, an imitation, his version of sophisticated intimidation.

He sipped slowly. When the glass was empty, his pudgy fingers carefully set it down on the table. With the cigar clenched between his teeth, he stepped behind her and removed the gag.

"Well, Ms. Michaels?" His liquid voice dropped to an icy note. He glared at her with disgust. The pretense was gone.

TREVOR WALKED into the house and took the steps to the third floor two at a time, the ledgers in hand. After putting on dry clothes, he went to the kitchen and slapped ham and cheese on a slice of rye. And paused with the sandwich halfway to his mouth. Why was the house so quiet? Where was everybody?

He looked across the hall and saw Casey's door ajar, but when he called, she didn't answer. Where was she?

He walked downstairs, fully expecting to find her with Mina, baking cookies in the kitchen. Although the lights were on, the kitchen was empty. The offices, the storage room, the reception desk—all were empty.

An awful fear gripped him. Had the two creeps discovered C & C and taken her away while he was gone?

His fear bordered on panic. He mounted the stairs to the second floor and banged open every door looking for her. He called out her name, hoping he was wrong. His fear grew more intense.

Knocking. Someone was knocking at the front door. He forced himself to walk down the stairs to reestablish some control. Where would they take her? What would they do to her? He couldn't bear his thoughts. He threw open the door.

Mina jumped back and turned to go. He held tight to the knob and opened the door wide. Of all the people who didn't need to be scared unnecessarily, it was Mina. "What a surprise, Mina. Come on in."

Timidly, she stepped into the hall, her hands buried in her Windbreaker. "Casey back?" She held out her hand. She smiled and looked down at the floor. "I make necklace for Casey."

Trevor took the necklace and examined the colorful beads. He tried to slow the adrenaline pulsing through his body. Maybe Mina had seen something.

"You made this all by yourself?" He said it quietly, slowly, not wanting to spook her again.

She nodded, her smile in place. He had to remember their cultural differences. Her smile would be a sign of embarrassment. He had to go slowly.

"Casey's going to be sorry she missed you. Did you see her leave earlier?" Every nerve wanted to scream. His hand balled in a fist. The beads pressed against his palm.

She backed away. Her dark eyes widened, her smile creased her cheeks. She lowered her head, avoiding his eyes.

Too gruff, too coarse, Steele. Control your voice, damn it. But then, eye contact was considered rude in her culture. Maybe it wasn't his harsh voice that was scaring her.

He stooped down to her level and tried again. "I've been looking for Casey."

Her head shot up. "Casey lost?"

"No, no. Maybe I'm lost, and she hasn't found me yet."

She giggled. "You not lost."

In his softest voice, with his nicest smile, he said, "Did you see Casey leave?"

She put her hands behind her back and bowed her head before she nodded.

He struggled to go slowly. "I didn't see her when she left. Can you tell me what you saw?"

She shrugged her shoulders. "She leave."

He needed to be more direct. "Where did you see her?" His voice remained soft, his smile gentle.

Mina pointed to the hall leading to the back door.

"Out back?" She nodded. "Did she go by herself? Did you see anyone with her?"

She shook her lowered head. Casey had left by the back door. Alone. He was getting somewhere.

He looked carefully at Mina, her head still bowed. A tear trickled down her cheek.

"Are you worried about Casey?" he asked.

She nodded. "Casey gone."

He knew what she meant. This poor kid, who must feel like she'd been deserted by everyone she ever loved, believed Casey had deserted her too. God, how he wanted to hold this fragile child and tell her everything would be all right.

Hesitantly, sounding more confident and cheerful than he felt, he said, "Mina, can I give you a hug?"

She took a step back, her hands clasped behind her, and stood perfectly still, as if weighing his request.

He fingered the beads in his hand. He held them up and let the light reflect off the blue-and-red glass prisms. "This is the most beautiful necklace I've ever seen. Casey will love it. She sure is lucky to have such a pretty necklace and such a good friend."

Her mouth turned up in a smile, barely visible with her chin on her chest. She twisted her body from side to side.

"I'll give it to her as soon as I find her."

Her head popped up for a second, a look of hope in her eyes. Then she lowered her head again in respect. She paused for a second. Slowly, she came closer and wrapped her little arms halfway around his neck.

His surprise was so great, he was afraid to touch her. He didn't want to break the delicate bond of trust between them.

Slowly, he let his arms rest gently on her back. Her little hands clung to his neck. He hugged her for several seconds before he felt her grip loosen. Immediately, he let her go. She stepped back.

"Boy, I sure needed that hug, Mina. Thanks."

She hung her tear-streaked face. "You find Casey?"

"I'll find Casey. I promise." He wouldn't allow himself to think otherwise. "And now you'd better get back before Annlyn thinks you've disappeared into thin air."

A fleeting frown creased her brow before she turned and ran out the door.

Touched by Mina's display of trust, he straightened slowly and put the necklace on the reception counter.

Mina had relieved him of his greatest fear. He felt a bit of sanity return, knowing that Casey had not been forced to leave against her will. Where was she? He hoped with every shred of confidence in him that he could keep his promise and find her.

He sprinted across the backyard to the garage and discovered Moose's car gone. He ran back to the front yard and his car. He got in, but he didn't know where to go. Pounding his fist on the steering wheel, he closed his eyes to the streetlights. He blocked out the city sounds. Think, damn it, think, Steele. Where would she go?

He ruled out Aretha. He didn't think Casey would risk visiting her, and besides, they weren't close friends. No matter how much he racked his brain, he could come up with no other choices. He didn't know her other friends. She had no family.

Family. The house. She wouldn't go there.

Even as the denial formed in his mind, he was turning the ignition key and pressing on the gas. And almost hitting Moose as the car skidded on the wet street.

"Casey took your car."

"Man, I didn't tell her she could take my wheels. What the hell's going on?"

Trevor pictured the two cruds who wanted to get their hands on her. No, they could never catch her on the road. The danger came if and when she stopped.

"I don't have time to explain. Just do me a favor. Stay by the phones. Call me on the car phone if she gets back."

He ran a yellow light and cursed himself for skidding on the wet road. Had the surveillance team left Hallowing

Point? God, why hadn't he gotten the exact date from Barney? The slight relief he'd experienced after hearing Mina's story disappeared. In its place was an aching fear that tied his nerves in knots.

He wouldn't lose her. No, he couldn't. The thought made him shudder. The truth hit him suddenly, unasked and unwanted. He loved Casey Michaels. God help him, he loved her more than life itself.

He picked up his car phone and tried Barney's private line. When there was no answer, he called his secretary.

"If this is an emergency, I can send him a message in court," she said.

"All right," said Trevor, "but you hand-carry it yourself. Make absolutely sure Barney's the one who gets it. No in-betweens."

"Yes, sir, Mr. Steele, but it'll take longer for me to do it myself."

"Tell him there may be a problem at the Michaels house. I'm on my way there now."

He hung up hoping the secretary did exactly what he'd asked. Crowley and Jamison were always poking their noses in at the wrong time. If there was any trouble, he didn't want those two in the way.

The closer he came to Hallowing Point, the worse the weather became, and the more anxious he felt. The rain beat harder. The skies grew darker, grayer. He kept telling himself this trip was a guess, that probably Casey wasn't at her house. Most likely she'd returned to C & C. He moaned in pain. He knew Moose would have called if that were true.

He didn't bother hiding his car. Instead, he fought with the wheel as the car slipped over the wet gravel down Casey's drive. His sixth sense warned him to use caution. Be careful, it told him, but the warning barely penetrated his senses.

His one goal was to make sure she wasn't here at the house. And what if she wasn't? Where would he look next?

He rounded the last curve and spotted Moose's car. Hope surged through his blood. Some of the tension drained from his body. What he had to do now was get her out of here as fast as possible.

The house looked dark and empty, too dark for her to be downstairs. He rushed from his car through the soaking rain to the front door and pounded it with his fists.

"Casey." He yelled above the wind and rain. "Casey, open up." He reached in his pocket for the key and turned the lock. Twice. Something was wrong here. She would never leave the door unlocked.

He stepped back and pulled out his gun, his apprehension growing. The door flew open and a huge hand trapped his wrist, crushing it till it went limp. His gun dropped to the porch. With his good fist he power-punched the guy's belly. The man bent and groaned but never loosened his grip. Trevor struggled to get free. The man forced his arm behind his back. A cold muzzle jammed against his neck.

The man dragged him into the hall. "In there." He motioned to the living room.

A heavyset man with a bulging belly grinned at him from across the room. "Mr. Steele, I presume." He puffed cigar smoke into the air. "The boyfriend. We've been expecting you."

He felt his gut twist inside. He lunged for the man before an iron arm clamped around his throat. He felt the cold metal of another gun against his temple.

Chapter Sixteen

"Don't try it."

"Where is she?"

"All in good time."

The cigar hand waved to the familiar faces. "Bind him, Wally, while Burt holds him."

Trevor gasped for air and struggled to find the common sense to bow to the trigger finger five inches from his skull. He couldn't help her at all if he was dead.

"I came here to find Casey. That's what I intend to do." He winced as the rope cut into his skin.

"Perhaps we can strike a bargain." The man was on his feet. "Your girlfriend has something that belongs to me. And I have your girlfriend."

A lethal calm settled over the tips of his nerves. The thought of these creeps touching Casey had him seething inside. In a voice belying his rage he said, "She doesn't know where the bonds are. Let her go."

"Ah, then perhaps you do. Perhaps you've been playing against us trying to get her to lead you to them yourself. No more lies, Mr. Steele."

Inwardly, Trevor cringed. The truth hurt. Finding the bonds had been his original goal. The bonds would lead to information about Richard, and he had to know about his twin's death. Just when his purpose had changed, he wasn't sure. Casey was his goal now—her love, her safety. "Where is she?"

"We're ready to talk, then?"

"Believe me, if I knew where the bonds were, I'd tell you."

"Let me do this, boss. I can make him talk," said Burt, his dark eyes excited, his mouth a sick grin.

"We're not violent people, Mr. Steele. At least not all of us." He glanced at Wally and Burt. "Ordinarily, I abhor physical violence. But, of course, these are not ordinary circumstances. You, Mr. Steele, and Ms. Michaels have been the proverbial thorns in my side. It's time to remove those thorns."

He dropped his cigar to the floor and twisted the live ash with his shoe. "Burt, Wally, it's your turn to convince Mr. Steele to see the light."

He walked out of the room and up the stairs.

CASEY LAY on the pantry floor drifting in and out of consciousness. She'd hit her head on a shelf when they'd shoved her through the door. Yes, she remembered that now. She remembered thinking, watch out for that shelf, it sticks out farther than the others.

Thinking it hadn't stopped her forward motion or prevented her head from striking the edge. She remembered the sudden light streaks behind her eyes, like lightning in a coal black night.

She stretched her eyes wide in between each blink to help focus her vision. She tried to move. Pain crashed through her awareness. Her hands were still tied behind her back, and the rope bit into her raw skin. The rope was so tight around her feet that her ankles ached and her toes were numb.

She rolled to her side and cringed from the pain in her shoulder. She couldn't tell if it was cut or bruised. How long had she been here? Minutes? Hours? How long had her mind been drifting?

She moved again to ease the weight off her shoulder. A light caught her eye. A trick of the imagination? Maybe she was still seeing stars from her crash with the shelf.

She blinked hard and long several times. No, it was still there, and most important of all, she could see it clearly. No fuzziness, no fading, just a clean, clear line like the edge of a sword. She felt her energy start to flow.

She scooted closer, not trusting her own eyes. The light was like a beacon, her last spark of hope on a dark night. She reached the door. The sliver of light showed steadily underneath. She breathed a sigh of relief—even if the light disappeared, she now had a point of reference.

Thought fragments kept sliding around in her mind out of reach. One minute she had control of them, the next minute they were gone, but, thank goodness, her mind was beginning to clear. The pieces kept scattering like a puzzle on a lopsided table.

She held on to them and tried to fit them together. Some pieces stayed neatly in place, others didn't belong.

Victor seemed to be the name in this puzzle. He was the boss. All this time, her job at the courier service had allowed him to keep track of her, even to regulate her day.

What didn't make sense was Victor as boss of a setup like this. Never would she have imagined him capable of smoothly running an organization as big as this one seemed to be. And what was his connection to Richard?

She turned over onto her side. She had to get out of here. She searched her mind for some item in the pantry that could cut her ropes. The only possibility was an aluminum foil box, and that was in the kitchen.

She heard a commotion in the living room. Victor and his boys must be tearing the place apart. Suddenly, what she'd feared most pulled her from her thoughts and jarred her fully awake.

Trevor. Oh, God! That was Trevor's voice. "Try again, you fool. Try all you want. It won't work," he said, goading.

She had prayed he wouldn't come here. She had hoped he wouldn't charge into the house looking for her. Victor would have his morons go after him with a vengeance.

Trevor knew nothing. How long would it take them to believe him?

She listened as long as she could bear it, then raised her bound feet and battered the door, over and over, louder and louder. The noise blocked out Trevor's misery. It hid some of her pain.

She paused to listen. His voice sounded weak. His tone was still belligerent. Oh, God, they would never let up.

Tears streamed down her face. She pounded the door with all her strength. She hollered and shouted, most of her words drowned out by her feet stomping the door. Distract them, Casey, and let Trevor know you're here.

Every muscle and nerve screamed to be free. She strained with a fury at her ropes, twisting and turning, fighting against the impossible knots that kept her separated from him.

Breathless, she stopped shouting and lowered her feet to the floor. She strained again to hear his voice.

The house was deadly quiet. She couldn't hear him at all.

Panicking, she twisted around and put her ear to the door, focusing her attention to hear some word, some noise, any sign that he was alive.

She heard Victor and Wally and Burt murmuring in low voices that seemed so far away. My God, where was Trevor? Please God, let him be alive. Let him be okay.

A new sound filtered under the door. It was a shuffling sound, a smooth steady *swish, swish,* and faltering footsteps and heavy dragging. Oh, God, had they killed him? Why were they dragging him across the floor?

She turned back on her side and with all her might, she attacked the door. The raw pain was ripping a huge hole in her heart.

"Knock it off, lady." Burt's voice growled, gruff and impatient, right outside the door. She gasped through her pain. Was she next?

Suddenly, the door burst open. Light filled the tiny room, temporarily blinding her.

"You've got company. Move it." Burt grabbed the rope binding her feet and dragged her deeper into the pantry, the smoke from his cigarette wisping in her face.

She squinted—and there was Trevor. Her stomach tightened as her breath escaped in a gasp. They'd used his face as a punching bag. But he was alive!

Wally's beefy arm held him around the waist. Trevor's eyes caught hers—swollen orbs in a bruised face. She saw pain mixed with relief and a spark of rebellion. But the moment he saw her, he gave in to the pain and closed his eyes.

Wally held him while Burt tightened the ropes around his arms. Then both of them shoved his bound body into the pantry. He stumbled and fell across her. Burt's snickering made her sick to her stomach.

Wally broke out in a giggle. "Together at last. Ain't that sweet." Burt slammed the door shut. She heard him wedge a chair against it.

"Trevor?" She tried to twist around to pillow his head on her stomach. The ropes on her arms tortured her. If only she could hold him.

She felt responsible. His body was bruised and broken because of her. This time her impulsiveness could cost her the only man who mattered. "Trevor, can you hear me?" She was frantic to hear his voice.

She managed to turn over on her back. The floor and the extra weight smashed her arms and hands into her back, but when she felt him move, she welcomed the pressure.

He moaned and moved his head. "Casey? Casey? I can't see. Where are you? Oh, God." The words came slowly. His slurred voice faltered between words.

"It's okay. I'm right here."

He rolled off her stomach and groaned when he met the hard floor. "Did they hurt you?" he said. "God, I'll kill those bastards if they hurt you."

"I shouldn't have come here. This is my fault. I am so sorry I got you mixed up in this." Tears spilled down her cheeks, making her more frustrated with herself. Tears would get them nowhere.

When he kept moving around on the floor, she said, "Lean back on me. There's no place to go."

"Like hell. We're getting out of here. I have to sit up."

Each move brought a curse and a groan. She didn't want to imagine the pain he must feel. She'd seen his arm and the odd position of his shoulder.

When they heard voices in the kitchen, they froze. Wally and Burt were shouting back and forth.

"Would you knock off the booze," said Burt, his voice loud and angry. "We have work to do."

"Go stuff it," said Wally.

The noise grew louder. It sounded like pans crashing together and rolling onto the floor.

"I don't need to," said Burt. "You've stuffed enough for the both of us."

"Try to sit up," said Trevor, his words slow, his voice a hoarse whisper.

It took a few minutes, but gradually she pushed herself up and braced her back against the lowest shelf. The noise continued in the kitchen.

"Back to back, Casey, so I can work on your ropes."

"But your arm."

"Forget the arm. Just do it."

She felt his foot on her leg. Using that as her guide, she scooted along the floor to get closer to him. She ignored the pinching ropes and gritted her teeth to hold back any cries of pain.

At last she sat beside him, her shoulder against his side, her hip touching his.

"Okay, a little more now."

"Trevor."

She leaned her head against his chest and absorbed the feel of him. He felt so good and solid. Even in his battered state, she could sense his strength, his obstinacy.

His heart beat against her cheek in a steady *thump, thump,* sending her a message of hope. She raised her head against his neck. Lord, how she loved this man.

He lowered his head and turned and met her mouth. Gently, their lips met in quiet desperation. She kissed his swollen bottom lip tenderly.

The kiss lasted just a moment, but when she pulled away she felt stronger, more confident. She was ready to do whatever they had to do to escape. It was as if he'd given her a part of himself to strengthen her own will.

"We can do this, sweetheart. As long as we're breathing, we can beat them."

"Yes." At that moment she believed they could conquer the world. Together they could triumph over Victor and Wally and Burt and anyone else who got in their way.

She enjoyed one more blissful moment nestled into his neck, then pulled back. The racket had stopped in the kitchen. Without the noise to camouflage their movements, they made a point of shifting slowly to avoid knocking into anything.

Trevor had more flexibility because his feet were free, but by the time they were back-to-back, she could sense his exhaustion, his slower efforts. His injured arm had to be draining his strength.

"I don't know if this will work, Trevor. The ropes are pretty tight."

"We'll make it work." He was still slurring his words, but they had an icy edge to them that told her he would never quit.

His fingers hit her raw wrists, and she jerked away from him. He cursed under his breath. "Sorry," he said.

Even the slightest movement caught her raw skin. She clamped her teeth together hard enough to make her jawbone ache. If he could work with a broken arm, she could distract herself from the pain he was causing by moving the ropes.

"The knots are on top, closer to your back. Push against me harder and sit up as straight as you can."

She scooted closer. Braced against his back, she could feel the tremors rippling up and down his spine. This position had to be so painful for him. "Better?"

"I'm getting there." His fingers wedged between the ropes and her back. "I'm surprised they didn't use you to get me to talk. Not that I could tell them anything."

"Victor likes to think he's an old-school gentleman. He'd be sinking to Burt's level if he encouraged them to use me like that."

"Victor? As in Victor Pernell, your boss?"

"Ex-boss, the same one who wanted to keep me running out-of-towners."

"I'll be damned."

She could feel his fingers working against the ropes. The ruckus overhead told her Victor and his two henchmen were destroying her house piece by piece. She could hear furniture being moved.

Every now and then a heavy object dropped onto the floor like a deadweight. They were searching the small bedroom at the end of the upstairs hall.

Trevor's hands stilled. He let his head lean back against hers. His left shoulder drooped down her back a notch.

"They may be too tight to loosen, Trevor."

"No, just give me a minute."

To get to the knots, he had to maintain such an awkward position. She tried not to think about it. Dwelling on his pain wouldn't help either one of them.

"Casey?"

"Yes?"

Several minutes passed before he spoke again. She thought perhaps his strength had given out, but then he continued.

"I'm sorry you had to be a part of this."

He was making no sense. She was the one who had come to the house to look for the bonds. Otherwise, neither one of them would be here. The pain was overwhelming him.

"It's okay. We'll be free before you know it," she said.

She wished she believed her own words. His strength was fading, regardless of how hard he was fighting to endure.

"I want you to know that whatever happens, I never meant for you to be hurt," he said.

Chapter Seventeen

"Come on." She wiggled her bottom against his. "Time's a wasting, Mr. Steele."

To her relief he switched back to his former position and slid his fingers behind the rope.

"Talk to me, Casey."

His words were an incredible show of his vulnerability. Her heart wanted to weep.

"I could sing." She struggled to sound upbeat and sang a few bars of a popular song in her off-key voice. "On the other hand, maybe I'd better not."

His fingers hit a particularly sore spot, and she clamped down her teeth again.

"Tell me what you want. Tell me anything, just keep talking. What will you do after the bond issue is settled?"

What did she want? She wanted him. She wanted to love him and cherish him. She wanted to share his sorrow and to celebrate his joy. She wanted to give him children and build a future life that would last forever. But that would never be.

Even if they ever had a chance, her deception had ruined it. She had betrayed his trust by failing to tell him what she knew about the bonds. How could he ever believe in a future with her? Once he satisfied himself about Richard's death, he would disappear from her life, and she would be left to put her heart back together.

She took a deep breath and let it out slowly. She had to give him some kind of answer. The goals she'd set down for herself before he took over her heart still stood.

"I guess the first thing I'll do is find another job. I don't believe I'll be returning to Victor's courier service."

Her words made him chuckle, a light, soft laugh that slid over her like a magic balm.

"So what kind of job do you want?" It was difficult to understand his slurred words.

The tension eased on her left wrist and sent sparks of hope at last.

"Probably something in accounting or financial management, but before I look for anything permanent, I'll finish school. After this semester's exams, I only have three credits left. I might take my last course at the end of the summer, maybe in the fall. And then there's my knee surgery."

Again, his hands stopped working. Her muscles tensed. She was afraid that this time he'd blanked out. She concentrated on his movements to detect his state of mind and to understand why he'd stopped. Maybe she shouldn't encourage him. Maybe her kindest action would be to try her luck with his ropes rather than taxing his energy like this.

"How did Mina's doctor's appointment go? Everything okay?" The thought came out of the blue. She'd use anything to keep him conscious.

"I don't know. She gave me a hug. Promised to find you."

"She did?"

"Yes, ma'am." He slurred his words. His fingers moved against her back.

"Hugged you, huh? That's a big step for her. I guess you think you're pretty hot stuff."

"Yeah."

The crash in the kitchen startled her. Victor's voice boomed like a percussion out of control. "No more booze! Find the bonds, then we'll celebrate."

She felt Trevor shift. His fingers resumed their work.

"We've looked everywhere, boss. They ain't in the house." Burt sounded as frustrated as Victor.

"Then search the grounds, around the outside of the house, in among the trees. Dig up any soft spots that look suspicious."

"In this storm?" said Wally.

She could imagine the look Victor gave Wally. He'd raise his head and look down his nose. His flitting eyes would harden and settle on Wally's. She already knew Victor was an expert at intimidation.

Victor's response came slowly. "Is that a problem?"

"No, boss."

"I didn't think so."

"What if we can't find the damn things?" said Burt.

"Ah, gentlemen." Victor's control sounded complete. "I am convinced of two things. Number one, the bonds are here. Number two, our two lovers don't know where."

"You'd think ole Rich woulda told somebody," said Burt.

Trevor stiffened, his back rigid against hers.

"Yeah, all that filthy paper sitting around waiting to turn green. Don't seem right," said Wally.

"Well, now," said Victor, "thanks to your overzealous persuasion, we can't ask him, can we."

"Not me, boss, you know that wasn't me."

"He won't be a problem no more," said Burt. "That's what you wanted."

Trevor was thrashing his body behind her, moaning and fighting against his ropes.

"Exactly," said Victor, "but you could have delayed resolving the problem until after you had some answers. As a result, it's now up to you to find the bonds. Gentlemen, get busy. Get the power light from under the driver's seat in the van and use the spotlights."

Casey struggled with her ropes. She wanted ten seconds alone with Victor. Or Burt. She'd like to claw somebody's eyes out. The men were bigger and stronger than she was, so she wouldn't last long, but given the opportunity, she'd dish out what she could.

She and Richard had had their differences. He'd hurt her, emotionally and physically; whether intentionally or not didn't matter. Compared to Victor and his bullies, he was just a stupid kid. He'd been in way over his head.

Her reaction amazed her. She never thought her animosity toward Richard would change. She felt an aloof acceptance of what had happened between them. The anger had slipped out under the door without her knowing it. Most of it, at any rate. She wouldn't be in this situation if it wasn't for Richard.

Trevor waited until the sound of footsteps vanished before letting loose. "Damn them." The strength of his voice surprised her. "I don't believe this. I finally find out what happened to Richard, and I can't do a damn thing about it." He fidgeted with his ropes. He let out a yelp and slumped forward. "Damn this arm."

"Are you all right?" What a dumb question. Of course he wasn't, but that was the first time he'd acknowledged the pain caused by his arm.

"I made the mistake of turning my shoulder." He moved from her back. "I want to get closer to the door. See if you can follow with me about three feet closer. If one of them opens the door, they'll eat my feet for breakfast."

She pushed herself along the floor until she met his back. "It might be better if I tried to untie you."

"No, the bastards put double ropes around my hands. Yours should loosen more easily." He slid his hands against her back.

He was breathing harder. The ripples of pain continued like waves up and down his back. He sat closer to the door than she did. His feet were positioned to strike when the door opened.

"I'm sorry about Richard." She could say that now and honestly mean it. No one deserved to die at the hands of Wally and Burt. And Victor. The thought of him made her stomach curl.

"I'm sorry, too," said Trevor. "At least I know he didn't commit suicide. You were right. But he was a damn crook, and that doesn't sit so well."

The men walked in and out of the kitchen several times while he worked to untie her. His efforts took on a sporadic nature. His fingers tugged frantically for several minutes in one spot, then moved to another and hardly made any progress at all.

Every few seconds he leaned his head back against hers and said, "They're getting looser." Each time the pause lasted longer. He seemed to be holding on by sheer willpower.

The back door slammed shut again. Burt's voice sounded first. "Well, did you?"

"I checked the woods. What do you want me to do, dig up the whole damn country?" said Wally.

"Put the friggin' bottle back. And the food. The boss ain't going to like this."

"Like what?" said Victor, his footsteps coming clearly from the hallway.

"No luck, boss."

"You were thorough?"

"We looked everywhere." The pause was poignant. "Except that old shed back in the woods," said Burt.

"Would you mind telling me why you failed to search the shed?" Victor's voice boomed.

"It was locked," said Wally.

"I'll get it, boss, don't worry," said Burt, hurriedly.

"What's that noise?"

Footsteps clomped past the door.

"My God! Get some water. Move it."

Casey had a hard time following the conversation when they left the kitchen, but from the panic in Victor's voice, she knew something had gone wrong.

"Trevor?"

"Just listen."

The men raced back and forth past the pantry door. After several runs, she heard them scuffling around in the kitchen, choking and coughing.

"It's out of control," said Victor, his raspy voice frustrated and tired.

"Whoosh," said Wally. "I never seen nothing go up like them drapes."

"Those damn cigarettes of yours," said Victor.

"The cigar—"

"You'd better pray those bonds are in the shed. This place is a tinderbox ready to blow. Let's get out of here."

"What about them lovebirds? You can't just let them go," said Wally. "We could have some fun back in the garage."

His perverse giggle made her skin crawl. Trevor's hand rested against her back.

"Indeed," said Victor, "they do present a problem, but not an unsolvable one."

"I vote we take care of 'em the same way we took care of Tapp, but slower. They'd be good for a few hours," said Burt.

"You two don't have a vote," said Victor, the polish gone from his voice.

"I don't get it, boss," said Wally.

"The fire will take care of our problem very nicely. Get out to that shed and find the bonds. Now. The fire's spreading too fast to stay here."

"Burn, baby, burn," said Burt, rather gleefully.

Casey gasped. "Trevor." She swayed her back against his. "Trevor, hurry up. Oh my God, the house is on fire."

"I heard. Keep still."

He concentrated on the loosest knot. Whatever else happened, Casey had to live. He would beat these ropes.

He was fighting not to black out, fighting to forget the casual way Burt referred to the death of his brother. His head kept spinning and spinning. He swallowed constantly to control the nausea that wouldn't leave him alone.

He felt her working with him on the ropes. Those wrists must hurt like hell. He didn't have to see them to know how the rope had sliced into her skin, and she never said a word, never complained.

"Faster, Trevor, come on. I need time to untie you, too. I'm not leaving this room without you."

It was a miracle he was still conscious. If he'd never believed in the power of love before, he believed in it now. She'd kept him going. She'd prodded and poked and humored and, yes, demanded that he not give in to the blankness creeping through his head. He could not have kept going for anyone else. She would survive. She would be okay, damn it, if it took every ounce of his life to make it happen.

He twisted his bad arm to a different position and swallowed the gasp of pain. With two hands he could loosen the ropes faster. Time was running out, in more ways than one. Once she was free and clear, the case would come down hard and fast.

If Barney took the notations he'd made on the ledgers and combined them with the notes from Rex's files and the partial list from upstairs, he'd have his answers.

Barney would get his message and be here soon, and then Casey would know it all. He couldn't imagine a future without her. She would refuse to have anything to do with him, so what happened to him now didn't matter.

He had to tell her. He owed himself that much. She was the most precious love of his life. She was earth and sun and water to his very existence. Tomorrow, she wouldn't care that he loved her. Tomorrow, he might not be around to fight for her anymore. Today was what mattered. This was his last chance.

He kept his hands busy with the ropes and let his head fall back against hers. The pain stabbed his shoulder. He ignored it. The feel of her soft hair on his neck was soothing, a reminder of what he would lose.

"Casey, you have to promise me you'll walk out that door with or without me."

"I couldn't leave you, Trevor." Her voice was quiet, shaky.

"You have to promise me. I have to know right now that you'll make it."

"We'll both make it. The rope on my left hand is almost loose enough to slip off. Don't give up. Please."

His hands stopped their work.

"Come on, Trevor. Don't do this to me. I love you so much. I'd rather die than leave you behind."

A new kind of pain racked his body, a pain of love finally found and lost in a whisper. Regardless of their love, he was helpless to change what was to come.

"Oh, sweetheart, I love you. God, how I love you."

She turned her head to the side, and he shifted slightly until their cheeks touched. Her skin was warm and tender and wet. Her tears spilled onto his cheek.

He pressed his face against hers and smothered the tears as best he could. He longed to kiss them away. He wanted to feel her soft lips on his.

"God, I want to hold you one more time." But he couldn't. He couldn't even stay cheek to cheek with her. The pain was draining him, and most important of all, he had to get her free.

"I have to tell you something, Trevor. You're the only reason I came here," she said. He heard the reluctance in her voice and felt her body tense. "I came back to get the bonds."

"What do you mean?" His heart stopped beating. Had Barney been right? Had she been Richard's accomplice? My God, that couldn't be true. He felt his hope shattering.

"I love you, Trevor, please know that out of everything that's happened, that truth can't change. I know this doesn't make sense, but I have to try to explain. I knew Richard stole those bonds. I saw them. I even took a receipt for the bonds from his briefcase and hid it in my room.''

"You saw the bonds? When?"

"It's not what you think. I saw them by accident. Richard gave me his briefcase to take home.''

"When?" He held his breath.

"The last day I saw him. We had lunch together. I drove home alone because he had some work to do. I was looking for a pen. I went into his briefcase to borrow one of his, and I saw the bonds. I didn't know what they were at first, and when I figured it out I was shocked.''

He released his pent-up breath. Damn Richard. If she'd been caught carrying those bonds, she'd be up on charges now.

"I think the bonds are in the cellar, Trevor, beneath the house. I forgot all about the cellar. I was going to get the receipt and the bonds and tell you what I knew.''

"Did Richard admit he stole the bonds?"

"We argued when I showed him what I found, but then he bragged about how smart he was. It was an invincible scam, he said." She sagged against him. "I'm sorry.''

In his foggy brain a few missing pieces clicked into place. The last day she saw Richard, she asked him about the bonds. The last day she saw him, they argued. Eighteen months ago. The fall down the stairs, the knee injury, eighteen months ago. He felt his stomach turn inside out. That damn bastard.

"Richard hurt you, didn't he? Is that when you hurt your knee, when you asked him about the bonds? Did he push you down the stairs, Casey?"

He heard her sudden intake of breath and the quiet sob that followed. My God, he hadn't meant to hurt her more.

"I know he didn't mean to. He was angry. Richard never hit me, Trevor, you have to believe that."

Her body had slumped against his back. Loosening the ropes had become impossible. "It's okay, sweetheart, it's okay. Sit up straight against my back now so I can reach the rope. God, I wish there was some way to make up for all this."

His fingers twined with hers. He could smell the smoke mixing with the air. "We can't worry about what happened before. Richard's in the past. The bonds you saw are probably long gone by now, and I think the ledger analysis will help us find the ones we're looking for now."

"I'm so sorry I didn't tell you. I hid the receipt because I didn't want it to incriminate me. I was being selfish. I thought we could find the bonds without it. That's everything I know, I swear."

She was so upset she was choking on her words, and his mind was getting too fuzzy to think straight. He had to say something to make her feel better, to share the blame before he passed out. He was a federal agent and he'd acted like a damn fool. "It's all right, sweetheart. I love you, you must know that. But you're not the only one who made a mistake. I came rushing to the house without thinking. I should have known better."

"No, don't even think this is your fault."

"It makes sense they'd be here."

"It's not like you do this sort of thing every day," she said, shifting her back to a slightly different angle. "Let's just get these ropes off." She moved to her right. "Does that help?"

There was no more noise in the kitchen. He didn't want to think about what Victor was doing. He refused to think about Richard. Concentrate, damn it. Get her ropes untied.

The dizziness tormented him, swirling throughout his head. He closed his eyes and pressed closer to her side. She was his anchor to consciousness, the driving force that kept him going. His mind refused to work. Every time he loosened the rope around her left wrist, it tightened on the other wrist.

"Oh my God, look. The door." Thin wisps of smoke funnelled through the bottom crack. "Come on, just a little bit more and I think I can slip my hand out."

His fingers fumbled with the rope. The blankness had taken over most of his head. What little awareness he had left spun out of control. Speech was difficult, yet he had to tell her.

"Don't give up, Casey. No matter how bad it gets in here, don't give up. Help is on the way."

"If Moose doesn't get here soon, he'll be too late."

"Not Moose. A friend of mine. Barney."

"The guy who analyzed the ledgers?"

"He's a friend of mine. He'll bring plenty of help."

One thought dominated his muddied mind. He had to tell her. She would put two and two together once Barney arrived. He couldn't let her find out that way. If he told her now, he'd have a chance to explain.

"He's a government agent."

She stilled against his back. "You have a friend who's a federal agent?"

The smoke smothered his nostrils. He turned his head away from the door to avoid it, but the effort was useless. The fumes were singeing his lungs.

"We worked together years ago."

"But not now?"

Nothing he'd done in his entire life had been as gut-wrenching difficult as telling her he was an agent. The silence was deafening.

"Yes, Casey, I'm a government agent."

He could barely speak. His throat burned. He choked and coughed from the smoke and forced himself to hold on. He had to make her understand. He made one final twist of the ropes.

Casey was free.

Chapter Eighteen

"You're a federal agent?" A violent shudder attacked her. She drew away from him. "And I'm the job you're finishing before moving on to C & C. Oh, God, Trevor, all those lies." She coughed from the smoke. The white line of light had turned a hazy gray, but she barely noticed.

Trevor's coughing followed hers. "They weren't lies, Casey. I love you, damn it. I didn't plan to fall in love with you. I wanted to find out about Richard."

"Lies!" She pushed herself to the end of the pantry. "You know what, Trevor Steele? You *are* just like your brother!"

She heard his gasp from the other end of the room. She waited for him to deny what he'd said, to call it a cruel joke, but there was only a foreboding silence.

Hoping for some relief from the fumes, she shoved herself toward the corner and hit her shoulder on the shelf. She yelled out in pain. Smoke was everywhere. Tears streamed down her face. Her stomach was tied in knots. How could she have been so foolish twice?

She heard his feet scrape the floor. "Get out, Casey." He spoke very slowly, his words barely audible.

Her eyes burned. Every breath she took clouded her lungs with smoke. She stared at the dull line of light, at the thick smoke curling under the door. There was more of it now. Too much more.

There was no time to waste. Quickly, she untied her feet and rubbed at the numbness. At the first sign of feeling, she stood up. Her legs buckled and she grabbed the shelf.

Trevor's body thumped to the floor.

"Trevor?" He didn't respond. "Answer me, damn you."

Forcing herself to walk, she felt her way to the door. "Trevor?" She shook him gently, but he still didn't answer. Smoke billowed over his head and around his face. She pulled him back a few inches.

If they were going to make it, they had to get out now. The thick smoke was fighting to get under the door.

Not taking any chances, she took off her T-shirt and wrapped it around her hand before trying the knob. The handle turned, but the door refused to budge. The chair, she'd forgotten the damn chair.

She could hear flames roaring not too far away. The smoke cut into her throat. Desperately, she tried to remember what was in the pantry, what could fit under the door.

She couldn't panic. She had to stay calm. She felt along the pantry shelves. Cans. Boxes. An old roasting pan. Oh, God, there had to be something here.

In the back corner, she found a thin metal yardstick that might work. She felt her way back to the door. Trevor hadn't moved or uttered a sound.

She slid the yardstick under the door as the smoke smothered her face and made her choke. There was no escaping the deathly fumes. She grabbed her shirt and held it to her nose while she stabbed blindly back and forth, up and down. When she hit an obstacle, she gave a hard shove. She tried again at a different angle. The chair crashed to the floor.

She used her shirt to open the door and met the gray wall of smoke. She stooped down where the smoke was less dense, but she could barely see the far table in the middle of the room. It didn't matter. She'd get Trevor out that back door.

The kitchen light shone through the smoke onto his face. Her heart tightened in her chest. It was battered worse than she thought. His gray color frightened her.

She tested his ropes. She'd never get him free. There was no time to waste.

She tied the shirt around her mouth and nose, sat down, then grabbed him under his arms and began their slow journey across the kitchen floor. He was heavy, a deadweight, much more difficult to move than she thought.

Her wrists burned, her muscles strained. Her eyes were mere slits from the stinging smoke. She braced her feet on the cabinets whenever she could and used them for leverage.

Inch by inch she dragged him across the floor, lambasting him all the while, *liar, liar,* her anger fueling her strength. She was tall. She was strong. She muttered to herself between clenched teeth, I can do this, I can do this.

Trevor moaned and coughed. At least he was breathing. At least he was alive. Each move jarred his bad arm. She thanked heaven he was unconscious. This ordeal was almost over. She could cry later. She might cry forever.

The fire whooshed and crackled in the house. Smoke billowed in from the living room. Flames licked at the door frame. Something crashed to the floor, startling her, making her gasp for air, and she coughed so hard she wanted to stop trying.

But she couldn't. She was almost to the back door. Four more pulls, come on, Casey, only four to go.

The door was locked. For a moment the barrier seemed impossible to overcome. She wasn't thinking clearly. The smoke was overpowering her. Panic and fatigue fought together to take over.

"No!" The word croaked out of her mouth, her voice barely recognizable. She rolled Trevor aside, reluctant to let him go. She pulled the shirt from around her face to feel blindly for the knob. She had to turn the lock. She had to open the door. Air, they needed clean air.

She opened the door. Wonderful wet air bathed her face. She couldn't stop coughing. Her raw throat ached.

Crouching on the floor, wishing she could crawl, cursing her knee, she dragged him through the door and onto the porch. His feet clunked down the steps to the rain-soaked ground. She couldn't stop. She had to get him as far from the burning house as possible.

The fresh, moist air helped. The rain cooled her scorched skin. Trevor was choking and coughing. Still, she dragged him on, into the yard, through the wet grass, slipping in the mud and pulling herself back up until she reached the edge of the woods on the side of the house. When she was satisfied they were clear of the smoke and far enough away from the flaming house, she collapsed on the ground and gave in to a severe coughing fit.

Beside her, Trevor stirred. Gathering her strength, she worked on his ropes while her tears flowed freely. She loved this man—but she could never trust him again. The loss was overwhelming.

Three people rounded the corner of the house, vague shadows in the smoky, flame-washed dark. Her stinging eyes wouldn't stop watering. She saw only images coming toward her.

A new fear took hold. Had all their efforts been in vain? Would she and Trevor die, anyway?

She tried to hide him from their view and realized how impossible that would be. She kissed his face, his eyelids, his nose and smoothed the hair away from his face. He no longer coughed. He hadn't moved or groaned for so long, she feared the worst. He was breathing in short, shallow breaths. She put her cheek on his and whispered, "I love you, Trevor."

A jacket was wrapped around her shoulders. Ready to do battle with what little strength she had left, she spun around, swinging her arms. Instead of Victor, she met clear blue eyes in a kind, wizened face.

"We'll take care of him. Don't worry." He helped her to her feet and led her aside with his arm firmly wrapped across her back.

The two other men appeared. Mr. Crowley and Mr. Jamison stood before her. She pulled away from the protective arm, her mind finally working up to par. "You're Barney," she said to the blue-eyed man with the gray beard.

"And you're Casey Michaels, I presume." She nodded. "The ambulance should be here any minute. We'll get you both to the hospital."

"I don't need a hospital. Trevor's arm's broken, though. He's in bad shape." The words croaked out of her raw mouth. Then she stopped, her jaw slack.

Across the yard, her house was ablaze, the flames filling every window. Beside her, the men were trying to revive Trevor. Her knee gave way, and she sank down to the ground.

"Why don't you wait in my car?" said Barney. He reached down to help her up.

She shrugged his hand away. "I'll wait here."

"You brought him out, didn't you?"

She nodded.

"How?"

She looked up into his eyes, but didn't answer. Trevor was a big man, tall and well-built, and somehow she'd dragged him across the kitchen floor unconscious. She wasn't sure how she'd done it herself, but how wasn't important.

If he hadn't spent his last bit of strength loosening her ropes, they both would have perished in the fire. She told herself she'd owed him, but deep down inside she knew that was a lie. She never would have left him behind.

She pulled the jacket tighter around her and hugged her arms across her chest. Her aching body and injured wrists would heal, but the hollowness inside would last a lifetime. The deepening well of emptiness and despair could only be filled with Trevor's love, a love she could never accept. Trevor Steele, like his brother Richard, had betrayed her. She would not knowingly make the same mistake twice.

"We'll need a statement."

Barney's voice startled her, but she only nodded, knowing there was something she should tell him.

"When you're better. At least let me drive you to the emergency room so they can check your throat."

And then she remembered how this had all started. "The bonds might be in the cellar."

The ambulance arrived, followed by three fire trucks. She watched the attendants load Trevor onto the stretcher and check his vital signs. Their thumbs-up sign to Barney brought relief.

Barney walked to the stretcher as the attendants lifted it into the ambulance. Trevor tried to raise his head, then frantically fought against the straps that bound him. He tried to see through squinted eyes. He twisted and turned to see the house.

"Take it easy," said Barney.

"Where is she? My God, the house. Where is she?"

"She's okay." Barney pointed. "Over there."

He saw her through hazy eyes and smoky air. She turned away as soon as he looked at her. Feeling totally defeated, he collapsed on the stretcher. "I really messed up this time, Barney."

The firemen attacked the house with their hoses. The flames crackled and hissed. The side wall collapsed, and with it, the only home Casey had ever known.

She was surprised at how calmly she could watch the flames consume her past. The house held many old memories. Her parents, her sister, good times, loving memories the fire could never take away.

But what had the house held for her since then? Aunt Maude. Richard. And now, Trevor's deception. "Let it burn," she said bitterly.

Numbness settled around her like a shroud she might never shed. The fire was destroying her home. Trevor had destroyed their love. She'd never felt so hopeless, so utterly defeated. So alone.

THERE WAS NO PEACE in this hospital. It seemed like forever since the fire, since Casey was a part of his life, since the future held more promise than he'd ever dreamed possible. His body was healing. The rest of him, that was another matter.

The door opened and Barney walked in. The grin on his face was ridiculous.

"I see you've got your usual friendly smile in place," Barney said sarcastically. He sat in the chair beside the bed. "How're you doing?"

"Great, Barney, fantastic. How do you think I'm doing? I can't sleep. These idiots wake you up all night long to ask you if you need a sleeping pill."

"Yes, sir, Steele, you're in good form."

"I haven't even seen my doctor in two days."

"Think you can handle some good news?"

"Try me."

"The 'goons,' as you call our men, have been busy. We got them all, Trevor. Victor Pernell, his henchmen, even the big boss in New York. The list you left in the car cinched the case. They even found Rex Alcorn drugged up in a warehouse."

"Hot damn, Casey will love it."

"That's something else we need to talk about. But I'll get to that in a minute. First, you've got a few points to clear up."

"Rex's wife's a sweetheart. We wouldn't have come this far without her."

"I met her. She couldn't keep her hands off the guy, she was so happy to see him."

"What will happen to him? Can you do anything to help him?" He knew Rex was a hapless victim of all this.

"I'm working on it. He and Tapp were part of the ring, only Rex didn't know it. He's helped us a lot. I think the judge will go easy on him."

Barney stood up, stretched and walked to the window. The setting sun lit up the sky in streaks of orange. "Not a bad view, at least." Barney turned from the window. "You should have told me right off the bat that Richard was your brother. You know the department's policy as well as anyone else."

Trevor had never blushed, but right now he felt his face flame with red heat. He shifted uncomfortably in the bed.

When Trevor was rushed to the hospital, Barney had waited outside the emergency room while the doctors taped his ribs and set his shoulder. Patching up his arm had taken longer, but Barney had waited. And when they'd wheeled him to his room, his old friend had followed to make sure they settled him in just right. Groggy with painkillers, he'd blurted out his relationship to Richard the minute they were alone.

"Well, yeah." What else could he say? He felt like a kid caught with his hand in the cookie jar—guilty. Barney'd always had that effect on him. Maybe that's how sons felt with their fathers.

He looked away, sorry again for deceiving his old friend, but sure he'd had no choice. "You never would have put me on the case if you'd known."

"That's right."

"If you know that much, then you must know the rest. I was supposed to meet Richard for the first time the day he died."

"That I didn't know." Barney sat down and stroked his beard.

"I had to know what happened to him, Barney."

"I hope you didn't get more than you bargained for."

"It wasn't suicide," said Trevor. "Knowing that helps."

Barney held up Richard's journal that he'd found with the bonds—just as Casey thought, they were hidden in the cellar. He'd given the journal to Trevor to read as soon as he'd found it, and yesterday Trevor had returned it to him.

He set the journal on the bedside table. "Even though your brother left this with the bonds," said Barney, "he probably would have wanted you to have it."

"Yeah, well, he could have made his move before, when his mother wrote him that letter. Two years, Barney, come on."

"You don't have to like him, Trevor. Twin or no twin, he was what he was."

Yes, he knew. From the moment he found out he had a brother, he'd loved him, but events had sped by so quickly, emotions had shifted from low to high to low so fast, that, even now, he felt the loss of something intangible, something he'd never known.

He wanted to be proud of this new brother, but he wasn't. He felt betrayed by the person Richard became, and that was difficult to accept. God only knew if he could ever forgive him for hurting Casey. His friend was right, though. He had to accept the past. He had to settle for a brother he'd never known and be thankful he'd discovered him at all.

Barney watched him closely. "And you never mentioned Collins & Company. I stumbled on that by chance when I met your assistant manager—what's his name, Moose?—yesterday in the hall."

"I thought Ned might have told you he turned the place over to me. Hell, Barney, I had no idea he planned to do that. I think he knew me better than I know myself."

Barney's eyes twinkled. A satisfied smile spread across his face, but he said nothing.

"It's time, Barney. Send in my resignation tomorrow."

"You're sure?"

Trevor nodded. He would miss his work. He'd miss the travel, some of the people, the excitement, but he was ready to put all of his energy into Collins & Company. With any luck he'd be so overloaded with work, he might be able to push Casey to the back of his mind. Maybe.

The last words she'd said to him hung heavy on his heart.

Maybe he was too much like Richard to make her happy. She was right, he had deceived her. He could only hope that down the road her pain would heal. She would forgive him. Eventually. He had to believe that.

Barney leaned back and put his feet up on the bed rail. "Got a request from a friend of yours a few days ago."

"And who's that?" Barney's visits always made the day easier to bear. He and Moose and Annlyn had been his only visitors.

The one person he needed to see hadn't been in. He'd called her morning and night at Aretha's, where she was staying, and she wouldn't answer his calls. She'd even sent him a check for the money he had deposited in her account.

No matter what time of day or night, no matter what he was doing, Casey's image, the memory of her touch, her lips, her caressing glance, stole into his mind to torment him.

"Casey Michaels wants to sift through the ashes at the house. She thinks she might find some family knick-knacks."

His heart balled in his throat. "Then she really is okay?"

"As well as to be expected, I guess."

Trevor jerked up in bed too quickly. The sudden movement had him wincing in pain from his cracked rib. "What the hell does that mean?"

"I guess it means she lost everything, but she's coping."

Trevor eased himself down on the pillow. He could see her, right there in his mind's eye. Her beautiful auburn hair that smelled like fresh lemon and herbs. Her blue eyes clouded with passion, her cute little nose, her stubborn chin.

"I told her the area was off-limits."

"You what? You can't do that, Barney. The case must be closed by now. Her whole life was in that house."

"Of course, if she had some official somebody with her, that'd be different, but nobody would volunteer to go."

Trevor stared hard at his friend, then laughed until his ribs hurt. "You're setting me up! You're actually sitting here in my hospital room using the most obvious ploy in the world. On me!"

"Is it working?"

"You're damn right it's working. Just get me out of here."

"It's already been arranged. The doctor's releasing you in the morning."

"Why didn't you say so?"

"You meet Ms. Michaels at two."

"She agreed to this?" Barney shook his head, and his new hope died. The one spark left burning was the fact that in less than twenty-four hours he'd see her again.

CASEY ARRIVED at her house before noon, Aretha's words ringing in her head. It was time to make some decisions. She had to see for herself if there was anything salvageable. She had to decide whether to sell her property.

She removed the orange tape stretched across the entrance to her drive. After capturing Victor, it had taken Barney three days to plow through the bureaucratic restrictions to approve her visit. No matter what Barney'd said, this was her property, her loss, and she needed the time alone. Mr. Official Government Rep would arrive soon enough.

She parked along the edge of the clearing where she could easily see the remains. The brilliant sunshine mocked the destruction before her. The front wall and the original back wall remained standing, like a death squad in their blackened stone. A metal support beam stood between them. It looked naked without the house to clothe it. The surrounding trees looked older and sadder with their singed trunks and missing leaves. Everything else was ashes, piled layer upon layer, as if waiting for its deceptive sameness to be removed. The remains looked worse than she'd imagined.

She had mixed emotions about the house. Years ago, she'd been happy here in this house filled with laughter. She'd been surrounded with love as a small child, and in her innocence had taken it for granted.

For a while Trevor had resurrected the laughter, the security, the love just waiting to be revived. His love had made her a new person. He'd pulled her out of her shell without either one of them realizing it.

No, she refused to think about him so specifically. His unwanted image haunted her constantly. Her heart ached for what could not be.

She tore her eyes away from the painful ruins and climbed out of her car, taking the new pair of extra-long gardening gloves with her. Her knee was still stiff from recent surgery, and she limped slightly as she turned away from the house.

Each day her knee improved, and each day as the visible reminder of Richard faded, the past slipped into proper perspective and insight crept in like the dawn of a new day. She'd actually forgiven Richard. The fire that destroyed her home had acted like a catharsis to bring that part of her past to a close. It seemed appropriate that the reward money from the bonds he'd stolen had paid for her surgery.

She could see the river through the trees, and the scene filled her with awe, as always. She loved this spot with its shades of green, the occasional deer, the duck family she watched grow every year by the edge of the shore. She didn't know if she had the heart to sell it. The house was gone, but the property would always hold her fascination.

She tucked her gloves in her pocket and meandered her way through the woods. She ignored the scarred trees and let her eyes scan the river and the opposite shore.

It felt good to be free of Richard. Yet she continued to feel lethargic, dejected, and to put off getting out of bed each morning for as long as possible. Trevor's deception plagued her, and her own blindness made her feel worse. How could she have been so trusting? Who else would believe Prince Charming could come galloping to the rescue just when she needed him? Who else would be fool enough to fall in love with him?

Soon she would leave Aretha's house and total independence would be hers. Maybe that would make the difference. She'd considered herself free and independent after Richard disappeared. Yet, looking back, she realized she'd restricted her newfound freedom to choosing goals. The rest of her life had remained stagnant.

She had a broader idea of independence now. Every aspect of her life was open to choice. She could even choose to forgive Trevor.

But she couldn't neglect the other side of the coin. Responsibility. The idea kept nagging at her and forced her to admit what she didn't want to hear. If she hadn't been so paranoid about federal agents taking over her life, Trevor could have told her the truth once he trusted her.

And how ironic. A federal agent *had* taken over her life. He'd captured her heart. No matter how hard she tried to block him out, she couldn't. His musky scent, the excitement of his touch, the wild, crazy way her body had answered his—he was in her blood, and she might as well face that, too.

She heard a car approaching and glanced back to see the official government car Barney had sent rounding the curve. She edged closer to the ruins, wanting a few more seconds alone to steal the fragments of memories from the ashes and bury them in her heart.

"Hello, Casey."

Chapter Nineteen

His deep voice hit her like a blow to the head. Her heart lodged in her throat. She turned around slowly, allowing herself time to erect a solid wall of wariness.

He stood right behind her, his blue-gray eyes intense and probing. "Why are you here?" she said.

"It's good to see you."

His voice was strong and steady, its rich timbre was music to her ears, but he looked awful. Fading yellow bruises covered one side of his face. His arm was in a sling. He wore faded jeans and a gray T-shirt. There was a noticeable limp when he stepped toward her.

"What are you doing here?" she asked again, stepping back. Then she remembered. "Ah, yes, still playing the clever government agent." She saw pain glide across his face and quickly disappear. His body looked tense. The light seemed to vanish from his eyes.

"This wasn't my idea."

"Right." She put on her gloves. "Let's get this over with."

"Please." He touched her arm. "I owe you my life, Casey. Let me at least say thank you."

Her heart twisted inside. The entire ordeal with Victor flashed before her mind. She was on the verge of tears and hated herself for her weakness. She turned away and continued walking. "You're welcome."

They sauntered around the perimeter of the ashes in silence, Trevor walking stiffly, Casey carefully controlling her breathing to bring her emotions under control. When she stopped and leaned over to start looking through the ashes, he joined her in the search.

"You don't need to help me," she said. Bending over obviously brought him pain. "You're just the authorized, official government presence." She hated the dripping sarcasm in her voice. This wasn't like her.

Barney had told her the case was closed, that there was no one willing to take time away from their other assignments to come here with her. Why the area was still off-limits if the case was closed, she didn't know. She couldn't remember what Barney had said when she'd asked him. But Trevor had come. No matter how she felt about him, she could at least be decent.

"Besides," she added, "you'll get filthy."

"I guess you know they caught Victor Pernell and his crew," he said, continuing to work beside her. "The *P* ledger? That was some distant cousin of Pernell's in New York. Embezzlement seems to be a Pernell family tradition."

"You should have kept part of the reward. You earned it."

"Having the bonds returned in Richard's name was enough."

She nodded and dug more intensely through the filthy ash. Barney had made her delay coming to the house until Victor was caught, providing her with the excuse she needed to stay away. But she had no intention of discussing any of this with Trevor. Her business was no longer his. She had cut him out of her life.

Easier said than done. From the corner of her eye she saw him pushing the ashes around, near what had been her front porch. Each movement caused him pain. He tried to mask the discomfort, but he couldn't hide it from her. She knew his body like her own. Why was he doing this? Obviously it was painful for him. And just as obviously, she cared.

Why was he here at all? He'd said he loved her, yet he'd deceived her almost as horribly as Richard had. She'd learned to ignore the similarities between the two brothers. The slight tilt of Trevor's head when he paused seemed natural. The raised eyebrow fit his personality, or what she thought was his personality.

To her dying day she would believe that he had loved her when they made love. She'd felt that truth in every touch, every whispered word. She'd seen the love in his eyes, felt it in every breath. He couldn't have been lying to her all that time.

"Did Aretha tell you Barney's trying to recruit Jon?"

She paused in her digging. This was news to her.

"He managed to get into Victor's safe and copy the records of his telephone calls. His information cinched Victor's tie-in with the New York faction. Jon carried it off like a pro."

He stopped working and stood and stretched his shoulders. She refused to look up at him, but she could see him. He never left her peripheral vision, not for a second. Each move drew her eyes so magnetically, she began to lose her determination to stay aloof. So far they'd found nothing, but she renewed her digging efforts rather than acknowledge that he was waiting for her to stop.

He backed away and rubbed his ribs. "I'm sorry I wasn't up-front with you, Casey," he blurted out. "I had to find out about Richard. If I'd told you I was with the government, you never would have talked to me."

She paused again, her muscles tense, her teeth clamped so tight her jaw muscle twitched. "You're absolutely right."

"If it makes any difference, Barney didn't know Richard was my brother and... oh, I almost forgot." He wiped his hands on his jeans before digging into his pocket. "Mina's with her mother now. I thought you'd want to know. She made this for you. She brought it over the day you came back here to get the bonds." He held out a bead necklace.

She removed her gloves and took the necklace. "The day she hugged you," she muttered aloud, thinking that, like it or not, he was a kind man with a good heart. Why did that thought cause her so much pain?

She raised her head, and Trevor's eyes captured hers. She felt a new spark of life in her she hadn't felt before. There was a growing frenzy within her to have him touch her, to hold her. To love her. If only that could be. If only she could give him all the love stored up inside her. She searched for her anger at his betrayal, but it had vanished, disappeared among the ashes of her home.

"Casey?" He reached for her cheek.

She sensed his intention before he raised his hand. Even so, she didn't move. Let me feel his touch one more time, she argued with herself. She stood stone still while his hand caressed her face, while his warm fingers trailed a fiery path across her chin, while they feathered her lips. Her whole body cried out in wonderful pain.

She wanted to... No, she couldn't, she wouldn't. Her wall of resistance was cracking, and she needed to shore it up quickly.

She stepped back abruptly and brushed off her jeans. "Just maybe the rakes escaped the fire. I'll be right back."

Trevor watched her disappear around the protruding stone wall still standing at the rear. Her jeans didn't caress her body as they had before. She was thinner, almost fragile-looking.

He brushed his thumb across his fingers to hold on to the silky feel of her skin. There was magic between the two of them. Couldn't she feel it? Couldn't she see that they belonged together?

CASEY FOUND THE RAKES tossed in the ivy on the other side of what used to be her lily-of-the-valley bed. The fire had not reached that far, but something had. More likely, someone.

Wally. He'd mutilated her garden searching for the bonds.

She picked up two rakes and banged them on a tree to loosen the debris. The destruction in the garden didn't matter half as much as the war raging inside her.

She loved Trevor with a fierceness that scared her. She wanted to feel his arms around her and see the passion simmer in his eyes. But she was through with him. Wasn't she? Her mind and body were totally out of sync. He had no business charging into her life and making her fall in love with him.

With the rakes now ready to use, she walked toward the man who occupied her mind, smiling to herself at the foolishness of her thoughts. Make her fall in love? No, she'd done that on her own. Those piercing, penetrating eyes capable of so much expression had drawn her to him even before she stopped comparing him to Richard.

He'd moved to another section by the time she returned. He stood on the fringe of the ashes, his back to her. She handed him a rake. "This should make the job easier."

He stood motionless, staring at her hands. "How are your wrists?"

She looked at the gloves that went halfway up her arm. "They're okay. They're almost healed."

"I'm sorry that had to happen," he said.

"Stop, don't even say it. Let's just get to work. Okay?"

They each took their rakes and began the arduous task of raking through the ashes. They worked steadily and methodically. She managed to smile at him once in a while, but she didn't dare let down her guard. Her wall must stay firmly in place.

BY THE END of the afternoon, with the sun casting shadows from the west, they completed their search.

"Well, that's it," said Trevor.

He attempted to brush the black soot off his clothes, but with little success. They were both filthy. He glanced at Casey. The filth hadn't deterred her. Her cheeks and nose were blackened, her clothes ruined. That cute little nose, colored beyond recognition, was more alluring than ever. The smudges made her more appealing.

It was hard working beside her hour after hour. He constantly struggled to keep himself in check, to maintain the distance she demanded. Dear God, he loved this woman. This cool aloofness was driving him nuts.

"Did you hurt your knee again?"

"I had the surgery recently," she said, walking more smoothly.

"Good, good," he said awkwardly, wanting to say more.

She nodded and moved away from him. He watched her anxiously. Her face was so pale it showed the slightest hint of a blush when she talked of her surgery. He felt awkward and embarrassed, himself. Here they were acting like strangers, being polite, impersonal, distant again, not at all like he'd imagined, or wanted. He longed to hold her in his arms and let her warmth flow through him.

He clenched and unclenched his fist. The reaction brought pain to his wrist, reminding him why he was in this predicament in the first place. Damn! He had to get past that stubborn wall of hers.

"THANKS FOR COMING out here today," she said, walking ahead of him around the rim of the ashes.

She sounded like she was talking to someone she'd just met, when in fact her heart was breaking in two.

"You're welcome," he called from not too far behind.

"Well." She opened her car door. "See you." She set her gloves inside, reluctant to leave, reluctant to walk away and live with the pain of loving him. She had a choice to make.

She tried to envision a new home here at Hallowing Point. She saw herself sitting on a front porch swing, lazing around on a deck with the dogwood trees in bloom and the birds singing. She imagined sipping a hot cup of tea in her new kitchen, or relaxing in the living room before a roaring fire after a hard day's work. She imagined the new bedroom with a sun balcony. And the bed. She knotted her fists and tried to hold back the tears forming in her eyes.

No, all the imagination and determination in the world couldn't erase him from her heart. She belonged with him, and he belonged with her. She loved him. It was that simple. She wanted to share her life with him. When she allowed herself to look into her heart, she realized she had already forgiven him.

Maybe he didn't love her. Maybe everything that had happened between them had served one purpose for him—to find the bonds and understand more about Richard. This could be true. Her own instincts could be way off target.

The old Casey would have backed off and shut him out. Her former self could not have forgiven him, and never would she have considered whether he loved her or not.

She had changed. The new Casey, the one with a broader view of life, a larger chunk of self-confidence and freedom, beat down the intruding thoughts and raised her tear-streaked face high in pride and turned around.

TREVOR WALKED TOWARD HER feeling awkward and clumsy. "Casey?"

His heart beat painfully inside his chest. His nerves were shot, his muscles strung tight. This beautiful woman could make or break him. He could see the irony after the life he'd lived and the brutal people he'd tracked down. This slender, captivating woman in her ash-smudged clothes held his future in her hands, and she didn't even know it.

Casey's skin tingled from his nearness. He was so close, yet so far away. How she wanted to reach out and run her fingers through his hair. How she longed to take just two steps and feel his body brush hers. And she could. She could. He was that close.

"God, I've missed you," he said, his voice raw with desire.

His hands on her shoulders made her heart explode. She melted against him, and he wrapped his arms tightly around her. His warm, strong, wonderful arms sent her head spinning in pleasure.

He tipped up her chin with one finger. "I love you, sweetheart. Stay with me."

His words were more precious than gold. They framed her heart and held it captive.

"I was ready to leave the agency when I got Richard's letter."

"You don't need to explain, Trevor."

"Yes, yes I do. Hear me out. Please."

She snuggled closer in his arms. His familiar musky scent had her pulse racing madly. The feel of him was so right, so perfect. How could she ever have considered the possibility of forgetting him?

"My position provided me with the perfect cover to find out what had happened to Richard, and I couldn't turn away. You were the only unknown link. Everyone thought you were involved. Wheedling my way into your life made sense. Once I took that first step, it was too late to tell you the truth."

She pulled away from his arms, the loss of his warmth causing chills down her arms. She couldn't let him carry the whole burden of guilt. "No, Trevor, you can't do that."

This was it, he thought, the moment he'd dreaded. His heart cried in pain. The pervading fear reasserted itself, and his whole body tensed in response.

"I'm responsible, too," she said. "I should have come forward with what little I knew, but I didn't." She paced along the edge of the woods. Her eyes locked on his. "I've thought a lot about what happened. If I'd known you were an agent, Trevor, I know I never would have let you in the house, much less into my heart. I'm sorry, too."

A ray of hope shone, unsure of its welcome, not daring to flame. "Are you saying what I think you're saying?"

She flung herself into his arms. Joy swelled his heart to the bursting point. He would never, ever have enough of her.

"I tried to erase you from my heart." She was kissing his face, his neck. "It didn't work."

"I'm here to stay, sweetheart, for now, forever, for always. You're stuck. If you'll have me."

"I love you, Trevor."

He kissed her nose, her eyelids, her cheeks, her chin. An amazing new energy flowed between them. His enchanting blue-gray eyes mesmerized her, their naked passion like burning beacons of his love. She lost herself totally in their compelling force. She could feel his love envelop her body and embrace her heart. It caressed her very soul.

His lips met hers gently, as if all the tenderness in the world was focused on their joining. His tongue slid sensuously around her mouth, teasing and dipping to taste her nectar. He deepened the kiss. She floated in a sea of sensual delight.

He drew his mouth away, reluctantly it seemed, but he held her close, binding her to his heart. Just having him hold her brought more pleasure than she'd ever dreamed possible.

"Casey, sweetheart, I want you with me forever. Will you marry me, Casey? We can build a good life together, you and me, and I promise to love you with every ounce of strength in me. Will you, Casey? Will you be my bride?"

"Yes, oh yes," she said, her voice husky in the aftermath of his kiss. Tears trickled down her cheeks. She tried to stop the silly grin that controlled her face, but there was no hiding her happiness.

"I have this fantastic picture in my mind of lots of little kids racing through the woods and climbing trees and feeding the ducks. A real family. And a new home. How about it, sweetheart?''

The pure joy in his eyes undid her. She let her laughter flow over them like the wellspring of happiness they both felt. Two hearts beat as one as his arms embraced her in a love greater than life itself, an everlasting love that would strengthen and grow and endure beyond time.

''As long as they all have your bewitching eyes,'' she answered before she lost herself to the magic of his kiss.

When the only time you have for yourself is...

Spring into spring—by giving yourself a March Break! Take a few *stolen moments* and treat yourself to a Great Escape. Relax with one of our brand-new stories (or with all six!).

Each STOLEN MOMENTS title in our Great Escapes collection is a complete and never-before-published *short* novel. These contemporary romances are 96 pages long—the perfect length for the busy woman of the nineties!

Look for Great Escapes in our Stolen Moments display this March!

SIZZLE by Jennifer Crusie
ANNIVERSARY WALTZ
by Anne Marie Duquette
MAGGIE AND HER COLONEL
by Merline Lovelace
PRAIRIE SUMMER by Alina Roberts
THE SUGAR CUP by Annie Sims
LOVE ME NO'i by Barbara Stewart

Wherever Harlequin and Silhouette books are sold.

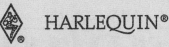

HARLEQUIN®

Don't miss these Harlequin favorites by some of our most distinguished authors!
And now, you can receive a discount by ordering two or more titles!

HT#25409	THE NIGHT IN SHINING ARMOR by JoAnn Ross	$2.99 ☐
HT#25471	LOVESTORM by JoAnn Ross	$2.99 ☐
HP#11463	THE WEDDING by Emma Darcy	$2.89 ☐
HP#11592	THE LAST GRAND PASSION by Emma Darcy	$2.99 ☐
HR#03188	DOUBLY DELICIOUS by Emma Goldrick	$2.89 ☐
HR#03248	SAFE IN MY HEART by Leigh Michaels	$2.89 ☐
HS#70464	CHILDREN OF THE HEART by Sally Garrett	$3.25 ☐
HS#70524	STRING OF MIRACLES by Sally Garrett	$3.39 ☐
HS#70500	THE SILENCE OF MIDNIGHT by Karen Young	$3.39 ☐
HI#22178	SCHOOL FOR SPIES by Vickie York	$2.79 ☐
HI#22212	DANGEROUS VINTAGE by Laura Pender	$2.89 ☐
HI#22219	TORCH JOB by Patricia Rosemoor	$2.89 ☐
HAR#16459	MACKENZIE'S BABY by Anne McAllister	$3.39 ☐
HAR#16466	A COWBOY FOR CHRISTMAS by Anne McAllister	$3.39 ☐
HAR#16462	THE PIRATE AND HIS LADY by Margaret St. George	$3.39 ☐
HAR#16477	THE LAST REAL MAN by Rebecca Flanders	$3.39 ☐
HH#28704	A CORNER OF HEAVEN by Theresa Michaels	$3.99 ☐
HH#28707	LIGHT ON THE MOUNTAIN by Maura Seger	$3.99 ☐

Harlequin Promotional Titles

#83247	YESTERDAY COMES TOMORROW by Rebecca Flanders	$4.99 ☐
#83257	MY VALENTINE 1993	$4.99 ☐
	(short-story collection featuring Anne Stuart, Judith Arnold, Anne McAllister, Linda Randall Wisdom)	

(limited quantities available on certain titles)

	AMOUNT	$
DEDUCT:	10% DISCOUNT FOR 2+ BOOKS	$
ADD:	POSTAGE & HANDLING	$
	($1.00 for one book, 50¢ for each additional)	
	APPLICABLE TAXES*	$ _____
	TOTAL PAYABLE	$ _____
	(check or money order—please do not send cash)	

To order, complete this form and send it, along with a check or money order for the total above, payable to Harlequin Books, to: **In the U.S.:** 3010 Walden Avenue, P.O. Box 9047, Buffalo, NY 14269-9047; **In Canada:** P.O. Box 613, Fort Erie, Ontario, L2A 5X3.

Name: _____

Address: _____ City: _____

State/Prov.: _____ Zip/Postal Code: _____

*New York residents remit applicable sales taxes.
 Canadian residents remit applicable GST and provincial taxes.

HBACK-JM

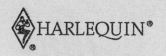

HARLEQUIN®

Harlequin proudly presents four stories about *convenient* but not *conventional* reasons for marriage:

- ♦ To save your godchildren from a "wicked stepmother"

- ♦ To help out your eccentric aunt—and her sexy business partner

- ♦ To bring an old man happiness by making him a grandfather

- ♦ To escape from a ghostly existence and become a real woman

Marriage By Design—four brand-new stories by four of Harlequin's most popular authors:

**CATHY GILLEN THACKER
JASMINE CRESSWELL
GLENDA SANDERS
MARGARET CHITTENDEN**

Don't miss this exciting collection of stories about marriages of convenience. Available in April, wherever Harlequin books are sold.

MBD94

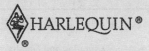

HARLEQUIN®

COMING SOON TO
A STORE NEAR YOU...

THE MAIN
ATTRACTION

By *New York Times* Bestselling Author

This March, look for THE MAIN ATTRACTION by popular
author Jayne Ann Krentz.

Ten years ago, Filomena Cromwell had left her small town
in shame. Now she is back determined to get her sweet,
sweet revenge....

Soon she has her ex-fiancé, who cheated on her with
another woman, chasing her all over town. And he isn't
the only one. Filomena lets Trent Ravinder catch her.

Can she control the fireworks she's set into motion?